CAFFEINE NIGHTS PUBLISHING

K.A Richardson

With Deadly Intent

...art

and ...ad...

Published in Great Britain by
Caffeine Nights Publishing
4 Eton Close
Walderslade
Chatham
Kent
ME5 9AT

www.caffeinenights.com

British Library Cataloguing in Publication Data.
A CIP catalogue record for this book is available from the British Library

ISBN: 978-1-910720-35-6

Cover design by
Mark (Wills) Williams

Everything else by
Default, Luck and Accident

For my Grandad

Maurice Arthur Hammond, 1930-2011

always loved and missed

Acknowledgements

I'd like to say a massive thank you to the team at Caffeine Nights – particularly Darren Laws for believing in me and this novel enough to give me a contract.

My thoughts go out to the friends and family of my first ever editor, Jenny Drewery, who sadly passed away in July 2015. She pushed me to my limits and beyond, and believed unfalteringly that I would land a contract. Her friendship and influence live on through this novel.

Crime Scene personnel and police officers who have put up with me constantly double checking facts, thanks for the unwavering belief in my writing, and for regaling me with endless tales of crime scene gallows humour. To my own Inspector, Rachel, I give thanks for beta reading and also for the numerous questions asked about the police side of a crime novel.

Special thanks to my amazing mum Jeannet, who has encouraged and believed in me my whole life. My dad Derek for being a steady presence believing whatever I do is the right thing. My amazingly wonderful and patient husband, Peter, who ensures a steady stream of coffee is present while I write, my Aunty Mary for her utter joy at knowing she'd finally be able to read my novel, and my brother Michael, for his constant questions about whether his name would feature in my book (it does now bro). They all make me so proud every single day.

My friends are my rocks – constant support through good and bad, and not being too shy to tell me when I'm doing something I shouldn't be! You know who you are – but to mention a few names (by no means all) Claire, Angela, Dionne, Rachel, Vicky, Eileen and Char. Keep filling the world with your outstanding sparkle.

Finally, I'd like to thank YOU, the reader who has bought this novel. Writing really wouldn't be possible without each and every one of you, whether I know you or not, you make my dreams a reality. It makes me very proud to admit I'm a member of *The Book Club* on Facebook – interaction, banter, and suggestions for books to read, characters and plots to write. I look forward to meeting more of you at the various events planned over the next year.

Prologue

It was dark inside his mind. The kind of dark so black no number of lights could illuminate it. His hopes and dreams had been crushed by the weight of a thousand sins. Yet despite this he smiled, the corners of his mouth curving upwards towards the still, cold depths of his icy blue eyes.

He could be charming, when he wanted, to men and women alike. But one look into those eyes, and you pulled back quickly, like a hand burnt by fire. The tiny hairs stood to attention on the back of your neck, and a shudder passed down your spine.

And you knew that something just wasn't right.

They say the eyes are the window to the soul, so what do you see when there is no soul? He had lost his, somewhere along the way. Or maybe it had just been replaced with something else. He had needs like everybody. He craved human contact at times; he ate and slept. But that was where the similarities ended.

Physiologically he was human.

Mentally he was something else.

Dark desires filled his mind, ruling his every thought and whenever the need overtook him he acted on them. He loved, but he loved the things most people hate: pain, fear and death. And now, years after the animal torture, truancy and lies of his early life, he was finally free to do as he wished. At the learned age of forty-two, he was finally ready to re-enact all of his deepest fantasies.

He had done his research, perfected his methods. Years of training had prepared him for this moment. He needed to *feel* – and he would do anything to make that happen.

He carefully packed the rusted, red metal toolbox with the items he knew he would need. Then he went to the bathroom to prepare himself. There would be a wondrous show tonight – the first of its kind. A premiere.

He smiled into the mirror at his theatrics. It would be a good show; a fantastic show, in fact. At least for him. He wasn't naive enough to believe his victim would enjoy it for one second. Well maybe *one* second: the instant when he chose to finish the performance with one last act. Another shiver of anticipation ran through him; this was the most excitement he had felt in forever.

It felt good.

He put on his dark jacket, tied his standard lace-ups, grabbed the toolbox and left.

Chapter One

'Fuck off, Brian,' muttered Scott Anderson.

'Scott, enough with the attitude already. You've been warned about your language. I can't keep you in the programme if your behaviour continues. You're disrupting other kids,' said Brian Mackintosh sternly.

He paused, and sighed in exasperation.

'Look, you're a good kid, Scott. I know that. When you admit and deal with your problems you'll be a great kid. Please, just try and keep your attitude in check, OK?'

'Whatever ... *Dad*,' said Scott sarcastically, shoving his hands into the pockets of his tracksuit bottoms. 'Can I go now?'

Brian nodded, watching as the teen practically ran from the confines of his office in the Outreach building. He was frustrated. He loved his job, but the kids in the centre sometimes came with too many problems for him to be able to deal with in the time he had them with him. And others just didn't want the help.

Scott had been kicked out of school for fighting, and assigned to the centre when he'd been caught breaking into a car. He was sullen, argumentative, full of himself and generally behaved like a pain in the arse. He'd recently starting hanging out with some older lads who exhibited a kind of gang mentality. They weren't part of the centre, but they hung about, pushing the younger kids around and trying to steal from them, and, worse still, getting the kids to steal for them. He had moved them on more times than enough: but obviously, not far enough from Scott, who had taken to leaving the centre to be with them.

Despite this, though, there was something about Scott that grabbed his soul. Behind the tough-guy act was a scared kid with haunted eyes. Brian had an idea what made him that way, the yellowing bruises he occasionally displayed giving him a clue. But despite Brian reporting it twice to social services, Scott still lived at home.

Quickly scribbling some notes in a barely legible scrawl, Brian decided he was going to speak with his boss about getting Scott some additional help. He didn't want to give up on Scott just because of his bad attitude. Every kid deserved a second chance. He just hoped Scott would take it.

He glanced up at the wall clock and frowned. It was gone 8 p.m. and Maureen, his wife's mother, hadn't rung him. She was looking after the kids, Abbie, who was three, and Michael, who was six. Michael wasn't well; he had a stomach bug and had been throwing up for two days now. Suddenly Brian wanted more than anything to be home with his son. Deciding the paperwork would still be on his desk tomorrow, he grabbed his jacket and wandered to the tuck-shop area of the centre.

'Hey, Gill. Would you mind if I sneak off and let you lock up? Stan's still out back if you need him. I just wanna get home to Mikey.'

'Yeah sure, sugar, no problem. You get yourself home to your babies,' said Gill Thompson with a wide smile.

'You, Gill, are an absolute gem. I'll owe you one.'

'Hell, sugar, you owe me way more than one,' she purred, flashing him a quick wink before turning and sauntering off, her bright orange heels clicking on the tiled floor.

Brian smiled after her. She had breezed into the centre six months before, made firm friends with the kids and then the staff, and established herself as a worthwhile member of the team virtually from the outset. She was a rare phenomenon – one of those mad, pretty, geeky women who lit the room up when they entered and turned the lights out as they left. Her blonde hair had coloured tips that changed on a pretty much weekly basis and she always wore her bright green-and-white spotted glasses. She was easy to get a feel for, though he had figured out early on that she only let you see what she wanted you to; and she cared more than anyone he had ever met. He had a lot of respect for her. He didn't know if she was aware of it, but she was an excellent fit at the centre.

He often wondered what her story was, why she had ended up at the centre. Maybe one day he would find out.

Grinning to himself, he pulled his car keys from his jacket pocket, headed for his beat-up Fiesta and drove home.

Susan sighed her frustration as she checked her mobile for the umpteenth time that night. She did it discreetly, hiding it under the counter of the cigarette kiosk and checking to make sure no one was watching. Mobile phone use was forbidden at work, especially on the shop floor.

He still hadn't texted.

It was only an hour until she was due to finish her shift. She couldn't leave it any longer to tell her husband the lie that she had been asked to work late.

Besides, how dare he not text? He wasn't the only one with a life; a separate life from the few stolen moments they shared together, at any rate. It was hard to believe it had been going on for three months now. She did feel guilty for her husband, but it seemed like forever since he had shown her any affection. All he ever did was talk about the kids or work. And the kids? They made her feel guilty too, but sometimes she needed a moment when she could forget about all the worries at home and just live in that moment. That's what he gave her: a release, of sorts. Somewhere to go where she was more than just a mum and a wife. He gave her a place to be her again. Even if it was only for a little while.

He had an aura of danger about him, his clear eyes holding a hint of sophistication. Susan firmly believed that when she spoke, he truly listened.

But their relationship had become a little strained lately. Their meetings had become less frequent and he had begun to leave her hanging. Like tonight. He had promised he would ring. He knew she needed to talk to him. But he hadn't rung, and now she would have to go home to face the kids and her husband, and listen to the squabbling and the moaning.

None of them knew her secret. They didn't suspect.

She sighed again, pushing the section of her fringe that had dropped back to its place behind her ear, and then jumped as her eyes focused on Sheila, her supervisor, who had appeared in front of her from nowhere.

Uh-oh, what the hell have I done now?

'Ann's going to cover you for a minute. Can I see you in the office?'

Susan groaned inside as she quickly signed off the till and followed Sheila, wondering which cardinal rule she had managed to break this time.

Once they were seated, Sheila said, 'Is something wrong, Susan? You've been distracted for a couple of weeks and we've had some comments from other staff that you're using your mobile on the shop floor without permission.'

Susan managed to stop herself staring in surprise. Thinking on her feet she said, 'Michael's not well. He's got some sicky bug from school and I was expecting Mum to ring me but she hasn't. I should have asked to use my phone, though. I'm sorry, Sheila.'

'Aw, the poor wee love. Listen, we're OK for staff tonight. Why don't you get yourself home and look after him?'

'Thanks, but I'm OK honest, just thought Mum might have rang. But if she hasn't she must be coping fine. I'll stay until 10 p.m.'

'OK, if you're sure, Susan. But take five now and go ring your mum. It'll put your mind at rest.'

Susan thanked her and wandered out to the loading area. She really wasn't good at lying, though Mikey *was* ill so it wasn't a complete lie.

Her mobile suddenly buzzed in her pocket.

'Oh *now* you text,' she muttered as she pulled the phone out and flipped open the top.

'Sorry, can't make tonight. Maybe tomorrow.'

'For Christ's sake,' she said, quickly typing out her reply: 'I need to speak to you. It's urgent.'

Almost instantly her phone buzzed again with the response: 'I said sorry. GTG.'

Susan stared, wondering what GTG meant. Then it clicked. She shook her head. A single tear rolled down her cheek. Angrily she swiped at it. Fine: tomorrow it was, then. She really did get herself into these predicaments. Brian was going to kill her when he found out.

How did my life become quite so shit?

Susan wiped her eyes with a tissue before heading back inside.

The moon was bright and full as he made his way purposefully to his car. He knew it was time; he had done his homework and knew her routine almost better than she did.

In no time at all he was parked in the car park to the supermarket where she worked. His breath almost caught in his throat as she came out of the doors, the moonlight glinting off her hair giving it the appearance of spun gold.

'Yes,' he thought. 'She will do nicely.'

As she climbed into her bright red hatchback, he turned the key in his ignition and felt the powerful engine roar to life. His hands remained perfectly steady as he put the car into gear and pressed his foot on the accelerator.

The woman had no idea of his plans for her, didn't register his car following behind her. But he knew. It had taken months to plan every detail of what he would do to her when he finally had his hands on her, working out the kinks and imagining any potential problems.

Not that there would be any.

He followed her car for several miles, keeping back a safe distance, patiently awaiting the point when he would gain control. He didn't have to wait long; he watched with a grim smile as her car began to speed up on the incline, just as he'd known it would. His eyes glinted in the darkness as he imagined the horror on her face when she registered her brakes weren't working. Her car jerked a little, still speeding down the steep hill towards the sharp bend at the bottom. He watched, smiling widely now, as she lost control at the bottom and slammed into a tree with such force that one of her wheels detached and rolled round the bend out of sight.

Now his work would begin. He hoped the impact hadn't done his work for him. He pulled in slowly at the side of the road, taking great care not to skid, stepped out and removed the toolbox from the boot. He carried it to the mangled car, placed it on the ground and opened it. He took a breath, surprised once more at the rush of adrenaline that overtook him. Calmer now, he walked over to the driver's side of the woman's car, bending slightly to stare inside the broken window. Blood streaked her face and hair, dripping steadily from a laceration across the front of her head, caused by the impact on the steering wheel. She wouldn't have the chance to wonder why her brakes had failed, let alone her airbags.

He watched her face intently, waiting for the split second when the look of recognition in her eyes died and turned to fear; and then he set to work, whistling softly and smiling – there really was some merit in enjoying one's work.

Chapter Two

The wind was howling outside in the courtyard. Cassandra Hunt stood at the window, slowly hung up the phone, and stared out, taking a moment to think, as she always did when she was called to an incident. The walls of her office provided little comfort, with posters advertising blood spatter information, rules for recovering footwear marks and entomology guidelines.

It was the worst feeling, being called to an incident when you'd left work for the day. Most people get to leave work behind, but not a Crime Scene Manager. The whirr of the printer in the corner stopped, pulling Cass from the momentary daydream she always had when she had this feeling in the pit of her stomach – the one where she was on a beach somewhere hot, without a job to do. She turned and stared at the printer, willing the now printed pages to disappear. But they remained.

It wasn't often that forensics was required at a fatal road traffic accident, but it wasn't unheard of. It was the first time Cass had been called back to work to attend one, though, and with the wind blowing a hoolie outside, it wasn't one she was looking forward to.

Cass sighed and grabbed the hair bobble off her computer base unit. Deftly, she twisted her hair up and secured it in place using the elasticised piece of material. She pulled two pens from the pen pot beside the computer and drove them through her hair Chinese-style. Years of experience doing the job had taught her that, strangely, the one place she wouldn't lose things from was her hair. As she worked a scene, she often ended up with various other items secured within the folds of her ponytail. Fingerprint brushes, pens, even swabs had found their way there at some point in her career.

Cass checked the stock on the van, plugged the information into the waiting satnav and set off towards the countryside to the north of the large town, Ryhope. Following the automated voice, she arrived at Burley Bank in no time, shivering slightly as the wind buffeted the van from side to side on the open stretches of her journey. She took the steep hill carefully, aware of its hidden dangers, and pulled to a stop at the base, behind the marked car and ambulance. The flashing blue lights of both illuminated the road, highlighting the large tree and mangled car now in view.

She jumped out of the van and approached the uniformed officers, noticing that the paramedics were still inside their ambulance. She glanced quickly at the collar numbers of the two officers, committing them to memory. They were talking together in hushed tones, and pulled apart slightly as she approached.

'Hey, Cass, sorry to pull you out of bed on a night like this. The incident support unit is at a road traffic collision on the A19 so they've been held up. Looks like she hit the bend too fast and wrapped herself round a tree,' said the older of the two men. She recognised him as one of the nightshift sergeants from her depot, Harry Green. He'd worked traffic for years, so she purposely didn't speak, waiting for him to finish.

'Something just isn't sitting right. There's no skid marks, she didn't try and slow down. Also there's just something about her positioning in the car.' He shook his head, 'I dunno. Maybe it's nothing but I figured better to be safe than sorry. Paramedics have proclaimed life as extinct on arrival.'

Cass nodded. 'OK, Harry, thanks. I'll just grab some lighting and have a look.' She went to the van and pulled out a couple of heavy-duty lamps. Working silently, she set them up and plugged them into the portable generator in the back of the van. She started on the incline, noting that Harry was right: there was no evidence of skid marks, nothing to say the victim had even attempted to apply her brakes. A fleeting thought of possible suicide crossed her mind, but she pushed it back. It wasn't her job to assume; she needed facts. She felt her gut grow heavier, however. The bad feeling from the office had followed her and she knew that that was never a good sign.

She carefully approached the side of the vehicle, sweeping her handheld Maglite torch from side to side across the ground. She saw a slight indentation in the grass at the foot of the tree, as though something heavy had been set down there for a while. The front of the vehicle was wrapped around the base of the tree, almost hugging it from both sides. Her torch hovered on the red spatter on the inside of the cracked windscreen, and something about the distribution made her pause. She would expect to see blood from an impact, possibly an upward spatter effect as the head was thrown backwards from the collision. That was there.

But there was other blood too. Cass frowned as she realised the airbag had failed to deploy.

Her gaze moved to the victim. A female, her face coated in a sea of red, her lifeless eyes staring out like small islands. Squinting as her eyes adjusted between artificial light and darkness, Cass guessed the woman's age to be around mid to late twenties. A large laceration spread across the woman's forehead, consistent with an impact on the steering wheel. Her face showed bruising to the right-hand side, and Cass furrowed her eyebrows, concentrating on the bruising.

It didn't seem plausible that it was caused by the crash. It looked more like someone who had been beaten.

She carefully moved the torch down towards the neckline of the victim, and that's when she saw it: a wound, heavily disguised by the amount of blood but there nonetheless. A neat but obviously deep laceration over the jugular area, which most definitely explained the additional arterial blood presence on the windscreen.

Cass pulled back quickly, retracing her steps to where the sergeant waited patiently.

'Harry, you need to get this road closed off and outer cordons put up immediately. We need a major incident log starting and the Murder Team down here, now.'

Harry paled slightly, but trusting her judgement he turned and started barking orders into his radio.

Cass paused, contemplating her next actions. She felt a chill crawl up her arms, as though someone was watching her through the darkness. Pushing the uneasy feeling to the back of her mind, she decided she would move the van and start photographing the area.

She had taken most of her shots when suddenly she looked up, unsure of what she was looking at in the pitch black of the night sky. Dark clouds scurried across her view and she felt a heavy drop of cold water hit her cheek with a splash. She cursed loudly, and moved quickly back to the van.

The younger officer heard her. 'Is everything OK?' he asked. She stared at him blankly for a second, not comprehending. 'You need to help me,' she said, turning and grabbing the tent from the partition at the back of the van. She briefed him quickly on putting up the tent, and in just a few minutes, the large green expanse of material covered the vehicle completely. Cass hammered in the last peg just as the heavens opened and the rain joined the wind in an awe inspiring battle of the elements.

It seemed like forever, but in reality it was only around thirty minutes until the Murder Team rolled up at the scene in their unmarked Ford Focus. Cass and Harry had set up a cordon round the crash site, and Harry had posted the younger officer at the lower cordon at the bottom of the incline while he managed the upper cordon at the top. All the vehicles were parked at the top, and Cass was sitting inside the cab to her van. She had phoned her boss, Kevin Lang, the Area Forensic Supervisor (AFS), and given him a brief on what was happening. Kevin was one of those rare bosses who had complete faith in his staff. He told Cass to keep him updated and to make sure she used the call-out system as soon as she needed additional staff. She said she would wait until after the briefing with the Murder Team Cadre, who would be heading up the investigation, and get back to him then.

Cass pulled her hood tightly around her face and jumped out of the van. She was standing beside the Focus as the three detectives clambered out.

She was pleased to see Detective Chief Inspector Alexander McKay heading up the team. 'Alex,' she said in acknowledgement as he gave her a quick smile.

'The MI van will be here in about half hour,' he said, placing his hand at the base of her spine and guiding her back to the dryness of her van. The touch made her skin prickle through her Gore-Tex jacket. Hurriedly she got into the van and turned the ignition, putting the blowers and heaters on for warmth as Alex climbed in beside her.

'So what have we got, Cass?' he asked, knowing her well enough to expect a straight answer. She explained quickly, giving him speedy recommendations. Cass had already heard from the radio dispatcher that the Pathologist was en route from Darlington so would be at the scene in around an hour. Alex nodded as she finished her summary; he had worked with Cass on a number of cases and had a lot of respect for her knowledge and methodology. He jumped out of the van and made his way back to his team to advise them of his action strategy, emphasising the importance of forensic awareness.

Cass phoned Kevin again. 'Hiya, boss. I'm gonna need at least two more CSIs here tonight. Faith is on duty tomorrow and has a doctor's appointment with Joey first thing, so don't call her. Can we use Johnny from Silksworth? He's on a mid-shift tomorrow so can just carry through, and Carla from Sunderland City? I've got the car tented, but the rain's still coming down hard. The sooner we get the victim out and the car uplifted the better. I've got SL Motorbods on standby for the uplift with a full-curtain truck.'

'No problem, Cass. Do you need me down there too? I can call the nurse to look out for Madge. I'll be there faster than Johnny at any rate.' Cass heard the silent plea not to need him. She knew how hard his life was at the moment. His wife had cancer and was losing the battle daily. Kevin had backed off from doing on-calls, and understandably did not wish to leave his wife in the hands of a nurse at silly o'clock in the morning.

'No, Kevin, you need to stay there with Madge. I can manage fine until Johnny and Carla get here. The RV point is at the top of Burley Bank. The MI Team have the lounge all set up.' Cass smiled into the phone, knowing Kevin would understand the slang term they all used for the mobile truck the MI Team used at major crime scenes. It consisted of an adapted moving truck, which housed a section formed and secured into a mobile office, and a refreshment area for the staff on scene. It had been a large investment for the force when it had been purchased a few years before, and there had been worries that it wouldn't be used as often as it should, especially with younger people joining the force. The driving licence requirements were old school and required a D-classification for the truck to be driven. But it had turned out to be one of the best large purchases made and was deployed frequently, both for major incidents and training days.

'Thanks, Cass,' said Kevin. He knew she could handle the scene and reminded her to phone him if there were any issues.

Cass ended the call just as Alex approached her van. She clambered out, shivering at the sudden temperature change. The wind buffeted around them, pulling her hood back from her head and causing the rough zip edge of her lapel to slap her cheek sharply. It drew a little blood and she saw concern on Alex's face. He reached out to touch her cheek just as she stepped back, stopping him before he made contact.

'I'm fine, Alex,' she yelled above the wind, not intentionally abruptly and unaware of how rude she sounded. She used a thumb to swipe at the scratch, before pulling her hood tighter and securing the fastener. Then, catching the rapidly disguised flash of hurt on his face, she smiled at him in apology for what she now realised had been a sharp retort. 'Sorry, Alex, I was a little distracted. I'm fine, honest. Have we got a plan of action?'

Alex nodded. 'Come join me in the lounge. How long till your staff get here? I'm thinking the weather is becoming a problem. Even the sided tent isn't going to hold for long in this wind.' He was almost shouting to be heard over the horrendous weather.

The temperature had dropped sharply. Shoving her hands inside her jacket pockets, Cass followed Alex into the shelter of the lounge. The experienced detectives already had two whiteboards set up with the beginnings of pertinent information starting to show. Two computers whirred on the desk to the left, set up to connect wirelessly to the force's computers via the mobile 3G service, also used for front-line officers' personal radios. Three uniformed officers sat at the small round table to the right, their cold hands wrapped around steaming cups of fresh coffee. Cass inhaled deeply, and didn't notice the groan of appreciation that escaped her lips at the scent of the fresh brew.

Alex heard and quickly poured her a cup, topping it up with milk. He remembered how she took her coffee from the odd time he'd made it in the past, which he found a little strange since he couldn't remember how his sergeant took it, half the time. But he pushed the stray thought to one side and handed her the mug, nodding as she thanked him and took a huge gulp.

'So, when are your guys getting in?' he asked again, getting straight down to business. Cass explained that she had a couple of staff coming in and that they shouldn't be too long. She couldn't do anything until the pathologist had arrived: protocol was that the doctor had to examine the body in situ before anything else happened.

'Do we have a name for the victim?' she said, almost as an afterthought.

Alex nodded. 'Yeah, she's presumed to be Susan Mackintosh, twenty-six years old. She worked at the Asda store on Leechmere Road. She has two young kids, and a husband.' He paused, realising his slip. 'I mean, had. I've sent the Family Liaison round to the home to confirm identity and make the death notification. Did you notice anything initially about the cause of death, or should I wait for the pathology report?'

'Looks like her jugular was sliced, judging by the laceration to her neck and the blood spatter on the windshield. There's also some additional bruising and injuries inconsistent with the crash but the doctor will be able to tell better when he gets her cleaned up and starts the post-mortem, which will probably be later today,' said Cass. 'I'll have Jason Knowles attend the post-mortem with his staff. Faith and Deena can deal with the vehicle when they come in for shift. Hopefully it won't be too long before it can be uplifted which should give it ample time to be dried out in the forensic bay at SL Motorbods.'

'It's a strange one, Cass. In cases like this it's often the husband or someone she knows.' A deep frown furrowed his brow at his train of thought.

Cass frowned back at him, nodding her agreement. 'Definitely seems like overkill, and shows careful planning. How could the killer know she would crash into the tree?' she asked.

A moment of silence passed between them as they sat contemplating the implications of the killer's actions.

20ᵗʰ September, 0335 hours – Hill overlooking Burley Bank

From his vantage point high above the crash site, he watched.

The cold wind had seeped into his core and he shivered, but he knew it was worth it. He needed to see what happened. He smiled as they scurried about at the bottom of the hill, erecting their tent to preserve the forensic evidence he *knew* he hadn't left behind. It was a shame they were working for nothing.

Stretching, he pushed his shoulders back, feeling the pinch as they protested.

He could be patient though; he'd had plenty of practice at waiting. Settling back into position, he pulled a box from his backpack and removed a foil wrapped square and a small flask. A slice of malt loaf and a cup of hot coffee would do for now; he could have a full meal later when he got home.

His tummy grumbled as he took his first bite and watched as yet another car arrived at the top of the hill.

20ᵗʰ September, 0340 hours – Burley Bank

Time passed quickly, though it felt slow to Cass as she drank her coffee in the lounge. Lost in thought, she jumped as the rear door was flung open and the pathologist entered. She was relieved to see Nigel Evans, and she smiled as he joined her and Alex at the table.

Nigel was an excellent doctor. He was efficient and had a dry sense of humour that could make the most horrific murder a little more bearable to deal with. A tall, kind-looking man, his eyes always sparkled whether with humour or with anger at lives taken too soon, and his hair permanently looked as if he had been dragged through a hedge backwards, though Cass was certain he must comb it. She also knew enough about him to know he liked to assess the scene and make his own judgements. She slowly rose from her seat and gave him a brief breakdown of information, before leading him out of the lounge and down to the crash site.

At the bottom of the hill, she stood back a touch and let him take the lead across the silver stepping-plates leading towards the passenger door. The intimate confines of the tent caused them to hug the edge of the vehicle tightly.

Nigel always worked verbally, his Dictaphone out of sight in his jacket pocket, but tonight his voice wouldn't be heard over the driving rain.

'Would you mind taking a few notes for me?' he asked Cass loudly over the wind. She nodded her agreement, and grabbed a pen from her hair and paper from one of the many pockets of her utility jacket. They worked deftly together, time passing quickly as Nigel commented on wounds and body positioning. Once he had finished his examination, Cass handed him the papers with her neat writing clearly legible against the stark white of the paper. Nigel then headed to the lounge while Cass found Alex to update him.

'Nigel agrees that this is a murder. There's no apparent reason for the laceration to her neck, or the bruising to the side of her face. He's going to book in the PM for tomorrow afternoon at Sunderland City General. We can get the body recovered now, but I think we may require the fire brigade. It looks like the crash has damaged the dash and steering surround and I think her legs may be trapped. We'll need to go in the passenger side to get her out – I don't want to lose any evidence by forcing the door the offender probably used to get to her. Once the body's out, the vehicle can be uplifted, and we can progress with the scene examination.'

Alex nodded his agreement and headed back to his team. Cass glanced up to the top of the hill, and saw two more crime scene vans parked by hers. She made her way up the bank to brief her team.

20th September, 0657 hours – Burley Bank

Daylight was just starting to creep through the dark clouds as the fire brigade finally freed the body. Cass worked comfortably with Johnny and Carla, bagging and tagging the hands and feet before moving on to the head. She paused for a moment, the plastic bag in her hand. She had always found that part difficult; placing a bag over someone's head seemed unnatural and alien to her. It was almost as if by doing this, a small part of her had helped kill the victim; the final dehumanising, irrevocable proof that the victim was indeed dead. It was also, however, the best way to preserve trace evidence. Cass tightened the bag with one last tug and tapped the side of the stretcher, indicating she was done.

The rain and wind had eased, and the birds had started singing in a dawn chorus that helped lift the solemn moods of the officers. Her colleagues knew it wouldn't be long before they would be relieved by the day shift and could head home to their families; and the relief showed.

'Hey, Kev, it's me. The body's out and on the way to Sunderland Royal. Carla's accompanying. Johnny and I will finish up here and get back to the nick as soon as we're done. I'll ring you when I land,' said Cass as her boss answered her call.

'No probs, that's brill. Thanks, Cass. Just spoke to Jason, he was called to a stabbing a couple of hours ago so I'll head up the PM. I've already spoken to dispatch and they're going to assign any minor jobs for the Volume Crime Team to deal with. They'll let us know if anything major comes in.'

'Great, that'll take a little off the load of the day shift. Dispatch said there are already five jobs on the command log. I'll speak to Deena and Faith about the vehicle when they get in.'

After ending the call, Cass watched as the others manoeuvred the black sack containing the young woman's body onto the stretcher and into the private ambulance operated by the on-call undertakers. As they both jumped out of the black van, Carla said, 'Anything else you need me to do once I'm done at the mortuary?'

Cass thought for a moment, before shaking her head. 'Get yourself off when you're done with your Socard entry.' All the CSIs were more than familiar with the database used to record any evidence and notes from a scene, and she knew whomever put in the first entry would let the others know the unique identification code allocated to the job. She gave a curt wave as the coroner's van made its way back up the hill and disappeared over the brow.

Alex looked up from his computer as Cass and Johnny entered the lounge, gave her a quick nod and turned back to his work, his long fingers tapping incessantly on the keyboard. She glanced over at Johnny, taking in the dark rings round his eyes and his pasty skin. He'd been in the job for five years, coming straight into the force from finishing his university degree. Cass had worked with him on several occasions now; with staffing issues the ever-present problem, staff often had to cover for one another when there were shortages. Cass knew better than to ask if something was wrong, though. He had been up since goodness knew what time at a crime scene. It was enough of an explanation for dark rings and pasty skin. She probably didn't look that great herself.

She glanced up as the officer nominated as scene loggist entered the lounge and headed towards her.

'SL Motorbods is here. Shall I let them through the cordon?'

Cass nodded before standing and following the officer out of the lounge. Johnny took a swift gulp of his now-cold coffee and caught the lounge door before it shut, jumping down the low step.

Eddie Conlon waited just outside his truck cab, the blue and white insignia shining brightly in the dawn light. Short in height anyway, he looked even smaller standing next to the large machine. His ever-present Bluetooth headset seemed glued to his ear. Cass didn't remember a time she had ever seen him without the portable device. He grinned widely as he saw her, large creases spreading through his well-weathered skin. 'Hey, Cass. How're things? Been a while since you visited for a coffee. You forgot your friend Eddie already?'

Cass smiled back at him warmly. 'Forget you, Eddie? Not possible. Just been busy. How's Elise and the baby doing?' She was glad he had picked up the call. Of the three companies the force employed to do forensic pickups, Eddie's was by far the best.

A look of pure pride washed over his tanned cheeks. 'Elise is more beautiful than ever and my boy's a little prince. He sleeps right through now, hardly ever cries.'

Cass grinned at him again. 'That's great. You need a different job, though, something that doesn't call you out at all hours of the night.'

Eddie shook his head. 'You know I wouldn't trust anyone else to do this job, Cass.' Becoming more solemn, he added, 'Heck of a hill, Burley Bank. I'll meet you at the bottom?'

She nodded, before turning and walking down the hill.

It seemed like only moments later that Eddie was heading round the bend at the bottom and out of sight, the crushed and mangled vehicle safely hidden behind the blue tarpaulin walls of his truck.

Cass stood back as Johnny took a new set of photographs of the scene now the vehicle had been removed. Crash remnants were scattered over the grassed knoll in front of the tree. The trunk was surprisingly still intact, though the outer bark showed damage and paint transfer. It almost looked as if the tree were crying bloodied tears through the cuts in its roughened skin. Johnny methodically placed markers at prudent sites around the crash scene, carefully taking long and short shots of all the visible evidence.

They couldn't start recovering anything without the images being taken first. The defence were sticklers when it came to evidence being able to be replaced in the exact same position it had been retrieved from, and it was becoming more frequent that solicitors were looking at what hadn't been done properly at a scene as opposed to what had.

Cass paused in her examination and said 'Johnny, what do you think of this?' as she motioned with her hand towards a rectangular indentation in the grass.

Johnny straightened and glanced over. 'A bag, or a case maybe? Looks heavy, judging by the depth. It's probably something the paramedics put down.'

Cass nodded thoughtfully as Johnny turned back round. She pulled a tape measure from one of the many pockets on her sleeveless utility jacket, and quickly measured the outline. 'Twenty-eight inches by sixteen. Strange.'

They had been processing the scene for almost an hour and were just finishing when Alex came down the hill. 'Have we got anything? The search team are here to do their bit.'

Cass shook her head. 'Nothing of value. We got a couple of cigarette butts but they're old and aren't likely connected. Nothing else for DNA. No footwear marks 'cos of the grass – there's indentations but no tread detail so they're useless. The best we can get from them is an approximate size. We've taken a paint sample from the tree bark, but it's pretty obvious it belongs to the victim's car. There are no tyre tracks, no other trace evidence and no scope for any kind of fingerprint examination. I think we're pretty much done, to be honest. Let the team have their look, but I don't think they'll find anything.'

Alex sighed. 'Can you make sure Deena and Faith update me as soon as they've completed the vehicle examination?'

Cass nodded as Alex turned and headed back to the lounge. 'Think that's us finished, Johnny. Get yourself back to the nick. Just put your notes through Socard and get yourself off. I'll check in with you later.'

20th September, 0740 hours – Hill overlooking Burley Bank

He stood, his form obscured by a large tree in the wooded area at the top of the steep hill and looked down over the scene of the crash.

He had maintained his position all night, watching the investigation unfold beneath him. They had been most helpful, putting up lights so he could see them moving around – so far away they looked like ants. He couldn't see who they were, but he knew who mattered.

The news crew had been hovering not too far from the fleet of police vehicles, their ever-hungry microphones sniffing the air wildly for their story. He would pick up a paper or two on the way home; a murder always made the front page.

He took in the comings and goings, noting with interest the arrival of the large truck that took the woman's car away. He couldn't see the logos from his position, but he saw the colours. He would have a look on the internet when he got home. There couldn't be that many companies that specialised in uplifting crash cars from a murder scene. It was paranoia that made him careful. If he found the company, he could double-check he hadn't left anything in the vehicle. Which naturally he knew he hadn't.

But as it paid to be prepared, it also paid to be cautious.

He checked the area around him carefully, making sure he hadn't forgot anything, and headed through the wooded area to where he had parked his car. He was tired now; it had been a long night. He was looking forward to a satisfying sleep, one which he hoped would clear his mind. He knew he needed to lay low for a while, and he knew he would use this time to plan his next show.

He liked comparing what he did to a show. Or maybe a sequel. Either way, it would be spectacular.

Chapter Three

20th September, 1005 hours – Ryhope Police Station

Danny White was annoyed. He glared at himself in the large mirror on the rest room wall, taking deep breaths to calm his temper, as his troubled brown eyes stared back.

His ex-wife had some nerve, ringing him randomly and ignoring him when he'd told her he was at a scene. He'd made the mistake of telling her his job was up for review, thanks to the government cuts. Granted, he was pissed at the time; but that was no excuse. She'd left it two whole weeks, just long enough for him to believe she wouldn't make an issue of it, before ringing him to discuss his child maintenance payments. He hadn't even lost his job yet and she was already demanding to know how much he'd be paying towards their two girls. He had no intention of not paying maintenance: his girls were all he worked for.

But she spoke as if money was the only thing that mattered. She'd been talking of upping sticks and taking the girls with her, all because of the new man she'd met: a solicitor, of all things. She wanted to take *his* girls to the other end of the country and she was the one screaming at him down the phone while he was working.

He'd felt like a complete prick in front of his team – he couldn't get a word in edgeways through her damned ranting. He'd finally pulled the phone from his ear just as she had slammed the receiver down.

He had his meeting with Human Resources (HR) later that afternoon when he would be told whether he was at risk of being finished, and he wasn't looking forward to it. He knew no one else was, either. There used to be a time when the police force was a job for life, a family. Now he felt like nothing more than a number in the lottery of politics.

First, though, he had to update the boss. He sighed deeply, feeling his anger dissipate as he wished he had more to report. Quickly he splashed his face, patted it dry and strode towards the Major Incident Room.

The door to the office slammed shut and Alex looked up. He sighed as the sergeant of the search team entered the expansive room and purposefully strode towards him. The weedy-looking sergeant didn't look the type to manage himself, let alone the staff he had under him as a search team. His floppy hair gave him an almost cartoon look and he was almost short enough to be comical, but Alex had worked with him before. He knew Danny White ran the best team in the department.

'Alex,' said Danny, pulling up a chair and sitting down quickly, 'In all honesty, I've never seen such a clean murder. The team haven't found anything that could prove useful. Here's the report.' He handed Alex a couple of sheets of paper.

'It's OK Danny, it happens. We're waiting on forensics from the vehicle. Hopefully that will bring something to the forefront.'

Danny nodded, before jumping to his feet and leaving the office as quickly as he had arrived.

Alex rubbed his tired eyes, longing for the bed he knew was a way off yet. There were days when he thought he was too old for this job, and this was one of them. At thirty-seven, he was hardly past his prime; but long shifts, lack of sleep and the cases he worked sometimes took their toll.

He glanced at the photo on his untidy desk, taking a moment to allow the smiling faces to bring him a feeling of calm. He missed his family. They all still lived in Edinburgh, except him. In the photo, his mum had her arm around his waist, smiling up proudly at her son. His five brothers and two sisters all stood around them, white teeth showing in their wide grins. He was the eldest of the family. The photo had been taken on the day of his graduation from probationer to police officer. His then fiancée, Helen, was also in the photo. Alex had moved to Sunderland with Helen just after the photo had been taken. It was where her family came from; and not aware at the time of how many marriages involving police officers fail, they had swiftly fallen into the trap. Sure enough, his now ex-wife had eventually got sick of the endless work calls, the overtime without notice and never having him there. They hadn't got around to having kids, so the break-up had been swift; but painful for both of them. Helen couldn't speak to him now without trying to start an argument. Nowadays, she only ever phoned when she wanted something.

Alex shook his head, wondering where this sudden pang of emotion had come from. He forced his thoughts to the back of his mind, and looked again at his desk. It resembled the scene of a ransacking, with paper strewn everywhere. He was a tidy person by nature and this stage of the investigation had always bugged him. He was busy organising the information to hand over to the department's document reader.

He'd just finished giving his first briefing to the day-shift staff after returning from the scene at around 8.30 a.m. The various sergeants had been allocated the numerous tasks required. He had once been one of those sergeants, and didn't envy them the job of rushing about all over and getting what they needed. He pulled out his Policy Book, essentially his job bible, from under an overhang on the mountainous pile of papers and jotted down his updates on the briefings.

He glanced at the clock and cursed under his breath. He hated the clock on the office wall, the same as everyone else, he guessed. It taunted him with its ticks and tocks, always stealing time away when he was busy and adding time on when the job was slow. It read 10.30 a.m. and he knew the post-mortem was booked in for 1.30 p.m. which was a whole three hours away. It wasn't a necessary part of his job to attend, but he always did. With any murder comes a feeling of attachment to the body, a feeling of obligation to find out the truth about what happened. It made him want to come to work and do his job. And at times like this, when he was sleep deprived and his head felt as if it would explode, the feeling made him stay to ensure he was doing the best he could for the victim, in this case Susan Mackintosh.

He frowned; he had just read the interim report from the Family Liaison Officer, which indicated strongly that Brian Mackintosh, Susan's husband, had not been the one who murdered her. Susan's mother had vouched for his alibi; that one of the children was ill and he had been up most of the night seeing to the child while his mother-in-law had taken care of tidying up and putting the youngest child to bed before watching TV on the couch with him. The DC he had nominated to look into Susan's lifestyle would tell him soon enough if there were any problems in their marriage, or any other skeletons in Susan's closet. But thus far, it was looking decidedly like the husband wasn't involved.

Which obviously begged the question: who had killed Susan, and why?

Suddenly his stomach grumbled, reminding him he hadn't eaten since yesterday lunchtime. Over the years he had learned that eating before a post-mortem was the best thing. For some reason, if he didn't he always craved pizza afterwards. And pizza meant extra hours in the gym.

He grabbed his wallet and mobile from the desk drawer, checking that he had some cash, and then pulled a set of keys off the unmarked car rack before heading to the MIT office. Making a beeline for Laura, the document reader, he said, 'Get this onto HOLMES as quick as you can. It's for the Mackintosh murder. If anyone needs me, I'll be at the mortuary.'

Not intending to seem rude, he paused as he turned and added a thank-you.

20th September, 1040 hours – Ryhope Police Station

Cass glanced at the clock in the corner of the computer screen and pushed back her chair, stretching in an effort to un-kink her back. She had managed to log the exhibits through Socard, had transferred her scene notes, checked the notes done by Carla and Johnny and printed off the photo thumbnails she knew she would need. She was just about to get up when the phone rang.

'Cass, it's Kevin. Johnny's going to finish his nine hours then go home instead of claiming the overtime. Carla's due back in at 2 p.m. so we shouldn't be too short-staffed. How's it going your end?'

'Not too bad. You got a pen? The Socard reference, in case you don't have it is SEP1532/13. I've already printed off Johnny and Carla's scene notes as well as the image thumbnails for the file. Johnny tell you there wasn't a lot of evidence?'

'Yeah, he mentioned it. Hopefully Deena and Faith will get something from the car. You haven't forgot the meeting with the dreaded Hartside tomorrow, have you?' Cass could almost see Kevin grimace down the phone at speaking the name of the Crime Department's Detective Inspector.

'No, I've not forgot. Not looking forward to hearing how the proposed cuts are going to affect us, like, but I shall be there nonetheless. I'm gonna brief Deena and Faith when they come in. Can you manage if I sneak home for a few hours shut-eye?'

'Yeah sure, Cass. You're on backs tonight, right?'

'Yeah I should still be in for 5 p.m. though. Fred's on tonight too. Who's covering central?'

'Penelope, but only until 10.30 p.m. – she has an early appointment with occ health tomorrow. You and Fred will be on your own until finishing but I'm sure you guys can manage.'

'Yeah, that's fine, Kev. Right, I'm gonna go put the kettle on for the girls. I'll speak to you later this afternoon.'

Cass busied herself in the small kitchen, quickly brewing the new blend she had picked up from Starbucks the day before, and by the time Deena and Faith walked through the door it was already poured into cups for them.

Before she knew it, they had both left to deal with the car and she was alone in her office once again.

20ᵗʰ September, 1205 hours – Ryhope Police Station

Cass looked up as Alex entered her office and sat down. He silently handed her a brown bag, then unwrapped his own sandwich and took a large bite. Cass was a little taken aback, not just by his presumption that she would be hungry, but that that he had actually brought her some lunch.

Catching her lack of manners, she said, 'Thanks, Alex,' and unwrapped the paper, revealing what appeared to be a chicken salad sandwich.

'Hope that's OK?' mumbled Alex with his mouth full. Cass nodded, taking a bite. It wasn't often she stopped for lunch at work, and it made a pleasant change. They ate together in comfortable silence for a few minutes, both lost in their own worlds.

Cass liked Alex; there was some kind of chemistry between them that she didn't quite understand, and in the rare moments of complete honesty it scared her. This, however, was not one of those moments, and Alex pulled her from her thoughts by crumpling his sandwich wrapper and accurately throwing it at the recycle bin in the corner. He knew she would have updated her staff and sent them on their merry way, and requested a quick update before filling her in on the investigation so far.

After the lunch with Cass, Alex found himself sitting at traffic lights en route to the hospital, pondering his reasons for buying her lunch. He had seen the surprise in her eyes, and he thought he had seen something else.

He frowned. Since Helen had left, there'd been no other women. He wasn't the sort to go to the pubs and clubs, trawling for one-night stands to fulfil whatever needs he had. He much preferred a night at the pictures, quite happy to be one of those saddos who sit there alone munching on their popcorn. Films had always given him a release. From the time he was a troubled teenager, he would wander down to the local cinema and sit for hours working through his problems as he watched the stories unfold. He still often found himself sitting in the dark alone, watching as stories were shown on screens bigger than he ever imagined as a child that they would be.

As he got older, he found dining out at one of his chosen restaurants in Sunderland or Ryhope alleviated some of the loneliness left by Helen, giving him the chance to talk to people who weren't colleagues. Alex often contemplated upping sticks and moving back to Edinburgh, going to work with Alistair or James in the Lothian Police Force. They were always on his case to do that.

But he never did.

A horn blared behind him and he realised the light had turned green. He gave his head a shake, deciding he was way too tired to be contemplating such deep and meaningful things. He had most likely imagined whatever he thought he saw with Cass. There was no reason for someone like her to go for someone like him anyway. He knew the rumours surrounding dating officers – a different girl in every station etc. He wasn't like that but the stigma was still there.

Pulling himself from his train of thought, he continued to the hospital and found a parking place. He had plenty of time before the post-mortem was due to start, but he always liked to check in with the pathologist prior to his intrinsic examination of the body. He had a lot of respect for Nigel Evans; he'd worked quite a few cases with the unusual doctor and always found him to be pleasant and open. He answered questions with ease and didn't mind Alex suiting and booting up to be in the room with the body. Alex always had the option to stand in the viewing area of the morgue, but he had always liked to be in the thick of things. It was essentially how he processed what was happening.

He made his way down the corridor, inhaling that metallic, chemical-enhanced smell that permeated the morgue. Pausing at the office, he signed the visitor register, noting that Kevin Lang and his team were already there. Alex nodded in satisfaction: early attendance might mean an early start.

In the next room, Kevin stood talking to Nigel, with two members of the CSI team that Alex didn't recognise.

'Kevin, Nigel,' he said. He waited to be introduced to the other members of staff.

'Boss,' said Kevin. 'Billy, James, this is DCI McKay.'

'Just call me Alex,' he said, making quick eye contact with the CSIs. He always ensured people knew he was approachable. Many inspectors and sergeants demanded they were addressed by rank. In that respect Alex was completely different. He accepted boss or sir, merely because he knew some people liked the rank structure; but generally most people called him by his first name.

Nigel shook Alex's hand. 'Shall we begin?' Alex nodded, and they all followed as Nigel left the room.

Once suited up, with blue plastic coverings over their shoes, and masks over their faces, they headed into the mortuary. Nigel didn't bother introducing the mortuary technician by name. He was the only one currently employed by the hospital.

Gordon Perkins was a funny little man. He had a shiny, balding head, with wisps of hair at the sides which he tried vainly to place strategically over his bald patch. The wisps however, were far too fine and gave him a comical, old-man look, when in reality he was in his mid-forties. He dressed for the occasion in blue hospital scrubs and was armed with his tools. He stood back as Kevin took photographs of the clothed victim.

Gordon then methodically undressed the body, encountering a little trouble as he removed Susan's top and unhooked her bra. 'Doesn't matter how much practice you get, sometimes these suckers are stubborn,' he joked lightly. The remnants of Rigor Mortis were still present and Susan's body was obviously stiff as Gordon manoeuvred her back into position on the table. Her injuries were stark against the illumination in the mortuary. The body was rinsed and then the horrible sawing noise filled the room as Gordon deftly made a Y incision across Susan's chest.

Nigel stepped forward and the post-mortem began in earnest. Alex stood out of the way, allowing the doctor and the CSIs to do what they needed to do. He still found the post-mortem process enthralling to watch; it worked like a well-oiled machine with the 'dirty' CSI handling the samples passed by the doctor and handing them in tubs to the 'clean' CSI, who quickly packaged up the doctor's exhibits. Kevin, as photographer, took snaps as he thought necessary and stood with Alex when he wasn't needed.

Nigel talked constantly throughout the examination, recording his thoughts on a Dictaphone. He lightened the mood slightly with his humour, but made his respect for Susan obvious.

Alex looked on as Nigel paused at the wound on Susan's neck.

'Tweezers,' he said to Gordon, who handed him a sterile pair, a frown showing on his face. Nigel inserted the tapered ends into the wound on her neck and drew out something small and metallic. As he popped it into a small metal dish it made an audible ping and Kevin leaned in with his camera, snapping away.

Alex moved forward, wanting to see what it was they were looking at. Inside the dish lay a small, silver, bloodied triangle.

'Looks like the tip of a knife,' said Kevin, looking up at Alex.

Nigel was frowning in the background. 'Looks like, but I don't think it is. It's a deliberate wound, cutting through the jugular. There's nothing in that section of the neck hard enough to damage steel.'

'Are you saying you think this was placed there after her throat was cut?' Alex asked.

Nigel shook his head. 'I'm saying it's unlikely to have been placed there by a knife breaking while making the wound. It's possible it was already in her neck; but if it had already been in there I would expect to see tissue growing around the object, which I don't.'

Alex nodded, concentration furrowing his brow. He continued to ponder the object as it was bagged and tagged, finding his mind wandering back to it through the rest of the PM.

He rarely waited around after the post-mortem; he usually had all the information he needed by the end and plenty of other things to do, as was the case this time also – but despite this, Alex waited. Eventually, Kevin and his team came out from the morgue, and he saw Kevin motion the others to meet him back at the station.

'Mind if I grab a lift back to the nick with you?' he asked Alex, already knowing the answer.

Chapter Four

He was there. She could feel his presence. She knew he was watching her for the smallest sign she was awake. Struggling to control her breathing, in and out slowly, she tried to look relaxed. She could already smell the sweet tang of stale alcohol on his breath and suddenly her instincts went into overdrive – he knew she wasn't sleeping. Her eyes flung open just in time to see his fist swinging towards her face.

Cass woke with a jump, sweat drenching her forehead as the remnants of the nightmare left her. Frowning, she tried to steady the pounding in her chest. She hated those dreams. They crept up on her out of the blue. Worse still, she hated him. Hated him for giving her reason to dream, hated him for never letting her forget.

Shaking, she drew in an unsteady breath and for a moment she let the memories flood through her mind. She remembered the sudden burst of pain as his fist had connected, and the warm flow of blood as it had streamed from her nose. She recalled the metallic taste as the red liquid oozed into the back of her throat causing her to gag. And she remembered the feeling of utter fear as he dragged her from the duvet by her hair. Cass had curled into a tight ball, trying to protect herself as he readied his foot and aimed for her ribs.

Her breath caught in her throat as the most difficult memories threatened to escape and Cass forced them back into the box at the back of her mind. Her therapist had taught her the trick, telling her it was important to remember sometimes, but on her terms, when *she* could control them.

Please stop shaking. She held her hands in front of her, trying to steady her breathing and slow the quivering.

Ollie whined suddenly, startling her, and she realised he had his head on the bed beside her, silently asking if she was OK. She stroked the downy fur behind his ears.

'I'm OK boy,' she whispered, looking into his chocolaty eyes. From the time he was a pup, she had always loved how full of expression he was. He understood her every word, and loved her with fierce loyalty.

A flicker caught her eye as one of the numbers on the digital clock changed and she groaned as she registered the time. She'd only been in bed for a couple of hours.

As exhausted as she was, she knew sleep wouldn't return. Deciding it was time for coffee, she dragged herself from the bed, stepped over Ollie who had already decided it was much too early to get up and had curled back up in a ball beside the bed.

The afternoon sun lit up the kitchen as Cass poured a large cup and inhaled the aroma gratefully. She couldn't remember the point in her life when she had first begun to enjoy the caffeine hit when she first got out of bed, but it had grown almost to the point of obsession. She allowed herself a moment to savour the rich, smooth taste of the first sip as it travelled down, warming her insides on its journey. Then she popped the mug on the side, and grabbed the phone from its charger.

As the slightly husky voice said hello, Cass smiled.

'Hey, Mama. I haven't woken you have I?' Her mother worked shifts and never knew from one day to the next what she'd be doing.

'No love,' said her mum, clearing her throat softly. If Cass had, she wouldn't have said anything.

'How are you? I got your voicemail last night. I hate it when you get called out to god knows what in the middle of the night. Was it bad?'

'Fairly. A woman was murdered. Not much evidence at the scene. I got home a few hours ago.'

'A few hours? How come you're not in bed? You're not infallible you know.'

'I was Mum. I woke up. I'm heading back to work soon anyway.'

Cass took a deep slurp of her coffee, already knowing what was coming next.

'You had the dream again didn't you? Cass, I really wish you would just move back home. It's not healthy living on your own in the middle of a forest. You need to be with people.'

'Mama, it's a wood not a forest. And I'm not on my own, I've got Ollie. I can't move back. This is my home. You know that.'

'I know,' sighed her mum, 'But I can wish can't I? Is it still OK for me to come up next month? I've got the leave booked in from work.'

'Yeah course it is, Mama. I'm looking forward to it. Might still have to work but I'll try and get some cover. You remember I told you Kevin's missus has cancer? Well it doesn't look like she'll last much longer. I think he's gonna need time off soon.'

'Aw, the poor man. Cancer is awful. I hope you get some cover though. I'm looking forward to spoiling you with pancakes and shopping, my daughter.'

Cass smiled into the phone. Calling her mum mama, and being called daughter in return was their little thing.

'Cass, that's the doorbell. Ring me later. Love you lots and lots.'

'Like jelly tots,' said Cass into the phone as she ended the call.

She wandered back into the bedroom with her coffee, grinning as she saw Ollie still flaked out beside the bed. It had taken her a while to wind down when she'd got home. She'd taken Ollie out for a well-deserved walk before crawling into bed.

Ollie had been handed in at the police station when he was just a shaggy grey-haired pup. Cass had happened to walk into the front office and saw him in a cardboard box, waiting to be picked up by the local animal shelter. He had been shivering in terror, looking at her with his huge brown eyes, and she was lost. She had taken him home that night, and stroked him comfortingly as he howled his fears every night for a week. She'd talked to him gently in hushed tones while stroking his downy puppy fur. Eventually he understood that she wasn't going to leave him in a cardboard box, or beat him as the constant cowering told her he had been. He settled in and Cass loved how he was always there when she got home. Because of her job, she had invested in state of the art technology for him: an electronic chip installed into his neck that acted as a swipe key for the hatch built in to her back door so he would have freedom of movement. The garden at the back was large and Ollie had never once tried to escape. He adored Cass with that unending loyalty that only dogs have. She could do no wrong in his eyes. For Ollie, life was perfect.

She smiled down at him. Lazy dog. She wished she could sleep like him, always happy and for solid lengths of time. Cass had never been a good sleeper. She functioned well on a few hours; anything more than four was a welcomed rarity.

Pulling on some joggers and a T-shirt, she grabbed the dog and headed out of the back door, walking him again before she returned to the office.

At the back of her overgrown garden was a large gate leading to a track. The gate was blocked in place by foliage and Cass and Ollie both used the nearby stile to exit the garden. Winding through a large wooded area, the path came to an end at a field. Ollie loved the wood, he chased sticks and dug for rabbits, though if he ever encountered one for real he just froze and stared in comical horror. Cass had always found it relaxing to walk him through the woods, walking for miles every day, probably a little out of guilt for leaving him on his own so much, but mostly because he loved the walks as much as she did.

An hour later she returned home, Ollie panting loudly as his large pink tongue lolling out of the side of his mouth. He took a drink of water from his bowl in the kitchen, left a trail of large wet drips all along the hall and stairs, and sloped back off to his bed. Cass glanced at him as she walked past to the bathroom. He really was the perfect dog for her, he loved his walks, was always there when she needed him and didn't grumble or destroy the house when he was on his own. Which was a good thing – because it wasn't long before Ollie was left to his own devices once more, as Cass headed back into the office.

20th September, 1515 hours – SL Motorbods, Sunderland

He was satisfied.

He'd come to the garage under the guise of having his vehicle fixed, and had been left alone enough to observe the proceedings within the forensic bay at the back of the garage itself. Not that his vehicle needed repairs. He knew pretty much all he needed to and usually did any work himself. He could also sabotage when required. He grinned to himself as he remembered how easy it had been to access Susan's car. He'd fed her a small untruth about an imaginary rattle, and she'd handed over her keys.

Women! So stupid.

Thinking ahead when he had left that morning, he'd worn a wig. Now sweaty and itchy, he had to resist the urge to scratch at the hemline.

Obviously warm in the rare British autumn heat, the two women had left the shutter open to the partitioned bay and he overheard them giggling like school-girls at the young, blond mechanic who kept wandering past the door, asking if they needed anything and offering coffee; and he overheard the things they had found, or hadn't found as the case may be.

He knew he hadn't been careless; he was too good for that. But it felt good to be certain.

The police had nothing to connect him to the crime. Well, nothing other than what he chose to give them. He smiled softly, finding humour in the puzzled looks he imagined on their faces at his little gift. He'd read in one of the many books he had perused throughout his lifetime, that leaving a signature was something most serial killers did. He hadn't really been bothered but he knew the metal shard would puzzle the police, and would continue to do so long after he had gone. And he loved the fact that they would never know what it meant. Especially seeing as how it didn't actually mean anything – nothing other than him saying 'I'm smarter than you are'.

The mechanic who'd been dealing with his vehicle suddenly appeared. 'Your pads were worn virtually to the metal. We've put you some new ones on but you'll need to give them chance to settle in so take it easy when braking for a few days. You can get your keys and pay at reception.'

He smiled back at the mechanic, and for a moment allowed himself to appear completely stupid. The flush of pink on his cheeks, forced through him biting at his inside cheek, portrayed apparent embarrassment at his mistake. He did as he'd been told and paid at reception, before wandering back through the garage and getting into the car left behind by his mother when she died.

He would never use his own car for reconnaissance work; it had potential to be traced back to him. His mother's reliable, boring Clio however, recently fitted with false plates to avoid detection, blended well into the background like so many other vehicles.

Driving steadily, well within the speed limit, he made his way to the Asda store in Leechmere. He wouldn't normally push his luck this far, but he had a hankering to overhear whatever rumours might be circulating the place where she had worked. And sure enough, as soon as he walked in the door, he was confronted with a picture of Susan smiling out from a board near the customer service desk. Flowers adorned the desk, and without trying he could smell their sickly sweet scent.

His eyes flashed slightly.

He hated flowers, didn't see the point in pulling them from the ground at all let alone presenting them in bunches.

For a moment he remembered his mother forcing him to cut thorns off roses as she prepared floral arrangements for the church. She had sneered as he cut himself, telling him to grow up and be a man, and then proceeded to soak the cuts in TCP, watching for the wince as the liquid burned and stung.

Yes, he hated flowers.

Realising his anger for what it was, he knew he had to calm himself. Breathing deep, slow breaths for a moment, he felt his blood pressure sink back down.

The sudden sneeze took him by surprise, causing the woman behind the counter to say 'Bless you.' He nodded at her in thanks, deciding she would be the one he would talk to.

Holding back his excitement, he feigned interest as she told him that Susan Mackintosh was dead, that she'd been a valued and much loved member of staff and he found himself phasing out slightly as she waffled on. He was almost impressed with the visible prick of tears in her eyes as she went on to tell him about the 'two wee babies' poor Susan had left behind.

His eyes grew dark, however, as the woman explained that Susan had been brutally raped and then murdered.

Raped? I'm no rapist.

The sudden onslaught of anger threatened his composure. Quickly, feigning trauma, he walked back out of the store.

Once settled in his car, he punched his fist hard on the dashboard, barely registering the pulse of pain in his knuckles. Raped? That was the rumour? That he was the lowest of the low scumbag who would rape a woman before killing her? Not that he hadn't considered it on occasion of course, there was definitely something about controlling the person you were having relations with, but rape? The papers hadn't mentioned rape. He was certain the post-mortem would show no evidence of such a crime. But just being associated with the word made him see red. He had some class, after all.

He'd already made a decision on who his next victim would be and was more certain than ever that he'd made the right choice.

The next one wouldn't be on the same scale. There was no chance that rape would be on the rumour mill headlines.

He knew he had to wait before he acted. And despite his breath hissing out from between pursed lips, he was prepared to do just that. It was all planned to happen in three weeks. The pitiful town of Ryhope would never see it coming.

First though, he had to get his anger out, before he did something stupid and made a mistake. That's what all the good self-help books had proclaimed after all. It was anger that made a person reckless.

And being reckless was something he would not entertain.

He drove over to the factory units and unlocked the central door using his key. Entering the unit, he locked the door behind him. He took in a deep breath, smelling the sawdust and machine oil, and he smiled as the scent instantly calmed his raging anger.

Turning on the large circular saw, he felt more of his anger dissipate and carefully, he began crafting his latest piece. The heavy oak was warm in his hands, and he felt the vibrations judder through him, helping him relax a little more as he became engrossed in his task. It would be hours before he moved now. The wood had to be manipulated well and handled carefully in order to be formed into the perfection he knew it could achieve.

On the wall to his rear, the large black cross looked down, waiting to be mounted onto his work when he was finished. Soon it wouldn't be able to judge him any more and a new cross would take its honoured place.

20ᵗʰ September, 1750 hours – Ryhope Police Station

Cass groaned as she stretched; the bland office chairs not the comfiest thing to sit on for lengthy stretches of time. Rubbing her blurry eyes, she glared at the computer screen for a moment.

She'd spoken to Kevin when he returned from the post-mortem and had frowned at the news of the metal shard. If Nigel believed it hadn't been left behind by a knife, that was good enough for her. A close study of the object had yielded no clues to its origins. One edge showed tool mark striations, but without a tool to compare it to, the marks were useless.

The exhibits had all now been handed to the dedicated Exhibits Officer, who had removed them into the Major Incident Store for the time being anyway. But the metal shard was bugging Cass and she couldn't seem to put it out of her mind. What was it and why was it there?

She looked up as she heard female voices in the corridor outside her office. Deena and Faith stopped at her open door and glanced in.

'Sorry, Ben, go ahead,' said Deena, her hand motioning towards the side.

Ben Cassidy entered, carrying a large box.

'First of three, Cass. If you're busy I've got cover in the front office. I can take them straight down to the lab and unpack them if you like?'

Ben worked the front desk at the station. She kept herself to herself and Cass had often wondered what her story was, how she had come to work for the police. 'That would be great, Ben, if you don't mind. Are they heavy? I can get Frank to give you a hand if you like?'

'Handyman's on his rounds. It's fine, Cass, they're not heavy. I'll take care of it.'

Cass watched thoughtfully as Ben's slender frame walked off. She thought she detected a slight limp in her gait, but filed the thought away before turning her attention back to Deena and Faith. 'How'd it go with the car?'

Deena shook her head and frowned, 'We'll update Socard in a sec, but there's nothing there except her blood and watermarks.'

Cass nodded, 'Good job anyway.'

Moments later, Deena returned and placed a steaming cup of coffee on the desk in front of Cass. 'The photos have been uploaded onto the central database. Figured you'd need them ASAP for the murder box.'

Cass shook her head at the dramatic name of her current task.

The term 'murder box' made the item sound much more interesting than it actually was. In reality, it was just a box, filled with information on the murder, but it was a job Cass loved doing. As hideous and stressful as any murder could be, compiling the information into a usable format allowed her mild OCD to be relieved slightly. Ensuring the box contained everything pertinent to the forensic side of the murder was her guilty pleasure, and she carefully looked over all the photos, not just from the scene, but also from the post-mortem and the vehicle examination, mulling momentarily over which ones were needed and which were essentially fluff. She took her time putting the photo booklet together; thumbnail sized images had been printed on photo paper and bound into a booklet, and these would later be used as a reference source when it came to pulling the case together. She also placed copies of the disks within the box, so that if Alex wanted to he could see all of the photos and not just what she had selected. Cass had already printed out a copy of the scene exam notes entered by her, Johnny and Carla and she filed them with the corresponding statements. Having the box ready meant the Forensic Strategy Meetings would run much smoother as all the information would be to hand.

20th September, 2330 hours – Ryhope Police Station

Engrossed in her work, Cass didn't notice the time passing. She took long sip of her coffee and grimaced as the cold liquid settled on her tongue. A thin film of skin from the top of the drink coated her lips and she gagged. 'Yuck,' she muttered and wiped her hand across her mouth in disgust.

She glanced at the clock above the doorway and jumped as Alex suddenly appeared.

'Hey, Cass, I'm gonna head off. I'm definitely in need of a shower and my bed. How about you?' he asked.

Cass looked at him, the implications of his accidental offer sinking in. She felt her cheeks flush and nodded, grabbing her warrant card from the slot in the computer and her handbag from its spot under the desk. Religiously, she locked her office door, and checked that the door to the CSI office was also secure. It was a habit instilled in her since she'd first started working for the force. While she'd been in her probation period, someone had managed to slip through the entrance door from front office and entered the CSI office, stealing various belongings before making off. It had been the station joke for weeks, the forensic department having to fingerprint their own office but the thought that one of the CSIs could have been present in the office had sent chills down their spines. They'd all taken to making sure the offices were locked up when no one was in.

Cass followed Alex down the stairs and realised she had unconsciously parked next to him. She flashed him a quick smile as she jumped into her car. Twisting the key in the ignition, she felt her heart sink as the engine sputtered but refused to turn over. She tried again but it made a pitiful sound and died.

Damn car, not again. Please work.

As it sputtered once more, Cass berated herself again for choosing this car. It had suffered one problem after another, and her bank balance had certainly suffered too after paying for all the repairs.

She turned as the passenger door opened. 'You OK?' asked Alex.

'Stupid car won't start. It's alright, I'll call the RAC. Get yourself home, you need the rest,' said Cass, trying to disguise the frustration in her tone.

Shaking his head with a frown, Alex said, 'I'll give you a lift. You'd be here hours waiting for recovery. The handyman can look at it tomorrow.'

'It's fine, Alex honest, I don't wanna put you out. I don't live in Sunderland. It's out of your way.'

'It's no problem. I'll take you home and grab you in the morning.' Alex was adamant but Cass felt torn, she really didn't want to put him to any trouble. He was tired, and to her it was a big deal for a colleague to know where she lived. She'd grown accustomed to keeping her private life separate from work and none of the CSIs had been to her home, let alone a police officer. On the other hand, she also didn't want to sit around waiting for hours for a mechanic to tell her he couldn't do anything and then have to make her own way home later regardless.

'OK,' she agreed finally.

'Check you out with your posh car,' she said as she settled into the plush leather interior of the new model Audi.

He grinned at her, 'It was the only one they had in the showroom. You think it says poser?'

'Well it definitely doesn't scream deadbeat like mine does,' she said with a grim smile

They fell into a comfortable silence, the radio playing quietly in the background and Alex followed her directions almost on auto-pilot. As they finally pulled onto a dirt track, darkened by trees growing on either side, his grumpiness became apparent. 'For Christ's sake, Cass, where on earth do you live? Timbuktu?'

'Sorry,' she said, 'We're almost there.'

Her breath caught a little in her throat as it always did when her cottage came into view. The moon was bright and full, casting a blue hue that gave the cottage an almost mystical glow.

'It reminds me of the little cottage in the woods of every fairy story I've ever read.' Alex said it quietly but she overheard and grinned at him, a little shy now he was at her home.

'I love it. I've had it for about six years. It still needs work doing but I'm getting it there slowly' she paused and then grabbed the bull by the horns, for once making a spontaneous offer. 'Would you like to come in for a quick cuppa before you head home?'

Alex nodded and followed her to the door and inside. He closed the front door and turned, his eyes widening as he caught the movement of something big and hairy that launched itself at him with a deep woof. Completely unprepared, he felt the weight of the thing hit him square in the chest and he flew backwards, landing hard on his backside. His eyes focused on the monster that was Ollie, just as the dog opened his mouth and started covering him with sloppy kisses.

'Oh god!' he heard Cass exclaim, 'Ollie, get off him.'

Reluctantly the dog pulled himself away from his new friend, gave him one last wet kiss and sloped off to the kitchen. Cass held out a hand, her eyes sparkling with silent laughter, and apologised as she helped pull Alex to his feet.

He smiled at her, 'You could have warned me you had a monster waiting to ambush me. Any other surprises?' he asked, jokingly checking underneath the cabinet in the hall.

A small giggle escaped as Cass led the way into the lounge and motioned for Alex to take a seat. 'Coffee?' she asked, her humour finally wearing down.

'Tea please, if that's OK? Coffee will keep me awake.'

Cass nodded and headed off to the kitchen.

Alex glanced around the room with interest. It was very homely, with wolf ornaments placed decoratively on the mantelpiece, a couple of Native American pieces of artwork on the walls, and the biggest bookshelf he thought he had ever seen jam-packed with books of all types. He sat down on the ample sofa, and without thinking, he kicked off his shoes and groaned as its plush cushions held him close in a tight hug.

Cass bustled around the kitchen, making a pot of tea. Her nerves were making her clumsy and she cursed as she spilt hot water from the kettle over the counter top. No one except her family had ever seen the cottage she called home. She'd had never been one for mixing business with pleasure and solidly maintained her personal side behind a facade of restrictions placed by being a 'supervisor' and 'having responsibilities'. And here she was with a man she barely knew in her cottage, a fact made worse by the way her insides went slightly fluttery whenever he looked at her.

When Cass finally calmed herself down enough to return to the living room, she stared in horror as she found him asleep on the sofa.

He's even took his shoes off, the cheeky sod.

Alex's long legs were tucked under him and his head rested on his hand on the arm of the couch.

What the hell do I do now? Wake him?

Shaking her head, she decided to let him be. She grabbed the tattered blanket from the back of the armchair and covered him over, closed the curtains and shut the door with a soft click.

Ollie had decided it was tea time and was crunching his biscuits loudly. Cass felt her tummy grumble in response to the thoughts of food. It was almost 8 p.m. and she hadn't eaten since the sandwich earlier.

She quickly popped some pasta in a pan and whipped up a bacon and tomato sauce, making a little extra in case Alex woke up hungry later. She let her thoughts jumble together her tired mind as she ate a bowl of the steaming food, then, deciding Ollie could wait until morning for another walk, she let him out to do his business.

By now she was pretty much working on auto-pilot and she undressed and fell into bed. The final thought she registered was a flashback to Ollie's over-enthusiastic greeting of Alex. A smile flittered across her lips as she fell into the world of dreams.

Chapter Five

21st September, 0640 hours – Cass's Cottage

Alex groaned as he stretched his aching neck slightly. His hands made contact with the soft blanket that covered him and, confused, he forced his eyes open. The impending dawn was just starting to send cracks of light around the room, and his eyes widened as he realised he was not at home. He rubbed his face and pulled himself into a sitting position.

'Crap,' he muttered under his breath as he realised he had fallen asleep in Cass's living room. The ticking clock on the mantelpiece read 6.40 a.m.

Pulling his legs round off the couch, he saw the note on the table in front of him and quickly realised it was too dark to read. He stood, moving toward the window and opened the curtains a crack. Glancing outside, he paused and stared. The whole area had that soft glow of light that only occurred just before the sun started to rise. It caught the shadows of the trees and magically transformed them from dull silhouettes to defined shapes. His car glinted like fairy dust when the light hit the beads of moisture.

A movement caught his eye and he felt his heart pound as Cass came into view on the drive. Her chest was heaving as she breathed deeper with the exertion, the sports T-shirt under her open jacket only enhancing the view. Almost as an afterthought, he noticed the dog, lolloping beside her, and realisation dawned that she was an early riser and had taken Ollie out. Alex pulled back from the window, a soft frown on his face.

How did she manage to sneak out without me hearing? Normally a pin dropping wakes me up.

He wandered into the hall, intending to say hi and apologise for falling asleep, but as Cass walked through the door, she jumped back violently as she registered his presence.

Her brown eyes darkened and he took in the instant look of fear on her face before she could rein it back in and hide it behind her normally steady composure. Her hand had flown to her chest and she had dropped Ollie's leash instinctively. The dog had been given a start, uttering a warning 'woof' until he realised who it was. He glanced at Alex through his huge puppy eyes and sloped off towards the kitchen.

'Sorry, Cass, I didn't mean to scare you,' he said softly, purposely keeping his voice neutral as he held his hands out in front of him. A sudden stab of anger shot through him; someone had hurt her.

Cass could feel her heart beating fast underneath her fingertips. She knew she had shown more fear than was necessary for the momentary shock, but she couldn't seem to stop her heart pounding in her ears. 'It's OK, Alex. I was away with the fairies. I'm fine, you just startled me is all.'

Forcing herself to look a lot calmer than she felt, she kicked off her hiking shoes, and smiled at Alex. 'Coffee?' she asked, walking past him to the kitchen. Cass berated herself silently, wondering how the past always seemed to dictate the present as she pushed open the heavy door to the homely room.

It was the very definition of a country kitchen. Yellow pine warmed the room naturally, from the cupboard doors to the table and chairs in front of the hall door and the large welsh dresser along the back wall. Cass had hung ivy pieces around the ceiling and tiles with various food related images adorned the walls behind the sink and stove. The floor was terracotta tile and added to the warmth of the room by appearance only – Cass shivered as the cold seeped through her socks, causing her toes to curl slightly.

She made a pot of coffee, breathing slowly to calm her shattered nerves, and handed Alex a steaming mug before sitting down beside him at the small table.

'I mailed you the vehicle examiner report last night. The brakes were cut and the air bag was disengaged. The examiner has made mention that it's only possible to do that by having access to the vehicle engine section. The killer had to have done it before Susan got in the vehicle.'

Alex nodded slowly. 'I figured that might be the case. I've already got Charlie, one of the sergeants on my team, digging into her life. Told her to check into when the car last had any work done. Did we get anything back off the vehicle?'

Cass frowned and shook her head. 'Nothing out of place. They've swabbed the blood but it seems pretty obvious it belongs to Susan and not the killer. I'll go over everything fully in the strategy meeting back at the office once it's all been compiled, but there's going to be very little we can do at this stage, forensically speaking.'

Alex nodded. He'd expected as much but was still disappointed. He had a lot of information to trawl through for the investigation, but forensics always progressed a case much quicker. He felt the coffee grow heavy in his stomach as he thought about the tasks ahead.

21st September, 0930 hours – Pallion, Sunderland

He made a sandwich and sat down at the kitchen table.

It had been there since he was a child, and the top had the look of well-worn mahogany, the varnish peeling in places. Some of his few fond memories involved this table; his mother peeling potatoes and singing to herself as he'd watched. It had been one of the rare moments of lucid normality. He'd learned not to interrupt her, letting her peel until she finished singing. His father had also left her to it, sometimes passing his son a piece of bread to chew on while dinner was cooking.

He felt his expression harden. His father had been weak. Pandering to him like that.

Unfolding the newspaper, he ate some of the food as he read. *Front page news. As it should be.*

He had always understood the need to stay ahead of the game. It wouldn't do for them to find out who he was. After scanning the article to see if there was anything else he needed to know, he refolded the newspaper and placed it on top of the small pile beside the back door before he wandered into the living room and paused at his toolbox.

He slowly ran a hand along the side, feeling the rough paint brush against his slightly callused palm. He remembered the day his father died. That weak man who had provided for his wife and child all his life in a manner that was proper and correct, had died suddenly and in a most undignified way. Naked as the day he was born, in a bath full of cold water, the ruined electric radio submerged with him in the freezing water. It had been ruled an accidental death.

But he knew differently. It was most definitely *not* an accident.

The toolbox represented everything his father had not been. It was strong, logical and practical. He'd found it in the garage among the items his mother had inherited from his grandparents.

And he'd claimed it as his own.

He had handled every item in the box, and added new tools as he came across them provided they were useful. His mother had always loved how strong his hands were. She had loved the wooden items he created, telling him over and over how he was such a good boy.

Even at forty she still thought I was a good boy. Stupid bitch couldn't see past the nose on her face.

The sudden rage that flowed through him shocked him. Despite everything he felt he had put up with from his pathetic father and god-fearing mother, he had always been very good at holding his emotion in check, at least when he was with others.

His mother had never been subjected to the temper he knew lurked beneath the surface. She had attended her church and forced her godliness onto him and hadn't once realised how condescending she had always sounded to him. She genuinely believed that by ridding him of sins she had raised him to be a good son and a good man. He grinned to himself, knowing it wasn't entirely his mother's fault that he wasn't – she hadn't known her son half as well as she had thought she did. His life had never been about pleasing her. Ever since he was a child, he had known he was different. Everything that he did was controlled, with the pros and cons measured up prior to him acting.

His penchant for working with wood had developed when he was a teenager. It had started as an escape – he could do odd jobs for the church and his mother would leave him alone, believing him to be doing 'god's work'. But he found he enjoyed the way the wood felt in his hands. He liked allowing it to develop and then seeing the finished article. He also enjoyed the way the wood withered and crackled when burned. Many a time he had produced a masterpiece, just to sit and watch the flames take it. It was more to do with the control it gave him.

Precision and forward planning were how he had managed to do such a good job of killing Susan. He had checked the papers and listened to the news. The police knew it was murder. But he was confident they didn't have a clue who was to blame.

Now, it was time for his research to begin in earnest. The old man was ripe for the picking. He was always on the same bench, the half-drunk bottle of cheap, white cider in his hand as he snored loudly or yelled random comments at people passing by. He had promised himself that his next show would be more spectacular after all. And he had every intention of fulfilling his promise.

Grabbing his sandwich and toolbox, he wandered out of the front door to his car.

21st September, 1120 hours – Ryhope Police Station

Cass looked up from her desk as Frank Reynolds knocked politely before entering. Aged in his forties with greying hair tidily swept back, he looked every bit the part in his blue police issue coveralls. Frank had been the handyman for the Ryhope station since well before Cass had started there. She had always found him a little lacking in personality, but he was reliable and always got the job done.

Today was no exception as Frank opened his mouth to speak.

'Sorry to interrupt you, Cass. I've had a look at your car. When I checked the connections they were corroded. I think you're probably going to need a new battery.'

He carefully placed her keys on her desk and stepped backwards.

'Thanks, Frank. Much appreciated. I'll sort something out.'

'I've let the engine run for an hour or so on the jump cables, so you should have enough power to get to the shop for a new one. Skippers on the sea front is reasonable if you don't have someone in mind. He'll fit it for free too.'

'I'll do that. Thanks again, Frank,' said Cass, turning her attention back to the screen.

Frank turned to leave, then paused and looked back.

'You seem busy. Nothing too serious I hope,'

'It was for the victim,' sighed Cass. 'Murder enquiry,' she added with a sweep of her hand over the untidy piles of paperwork she was attempting to compile on her desk.

'If you're busy I can pop out and get the new battery for you?'

'Thanks for the offer but I can pass the seafront on my way home,' said Cass, a little distracted as she shuffled a pile of papers, her brow furrowing in concentration as her train of thought returned to the investigation.

Taking the cue, Frank turned quietly and left the office.

Moments later, her mobile rang, the tone shattering the silence in the office.

'Cass Hunt,' she said into the microphone after swiping the screen to answer.

'Cass? This is Barbara Whitstead of the *Sunderland Echo*. I'd like to talk to you about the murder of Susan Mackintosh. I'm looking to quote the lead forensic examiner?'

Cass moved the phone away from her head for a moment, shocked at the call. She heard a faint hello and slowly placed it back to her ear.

'How did you get this number, Barbara?'

'Oh I have my sources,' said the reporter cryptically, 'A quote please?'

'No comment. And don't call me again.' Cass hung up quickly, taking a deep breath. She hated reporters; always there to twist words and print inaccuracies on cases. She was curious as to how Barbara had got her personal number though. She rarely gave it to anyone. It was on the force systems as her method of contact when out of work but no one in the force would give it out.

Chapter Six

'What exactly are you saying? Because it sounds like you are confirming that you are cutting the CSIs by six and losing two CSMs – am I correct in thinking that?'

Cass had paled slightly, listening to Kevin clarify with the woman from HR. She hadn't caught her name, but she really didn't like her. The woman was completely lacking in empathy, sitting there telling them about massive jobs cuts with as much emotion as if she were telling the stock girl to order more pencils.

Kevin's face was slowly turning a deep shade of red as he listened to her clipped reply.

'Yes Kevin, that's what I'm saying. It's not just your department you know. The job cuts are happening force-wide. You knew we had to cut costs and this is the only way to do it, unfortunately.'

'I don't care what's happening to other departments, I care what's happening to my staff. It just isn't plausible to cut the front-line forensic staff when we are already operating on reduced staffing levels due to sickness and natural wastage. Cut the vans, the equipment, hell cut the hours we work, but we cannot operate on fewer staff than we have now.'

'Well I'm very sorry but you'll just have to learn to cope. The long and short of it is that CSIs do not count as front-line staff. I'm sure your DI can arrange something whereby the attendance criteria for jobs can be re-assessed so your staff don't become overworked. We'll have a look at redeploying them into alternate roles in the force if this is at all possible.'

'Not front line? Redeploying into alternate roles? Where the hell's the benefit in placing a fully forensic-trained, experienced member of staff into a job where they lose their skill set and the force lose their knowledge and availability to work?' Kevin hit the desk with his fist in frustration.

'Well what's the selection process going to be based on? How is it possible to choose who will stay and who will go exactly?' interrupted Cass, watching as the HR advisor's cheeks flushed a deep pink at Kevin's sharp tone. She placed a hand on his arm in an effort to placate him.

'Your DI has the information on selection processes and I'm sure he will discuss this with you. I have another meeting to get to, so please excuse me.'

Cass and Kevin just stared as she got to her feet, grabbed her bag and walked out of the room without a backwards glance.

'Boss, tell me this isn't happening and we are going to fight this. Losing staff is the most ridiculous thing I've heard to date,' said Kevin, looking over at DI Hartside who until now had been silent.

'Kev, you need to take a breath and a step back. This has all come down from the powers that be. The cost reduction is government based, you know that, and Marilyn was right, it *is* force wide. You need to know I fought this every step of the way. They wanted to cut ten CSIs, two CSMs and the two supervisors. I personally compiled the figures that said the most we could lose was six and two.' The DI's voice had turned whiny as he tried his best to placate Kevin and the rest of the team.

Cass stared at the DI with disdain; Simon Hartside had never been what she considered a good choice as head for the department. He was a police officer, had never dealt with forensics, and had no idea what went on behind the scenes as he had been fast-tracked to inspector so had sat behind a desk for most of his career.

'You compiled the figures based on what data?' she asked, squeezing Kev's arm slightly to still the volcano that was about to blow.

Simon stared at her, almost not comprehending for a moment. 'Well, on the data from the Socard database naturally, the number of jobs attending offset by the time it took to deal with and the number of staff on duty at the time. It was all completely above board I assure you.'

'Did you take into account travelling time, note writing time, meal breaks, and additional duties that aren't required to be put onto Socard, such as putting exhibits through the property system, liaising with officers and giving advice, keeping the vans maintained and what-not?'

Simon backtracked rapidly, his eyes starting to twitch a little. 'Well all of that has an impact, naturally. There's nothing set in stone numbers-wise at this stage. We still have to go into consultation with the union and come up with feasible losses in all areas of the force.'

'You keep saying we. Just how involved are you in the force-wide cost-cutting, Sir?' asked Kevin.

'Well erm, I have been asked to assist HR wherever possible in the dissemination of the information, especially to all areas of the crime department. Look, I have your interests at heart. This isn't going to be easy for any of us. They are talking of dropping the DI wage bracket which will mean even I will be affected.'

'You lose a couple of grand where the staff could lose their job. Yeah, I can see how badly that would affect you. I'll be going to the union today, boss. This whole thing is a bloody farce.'

And with those parting comments, Kevin and Cass got up and left the room, leaving the DI shaking his head in apparent confusion.

21ˢᵗ September, 1540 hours – Ryhope Police Station

Cass was sitting in a world of her own, staring out of the window. Dark clouds scurried above shedding a dreary look on the normally pretty courtyard to the back of her office, and the rain began pelting the window in time with the pounding in her head.

She wasn't a born worrier, but the thought of her job being at risk while having to inform the staff and try and maintain a modicum of positivity was weighing heavy on her mind. First on her list was Gregory Parker.

Cass picked up the phone and punched in his number from memory.

She could practically see him in front of her with his half-mast trousers as he pulled his cart round the golf course. Greg was just entering his second week of annual leave, and any spare moment he got was always spent playing.

She had just scheduled an emergency depot meeting to inform the rest of the on duty staff, and letting Greg know by phone was only fair. One of the most experienced CSIs in the force area, Greg had been in the police for over twenty years. He'd seen people come and go, and had dealt with more than his fair share of crap. One of the things Cass liked most about him was his direct attitude. He said it as it was. But that didn't mean he'd take the job cuts in good form. He'd had a beef with the DI since he moved into the department and Cass wasn't looking forward to telling him about the news.

She felt her breath catch a little as he answered.

'Parker,'

'Hey, Greg, it's Cass. Sorry to bother you when you're on annual leave but I just need to make you aware of a situation. Do you have a second to speak?'

'Yeah sure, boss, what's up?'

'We've just had a meeting with DI Hartside and HR.....'

Greg had remained silent throughout her explanation but now he let loose, and Cass moved the receiver from her ear a little.

'You're fucking kidding, boss. The twats are shafting us again! They've already screwed us with our shift allowance and call outs and now that wanker is doing it again. I seriously hope we're going to fight this, Cass. Cutting the CSIs and CSMs is a ridiculous idea – we're already operating on bare minimum. It'll get to the point where everyone ends up off sick with exhaustion.'

'I know how you feel, Greg. We're standing together on this. We're going to be looking at Hartside's reports and the numbers. Nothing's set in stone at this point – it's a proposal. I'll keep you updated though.'

'Yeah I know you will, boss. Thanks. I'll see you in a week but ring me if anything changes in the meantime.'

Cass smiled a little as she hung up the phone, the mental image of Greg in half-masts now firmly implanted in her brain. Grabbing her paperwork, she headed into the other office to tell everyone else.

22ⁿᵈ *September, 0750 hours – Ryhope Police Station*

Dave Jones shuffled his way down the corridor of the station, pushing a trolley which was rapidly becoming filled with bin bags. For a man in his forties, he moved like one nearing his sixties, due mainly to the pronounced limp. It was an old injury he had sustained when serving for the army: 'thanks for your service, son, now bugger off and join the real world.'

Dave had been cleaning at the Ryhope depot ever since. He'd seen people come and go, had his share of crap from management, knew every nook and cranny in the station almost as well as he knew his own home, and had made it his business to know everyone in the nick. He was nice enough to folks, most looked forward to a cuppa and a chat when they passed his office. Apparently he made the best coffee in the whole of Sunderland and naturally the biscuits always helped seal friendships. If that's what they could be called.

'Hey, Dave. How's things?' Cass's voice came from nowhere, interrupting his train of thought.

'Not bad, Cass. Just gotta keep going.'

'Yeah I hear you. Could you do me a favour? We've been clearing out the lab in the yard, and have had to ditch quite a bit of stock that's gone out of date. Would you mind contacting the skip hire people and arranging for it to be picked up please?'

'No problem love, I'll move it out when they arrive. It'll probably be tomorrow though, is that ok?'

'Yeah that's fine. Up to anything tonight?' Cass leaned on the nearby door frame as he said.

'No, not really. I'll probably catch up on the soaps. Nothing interesting.'

'Oh I dunno, bit of time at home with the Mrs, can't be all that bad?'

'No Mrs at home for me, she left years ago. Am on my own now, and to be fair I prefer it that way. Just me and the cat. It's a lot quieter.' He winked at her as he tugged the cart and made his way down the corridor.

Dave sighed as he pulled the cart out of view. He was tired. He'd had enough of cleaning up other people's messes, and the early mornings were starting to take their toll. What he should do now though was his main dilemma. He knew changes were coming. There wasn't a whole lot of choice though, for someone his age whose only experience was serving his country and cleaning.

Still, onwards and upwards. Tomorrow's a whole new day, or so me old mam used to say anyway.

His thoughts didn't dispel the impending sense of unease he felt though.

Chapter Seven

22nd September, 0840 hours – Ryhope Police Station

Alex poured himself a steaming cup of coffee in the small but functional kitchen in front of the MIT office and headed for his desk. He was late getting in this morning, his longer-than-usual gym session a glaring testament to the pizza he'd lazily opted for last night. He'd eaten the whole thing while sorting through some of the information from the case and making sure Holmes was updated. He had also checked in on a few of the other cases he was handling, making sure nothing fell by the wayside.

He had a feeling of dread settling in his stomach today. Frowning, he revisited the brief conversation he'd had with Cass last night. She had been in her office, looking forlorn as he popped his head in, and he couldn't help but ask what was wrong. She had sighed deeply and then progressed to tell him about the proposed job cuts in the department. Shaking his head, he took a gulp of his coffee, acknowledging he had known something was up when HR had scheduled a meeting with the whole team today. It was practically unheard of to pull every available resource in. They had cancelled the rest days so everyone was in together.

The rumour mill had been working overtime, and his staff believed it to be everything from a pat on the back to life-altering changes. His coffee suddenly turned bitter in his mouth and he put the cup to one side.

Today was not going to be a good day.

Making the decision to at least try and start on a positive note, he picked up the phone and dialled in a number from memory.

'Hey, Ali, it's me.'

'You OK, bro? Kinda early for a phone call.'

'Yeah am good, just checking in. How's mum?'

'She's good, fussing over Mary like any proud grandma. You know she's due to drop any day now?'

'Yeah I know. I've already sent her a care package. A Kama sutra book, a curry recipe and some condoms,' he grinned into the phone as Ali snorted with laughter.

'She's gonna kick your arse, bro.'

'Aye I know. I've sent her the bank details too, for bump's college fund. That bairn's gonna be richer than any of us by the time she hits eighteen, same as her brothers. Especially with all of us putting in.'

'It was a good idea, Alex, I know Mary appreciates it. She's not been finding things easy with Hamish under her feet all day.'

'When's he back at hospital? I haven't spoken to him in a few weeks.'

'Next week, bro, it doesn't look good though. They reckon long term physio, possibly surgery. I guess there's a reason Mum never let us have a motorbike.'

'Yeah you're not wrong, bro. I'll give Mary and Mum a ring later tonight.'

Alex listened for the click, then placed the receiver back into its cradle, mentally making a note to get rid of the Triumph 500 he'd had in storage for the past couple of years. Ali didn't know about the impulse buy he had made when he turned thirty-five. OK, he'd never actually ridden it, he'd bought it intending to do it up and then get his licence. Luckily enough he'd never found the time to give it the TLC it needed to become a spectacular machine again.

One of the DCs entered and he pulled his head back into work-mode, loaded up his email, opened the Vehicle Examiner's Report from Cass, hit the print key, and then did the same with the copy of the report from the post-mortem.

22nd September, 1520 hours – Ryhope Police Station

Alex had never felt quite so bewildered or angry. The meeting with HR had not gone well. The force in its infinite wisdom had deemed it necessary to cut the Major Incident Team by half. This was across the whole force but still, losing twenty-three members of staff was ridiculous.

He had tried to explain that having half the staff, who would still be working shifts, would mean that the force would be under manned at the best of times. All it needed was for two or more major incidents to occur at the same time in different areas and they would all be up shit creek without a paddle.

But HR had refused to acknowledge his concerns, His boss, the Superintendent, sitting there meekly as he tended to do. The Super was one for letting the ball roll and stop where it may. He was OK in the respect he kept out of the major decisions, but as a boss he was the worst. He was almost at the end of his thirty years. Hell, he'd probably already submitted his request for early retirement. Alex wondered how many of his team he would lose to the proposed Voluntary Redundancies. The words shuddered in his brain; it was hardly voluntary when they were telling staff that they would lose their jobs after three months' consultation, followed by six months on the redeployment register if some of them didn't consider VR.

Sometimes this police force did things completely back to front but Alex knew enough to realise they would do as they pleased. The government had said cut costs in the police force, given a time limit of three years in which to do it, then sat back on their heels smiling in that 'we're doing this for the good of the country' way as every police force went into a complete state of panic and began implementing immediate strategies to make the cost reductions happen.

Alex had only been out of the meeting a few hours and he was aware that some of the older members of staff had already looked at the figures, and submitted their requests. He had tried to reassure the staff that they would stand together and fight, but he knew for many this was the last straw that would break the proverbial camel's back.

He sighed deeply, this was one of the few times he wished he had stayed a lowly DC and let someone else have all the responsibility. His staff were already stressed with the amount of cases they were handling, he already had three off on long-term sick. In one hour, HR had managed to increase the stress by a level he didn't quite know how to address since they were all in the same boat.

He held back the grimace as the annoying jingle of his mobile ringing interrupted his train of thought. Looking down, he felt his heart lurch a touch as it flashed 'Mum' calling. His mum never rang his mobile.

'Ma? What's the matter?'

'Alex, it's Mary. She went into labour a couple of hours ago. The hospital told her to wait until the contractions are five minutes apart, but she's in agony. She wasn't like this the last two times, I don't know what to do, son.'

Alex heard the desperation in his mother's voice, rapidly followed by an agonised scream in the background.

'Ma, phone an ambulance now. Tell them she's having problems, hell, tell them she's bleeding, anything. She needs a doctor, now.'

He could almost see his mother's face, pale with the worry he knew she would be feeling. It was always the same when any of them were hurting, that feeling of complete panic knowing she had to let her child get on with the pain themselves while not being able to do anything to help.

'Where's Ali?'

'I don't know, son, I phoned you first.'

'I'll call him – call the ambulance, Ma.'

Before she had clicked off the call he was dialling in Ali's number for the second time that day.

'Hey, bro, two calls in one day, I'm privileged.'

'Ali, it's Mary. You need to get home now, mum just called. Can you blues it?'

'That bad? OK, I'm en route. Call you when I know more.'

Alex tried to swallow the lump that had appeared in his throat. Right now he wanted nothing more than to go home and see his baby sister, feel his mum wrap her arms around him and kiss his cheek as she had when he was a kid, telling him everything would be fine.

But he had staff to deal with, meetings to attend and several active murder cases to solve. He knew Ali would keep him updated, would let him know if he needed to get home urgently. It didn't make it any easier to be miles away though. Feeling a sudden need to talk, he made his way down the stairs to Cass's office.

22nd September, 1705 hours – Ryhope Police Station

Worry lines marred the faintly tanned skin around Alex's eyes, and he realised he had been biting his lip while he worked. It had been a long day and he was tired, but he knew he wouldn't get a great deal of sleep tonight. He was almost tempted to ring the Super and tell him he had a family emergency. Susan's case wouldn't fall to the wayside; he had plenty of people he could delegate to. But his sense of responsibility forced him to reconsider. Mary was in the hospital, the best possible place for her. His family were there and would take care of her. And he knew Ali would let him know the second he knew anything.

Besides he had a set of three rest days starting in a couple of days, and he had already made the decision to visit before the phone call from his mum.

Tonight though, he would return home to his empty flat, and spend the night worrying about Mary, worrying about the job cuts and just generally keeping himself awake. He was too frustrated for the gym; for once he wanted company.

He could go to the local, he knew the DS and several of the DCs drank there, but he put this idea to bed. He knew they became uncomfortable when the DCI attended social events; he had often pondered over the change in people when he was with them. They became quieter, withdrawn even, and he understood it was to do with his rank, but it still niggled at him. It wasn't like he rubbed it in people's faces. He had worked damn hard to get to where he was, and he knew it. It did feel a little unfair however, when other people didn't realise it.

On the cases he had worked, and the social events they had been at together, he had never felt that way about Cass. She'd left the office before he had got there that afternoon. Deena had told him she had a dentist appointment so had taken a flyer. He knew he was probably being selfish; Cass probably had plans already; but he really didn't want to be on his own. He tidied his desk, grabbed his keys and headed to the car park.

He felt a sense of unease as he pulled onto the driveway that led to her cottage. What on earth was he thinking? He didn't just turn up at people's homes unannounced. Hell, he rarely went to people's homes unless it was work related. What if she didn't want him there? Would she tell him or be all polite and let him stay regardless, all on edge? Alex knew he was being irrational; he had no way of knowing how Cass would react. But still.

He shouldn't have come here.

Cass couldn't consider him a friend, she barely knew him. He pulled onto the gravel at the front of the cottage, spun the car around with the intention of leaving, and braked suddenly as Cass came into view through the trees, Ollie lolloping beside her, his pink tongue hanging out as he panted.

'Crap. You are such an idiot, McKay,' he muttered to himself.

He watched as Cass approached the vehicle, and smiled at him.

He felt his spirits lift slightly, maybe she wouldn't mind after all.

'Hey, Alex, what're you doing here? Everything OK?'

'Yeah, sorry for just turning up like this. I uh…' he paused, not knowing quite how to say what he felt.

Finally, he opted for the truth. 'I needed some company tonight, tough day, and I didn't think you'd mind. But if you've got plans it's no problem. I'll just leave you to it.'

'Plans? No I don't have plans, just walking Ollie as usual. Are you coming in for a cuppa or are you gonna sit in the car all night?'

Alex followed her inside, and strangely, felt calmer immediately. Her home was serene, it had an ambience of peace inside, and he knew it was this feeling that eased some of his tension. He remembered her reaction when he had startled her the morning he'd stayed over, and wondered if she had created the peaceful space consciously, an escape from whatever demons were following her. That morning already felt like a lifetime ago.

The kitchen smelled heavenly as he entered, and his stomach growled in response. She grinned at him as she heard the deep rumble. 'Hungry? I've made chicken and chorizo casserole. There's plenty if you'd like to stay?'

Alex just nodded. 'That would be great, smells amazing.'

After supper she led him into the lounge and they sat, and she finally asked what had made his day so bad.

'My baby sister Mary's pregnant. She's been rushed into the hospital today. Ma sounded absolutely distraught, she hadn't phoned Ali. It's been a tough couple of years.'

'Are Ali and Mary your only sisters?'

Alex coughed as the smooth coffee hit his throat. He chuckled as he put the cup on the coffee table.

'Ali is short for Alistair.'

Cass smiled widely as he continued.

'I'm the oldest, then there's Ali. Mark and Annie are twins, then there's Joseph, then James and Max, and finally our little Mary. She was a surprise.'

'Seven siblings? I can't imagine what that would be like, especially with twins too. There was only me and mum when I was younger. Bet your house was like a zoo at times.'

'Yeah,' he smiled fondly. 'I miss them. Especially at times like this.'

'What made you come to Sunderland?' asked Cass, looking at him intently. He let himself glance at her for a moment; she was sitting opposite him on the sofa, her legs curled up underneath her, her coffee cup grasped in both hands as she maintained his eye contact without hesitation. She looked comfortable, at home, and relaxed with him being there.

Taking her cue, he pulled his own leg onto the overstuffed seat, picked his coffee up and told her a little about Helen.

Chapter Eight

Charlie Quinn entered the office purposefully. She was acutely aware of the stares she received when she entered the room. She accepted it, she turned heads. People appreciated her form. End of.

She'd never let the fact that she looked more like a supermodel than a police officer interfere with her work; she knew appearances could be deceptive.

Striding confidently, she made her way to Alex's desk.

He had requested she dig into the life of Susan Mackintosh, uncover any skeletons hidden in her closet. And she had found said skeletons.

She paused at his desk, nodding silently as he indicated he would be another minute on the phone call.

He replaced the receiver, and turned to greet her. 'Charlie, how's it going?'

'OK thanks, Alex. You told me to come straight over if I found anything pertinent. Seems Susan has been having an affair. There were messages on her phone, not from the husband. I've checked with the network provider, and it looks to be an unregistered pay and go phone. I've tried ringing it but the mobile is turned off. The network have said it hasn't been used since the day of the murder. Could be motive.'

Alex felt his face convey the surprise he felt. Everything so far had leant towards a stable family environment. Now, despite an alibi, there was something that could potentially implicate Brian Mackintosh in his wife's murder.

'Thanks, Charlie, good job. Can you get the mobile to Jacob Tulley over in the Digital Forensics Department at HQ? I've already briefed him on the case and he's expecting you. We'll see if there's anything else on the phone.'

'No probs. Anything else you need, boss? I've got a few statements I need to prep for court. You're on rest days for a few after today aren't you?'

'Yeah I am. Nothing else at the minute though. Thanks again, Charlie.'

Alex watched as she sashayed down the office. He saw the leering glances from the male officers, and the hint of jealousy from the females. Charlie was a beautiful woman. A little young for his tastes but he could appreciate her beauty. He also knew she was very happily married. The door clicked behind her and the low murmur of people talking resumed in the office.

For a moment his mind pictured Cass. There was something about her shuttered eyes that made him want to pull them open and find the person inside. He frowned to himself; Cass deserved more than him. He had no idea where these sudden feelings had come from. He hadn't been attracted to anyone since Helen, and if he was honest, it scared him.

The phone rang suddenly, pulling him from his thoughts.

'McKay,' he answered, spinning the chair around to grab the file teetering on the edge of the filing cabinet behind him.

'Alex, Nigel Evans. Have you got a sec?'

'Yeah sure, Nigel. I take it the bloods have come back from Susan's PM?'

'Yes. Were you aware she was pregnant? Around six weeks along I'd say, based on the levels.'

'Pregnant. I wonder if her husband knew? Or if it was her lover's baby?' He paused, waiting for Nigel to comment.

'Well I'd say that ball's in your court. Nothing like having your cake and eating it. I'll take a sample from the foetus in case you need DNA for paternity reasons.'

'Great thanks, Nigel. Anything else I need to know?'

'No. I'll send the report straight over though.'

Alex hung up the phone thoughtfully. Susan being pregnant provided more motive for someone to want her gone.

It was time for him to visit Brian personally and speak with him. He had planned to do his cursory visit tomorrow, but this afternoon would do fine.

23rd September, 1345 hours – Pallion, Sunderland

He pulled apart the top shelves of his toolbox to get to the hammer in the space at the bottom. He remembered finding it years earlier, in the shed of one of his neighbours.

His teeth glinted as he smiled, remembering the look of horror on the neighbour's face when he came upon the mangled body of his faithful pet in his yard in front of the shed.

He had hidden behind the small, wooden building, wanting to see what the old man would do.

It had only taken five blows with the hammer to kill the West Highland terrier, its white fur quickly becoming stained with blood. But he had hit it a few more times, enchanted by the crack the bones made and the pattern of the blood. He didn't know what he expected when the man saw his dead dog, but he hadn't expected to see him cry.

His neighbour had knelt in the yard, with the rain pouring down on his bald head, and sobbed, pulling the broken body of the dog close. In between the sobs he had cried the word 'why?' before he had shakily taken a spade from his shed and painstakingly dug a shallow grave.

He had watched from behind the tree as the old man dug for an hour and buried his beloved pet, and he remembered being surprised that he hadn't felt something other than satisfaction.

The old man had passed away a few weeks later, pneumonia the rumour mill had said. And again he had spent time in his garden and wondered why he hadn't felt something.

Now though he understood.

He had read a multitude of psychology books, enough to understand he was what was categorised as psychopath. He was completely lacking in empathy, had no remorse for his actions and was emotionally detached from everything.

But he knew he felt *something*. Or maybe it was more the search for feeling something.

It was the reason he did what he did.

He was constantly searching to achieve *that* feeling. That same satisfaction he had felt when he looked at the sobbing old man and known that he was responsible for his pain. He felt enjoyment at the sorrow he could inflict, and a kind of peace in the knowing that when life ceased, it was because *he* chose to make it so. His favourite part of the kill was when the light of life and hope extinguished and the dim glow of acceptance appeared, the point they knew they would die. He'd seen it in the eyes of the small white dog and all the other animals he'd killed over the years. And now he'd seen it in Susan's eyes. He knew that was what he needed to see again.

The feeling was not a sexual release, but it gave him the ultimate sense of satisfaction. He knew that he was good at what he did.

He handled the hammer, feeling the grooved wooden handle weigh his hands down. He hadn't used it since the day with the dog. He was looking forward to listening to the old vagrant beg for his life as he made his bones crack in the same way the dogs had all those years before. He looked forward to making him pay for his life of ignorance, the life where he chose not to help the boy whose mother beat him, the meagre existence where fate had already intervened, rendering him an alcoholic bum with nothing better to do than drink his life away.

'*Yes, you saw me. You saw the bruises. You were friends with that useless arsehole of a father I had. You saw what she did. And now I see you.*'

He'd been surprised the first time he saw Albert, barely recognising him through the unkempt beard and hair. The years had not been kind.

But it was definitely him.

And it was time he paid for his ignorance.

He took a deep breath and put the hammer back, closed the shelves and fastened the clasp. He had the patience to wait until the time was right. The current news headlines would ease from first page down to the middle of the paper and then the city of Sunderland would be ready for his next great masterpiece.

Chapter Nine

23rd September, 1525 hours – Mackintosh Residence

Alex found himself sitting in the Ford Focus outside the house owned by Susan and her husband Brian. The front garden was well kept, the grass cut short and only just starting to sprout after the downpour at the weekend. He shook his head; it had been four days since the murder now, but it was all still so fresh that it could have happened that morning.

A blue plastic tricycle lay on its side on the grass and he felt a sudden deep pang to see his family.

I'll go see the Super when I get back, see if I can get a lieu day tagged on to my rest days. It'll be good to go home.

Mary had been given an emergency caesarean and his niece had been born safely but was in the special care baby unit. Mary had lost a lot of blood during the birth and was just being moved from ICU to a side room today. His mum had sounded dog tired when she had phoned him that morning. She needed him right now, and he wanted nothing more than to be there.

Since he'd left with Helen he had tried to get home regularly, but something always seemed to come up. He spoke with his mum every other day on the phone, was in constant contact with his siblings, but he knew that it was his choice to stay where he was. Being home reminded him of all the things he should have had with Helen but that he had thrown away on his job. He hadn't realised at the time just how awful it must have been for her, the wife of a police officer, waiting at home for that dreaded phone call or visit every time he was at work. The fact he did now just seemed to make Helen more bitter, and she never served to disappoint whenever she spoke to him, always making sure he knew everything was his fault.

He focused in on the house, distracting himself from the feeling of loneliness, and noticed a curtain twitch slightly. Realising suddenly that he must look suspicious just sitting in his vehicle outside the house of a murder victim, he unclipped his seat belt, grabbed his mobile off the dash and got out of the car.

The husband opened the door as he arrived, two small faces peeping out from behind the safety of his legs, their eyes wide as they looked up at Alex.

'Mr Mackintosh. Detective Chief Inspector Alex McKay. I'm here to express my sincere condolences, and speak with you about Susan if I may.' The well-polished lines fell from his lips smoothly, but in his head they sounded insincere and emotionless. He watched as a slow shutter of pain passed over the husband's eyes before he composed himself and stood to one side, silently granting Alex access to the house.

He led the way into the living room, the two children holding tightly to his legs as they moved back and forth with the stepping motion. He half turned and motioned to Alex to sit on the smaller brown leather sofa.

Alex remained silent as the two children clambered up the couch and clung to their broken father, one on each side.

'The Coroner's Officer said he can't release the body yet. When can I have my wife's funeral Mr McKay?' His voice trembled on the word funeral, and he pulled the children a little closer to him. It was obvious to Alex that the man had adored his wife. He was finding the transition difficult, and as was often the case, the children became his rock, his sense of strength.

'We have lines of enquiry ongoing at the moment that require keeping your wife's body for the time being. As soon as I can, I will have her released over to your funeral directors. Would you prefer to continue this conversation at a time when someone could perhaps look after the children for a while?' asked Alex.

The husband stared at him, not understanding that the conversation would likely prove too much for the innocent minds of his children. Realisation eventually dawned and he nodded. 'Susan's mother is upstairs; she'll have the children for a while.'

He got up and led the children away, and Alex heard muffled speech as Brian made his request.

When he returned, Alex explained all the points of the case honestly. He had learned over the years not to tell untruths, or sugar coat information when speaking with relatives. Invariably, they wanted to know the basic truth and what would happen next. He still paused over his next question though; it was never a pleasant thing to reveal a person's infidelity.

'Brian, did you know your wife was pregnant?'

'Pregnant? That's not possible. I had the snip after we had Abbie.'

'I'm very sorry to ask, but is it possible that your wife could have been having an affair with another man?'

Alex watched as Brian's face paled in shock. Tears pricked at his eyes and his breath caught as comprehension dawned.

'Oh god. Why? Why would she do that? We have everything. I mean it's not been easy lately, I've been doing more hours at the centre 'cos we've had a lot more people in needing assistance, but I thought we were OK. I thought she knew I was doing it for us. Was it him Detective? Did that monster kill my Susan?'

On his last desperate question, Brian broke down. Great heaving sobs caused his shoulders to shudder as he wept out his anger and grief. Alex wondered how long he had held it in, whether he had cried before today or just been in a state of denial. And he felt like a complete heel. Being the one to tell someone their wife was having an affair definitely rated high on the list of things he didn't enjoy doing. Silently, Alex handed Brian a box of tissues from the table.

An hour passed quickly, and as Brian walked Alex to the front door, his voice filled with emotion and tears shone heavy in his eyes. 'Please find who did this to my wife, Detective. Please. I don't care what she did with him, whether she was pregnant. She was my wife. If she strayed, then it was my fault. I should have been here for her more.'

Alex nodded, 'I will do everything in my power to catch this person, Brian. You have my word. I'll be in touch.' Always conscious never to make a promise he couldn't keep, his words were positive and confident. Brian nodded once, then closed the door with a quiet click. Alex could imagine him resting his head on the door frame in defeat.

As he walked back down the path towards the car, he felt a heavy drop of rain hit his cheek. Visiting those left behind was always hard, it left him with a heavy heart and today, a sense of unease. He wasn't one for making snap judgements where suspects were concerned, but his gut was screaming that Brian hadn't killed Susan. Which meant someone else had. And who knew what that person would do next?

He climbed into the car and brought the engine to life with a roar, just as the heavens opened, and the rain began lashing down in earnest.

Cass had made good use of her rest days, cleaning and finishing the decoration of the laundry room which was now fully kitted out with the washer from the kitchen. She had made up the spare room ready for her mum's visit, and finally headed to work for late-shift and was currently sat in her office with a hot coffee.

It had been a slow night.

Faith, Johnny and herself had cleaned all the vans, ensured they were all stocked, sorted out the DNA freezer and the other two were currently putting exhibits through the in-force property systems. It kept costs down to do as much as possible in house so the expensive cost of hiring external companies didn't mount up. This meant that there were always a large number of exhibits kept in the secure store. Every couple of months it got to the point where you could barely move for boxes of items.

Each CSI was supposed to keep on top of putting their exhibits through and sending them off to the main property store, however in reality this wasn't the case. Generally, when people got a quiet late shift they would start the arduous task of booking the items out on Socard and packaging them to be transported, usually by means of Frank the handyman. Frank only worked a thirty-hour week, the same as a lot of the police civilian staff, so if he wasn't around then whoever was on dayshift would take whatever items were required over to the main depot in the city centre.

Cass sat back in her chair, and felt a small shiver as she remembered her evening with Alex before he had left to go home. It had felt strange at first, having Alex's presence take over the living room. He had enjoyed her food, and said he had been in need of company. She had spent hours since then wondering about what that meant, whether he would want her company again. They had talked until late, mostly about him and his family, a little about the case, and not much at all about her. She couldn't tell him about the demons she had, making her reclusive and solitary in nature. Cass frowned to herself, acknowledging that she had wanted to open up and tell him why she had jumped so violently when he surprised her the morning he'd stayed over. She wanted to explain what gave her bad dreams and why she lived so far out of town.

But she couldn't.

Because to tell him was admitting that she hadn't moved on. She still lived in *his* shadow. And she always would.

Downing the last of her coffee and glancing at the clock, she wandered into the main office. Johnny and Faith were sat in silence, the radio playing quietly as they managed the bags surrounding them.

Looking up, Faith said, 'Hey, Cass. Come to give us a hand? Stupid RFID scanner has gone skew-whiff, I've logged it with IT and they're popping out tomorrow. I'll put a note on monitor before I go. I'm just putting the barcodes in by hand.'

Cass smiled, 'No I'm sure you guys can manage. I might do a pizza run though if anyone interested?'

'I'm good thanks, Cass, too skint for pizza. Might get some chips though?' Faith grabbed her handbag and started scrabbling for some change.

Johnny pulled the security tag tightly around the top of the latest property bag, pressed enter on the keyboard and spun on his chair to look at Cass. 'I'll go, Cass. I've gotta take these down to the mail room anyway and could use some air. What pizza you wanting?'

'Chicken and mushroom please. I'll shout you guys too, as a thank you for doing everyone else's property,' she added with a grin, knowing Faith would object. Despite never having any money she wasn't one for charity. Cass watched as Faith glanced at Johnny, who shrugged noncommittally.

'Thanks, Cass, would you mind if I got a chicken kebab then please?' she asked.

'No problem, Faith.'

Cass handed £30 to Johnny with a grin, 'See you shortly.'

An hour later they had all eaten, cleared up and Johnny and Faith had perked up a little with the end of shift looming. Cass had already returned to her office and had completed the last of the Personal Development Reviews for the staff. Sitting back, she glanced at the clock above the door.

'Faith, Johnny, you guys get yourselves off home. I'll cover if anything comes in before twelve.'

She didn't need to offer twice. Both of them had their stuff gathered and the office door locked before Cass had pressed save on the document she was working on.

Cass listened for a moment, the silence of the station almost deafening at this time of night. The nightshift were out on their patrols and the late shift had finished twenty minutes ago. Some people might have thought it a bit creepy, but Cass liked the quiet. She pulled her phone from her pocket, set the volume low and put her tunes on shuffle. For once, she was likely to finish on time.

28th September, 1535 hours – The Denes Park, Sunderland

Scott was really pissed off. Despite Brian's wife being killed, he had been at work today, on his case again, ranting on about second chances and opportunities. Brian and Gill had sat him down in the office like he was a frigging baby, telling him they thought he had potential and that he had been awarded more hours at the centre to help him get on track. It bugged the life out of him that Brian couldn't keep his nose out. He just wanted to be left alone.

He'd had enough of all the shit, and wanted to leave the centre. But, it was part of his probation terms to attend the centre daily. Scott scowled to himself as he walked through the back alley that led to the park.

Stupid bloke had seen him jemmy the car door. *He* was the only reason he'd been caught. He'd have been home free with the sat-nav if it hadn't been for nosy neighbours.

Being on probation had made him more popular though.

John-Joe and Jamie actually wanted to spend time with him now. Brian had said they were too old to want to spend time with him, and were trying to manipulate him, but he was wrong. He was going to be part of their gang now, all because of getting caught. They trusted him. All he had to do now was pass their damned initiation, and he'd be a fully-fledged member of the small gang. Then he would be introduced to the other members, the leader even.

Brian didn't get the honour involved in that. Brian didn't get anything.

Kourtney, his girlfriend, thought it was great. She was already hanging around with Jamie's girlfriend Sam, talking about whatever it was that girls talked about. He was pleased – it had stopped her being quite so clingy with him. He'd been on the verge of dumping her when he had been given probation. But the sex was good, and who was he really to complain?

Scott's dad was always at the pub, so more often than not Kourtney stayed over. Her parents had sent the police on more than one occasion to pick her up; they didn't get that she doted on him. They thought he was a bad influence.

Maybe I am a bad influence. But it's her choice to hang around with me. I don't make *her miss school. Maybe she's the bad influence on me.* He frowned slightly as the thoughts ran round his head.

Scott was due to start work shortly. Not that his job took up much time: he only did part time hours. But it topped his dole up so he could afford booze and fags, and the occasional bag of skunk. It was still a pain though. Pulling on the crumpled, black uniform shirt, he made his way towards the park.

Kourtney would be at the bandstand, skipping school as usual.

He figured if he grabbed her now he could get a quickie in before he went to work. There was a local garage block that had a few empty slots, and Kourtney was always up for it whenever he asked. As he neared the park though, he heard yelling, and turned the corner just in time to see the old drunk lobbing a lager can at Kourtney.

It missed and she turned back towards him, her eyes blazing and pure venom dripping from her mouth as she spat, 'Fuck off you alcoholic old twat.'

Scott watched as the old guy stepped back, the bench hitting the back of his knees and causing him to sit back down with a thump. A filthy looking dog barked at her loudly, not moving from his owner's side, and he heard the man mutter under his breath about the youth of today having no respect. For a moment he felt disgust at the way she had spoken to the old guy, registered the look of hurt resignation on his face. Then his loyalty set in.

'Kourt, you OK?' he asked, jogging over. Kourtney's cheeks were flushed with crimson but she smiled broadly at him.

'Yeah I'm fine. The old prick's been bitching on since we got here. Sam's on the bandstand. She's got some shit. You wanna share a smoke?'

Scott felt his stomach drop a little, so much for a quickie before work. Still, a few puffs would set him right. He followed her onto the bandstand, took the joint and inhaled a long drag, leaning back as he felt the glow.

Albert Grieves felt the edge of the bench hit the back of his legs as he stepped backwards, shocked at the way the girl had yelled at him. He'd seen a lot of bad things in his life, but he had never been spoken to in that manner before. He felt his creaky knees give way, and his bottom hit the bench with a thump.

Shaking, he ran his hand down the neck of his dog, Scruff, who had now stopped barking. The dog turned in a circle a few times before sitting down on the bench next to Albert's leg, and pushed his head back into his hand.

'It's alright, Scruff.' He heard the words fall from his lips softly, but he knew it wasn't alright, not really. There had been a point when the girl had been yelling at him where he had thought she might actually strike him. It scared him.

Kids these days have no respect. My daughter would never dare talk to anyone like that. She's such a good girl.

He felt his heart swell with pride, but then the other memories invaded. It was his fault, he should have kept a better eye on his boy, not let him buy that damned motorbike. But back then he had believed that kids needed to find their own way, grow into their own person. And because of that mistake, his Tommy was dead and gone.

The hurt was almost overwhelming. Albert reached for the bottle of White Lightening from the carrier bag on the bench, and took a long swig, feeling the liquid make its way down to his belly.

He felt tears shine in his sad eyes, and slightly embarrassed, he swiped at them. He felt guilty now; he really shouldn't have thrown the can at the girl. She was just a kid. He supposed her comments were warranted. Just like his daughter's had been. It had been years since he'd seen her now. The last exchange had been emotional to say the least; he could still remember her exact words.

'You need to get a grip, Dad. Tommy's gone, but it doesn't mean you are. What happened to him was not your fault. You're still here and you need to start living again, not sit staring into the neck of a bloody bottle. I will not stand here and watch you drink yourself into an early grave. You either give up the drink or you give up me.'

Tears fell from his eyes as he remembered his response to her ultimatum. He had walked away with nothing but the clothes on his back, a decision he had regretted ever since. Sometimes life just sucked.

He wiped the tears again, and took another long drink, shuffling in the seat until he found a comfy spot. Feeling sorry for himself, he laid his head on the back of the bench and closed his eyes. *Maybe I'll stop drinking tomorrow and contact Ellie. Maybe.*

Chapter Ten

29ᵗʰ September, 2020 hours – Cass's Cottage

It had been another long day. Cass had said her goodbyes at the office then picked up a Chinese takeaway on her way home, looking forward to munching her way through chow mein and salt and pepper ribs with something trashy on the TV.

She pulled up on the driveway, the smell of the hot food making her stomach grumble loudly, and grabbed the bag from the passenger seat. Pushing her key in the lock, she realised the door was already unlocked.

'Crap,' she muttered under her breath as she pushed it open. 'It's a bloody good job I live in the sticks. You daft bugger, leaving the door unlocked.'

She flicked the switch in the hall, and glanced up expecting to see Ollie bounding down the stairs towards her. But he wasn't there.

'Ollie?' she called, placing the food on the unit and kicking off her shoes. 'Time for dinner?'

Cass frowned slightly as she picked the bag back up and wandered into the kitchen. She gasped, dropping the bag of food as she saw Ollie on the floor.

His eyes were glazed and he was convulsing, his teeth gnashing together loudly, and there was a pool of strong smelling urine underneath him. Cass knelt beside him, refusing to let panic take over. Gently she stroked his neck, talking in hushed tones. She kept the motion up as she rang the emergency vet number on her mobile. Tears threatened to fall as she listened to the line connect and then ring.

'Park Lane Vets out of hours - how can I help?'

'It's Cass Hunt. I have Ollie registered with you and need to speak to a vet immediately. He seems to be having a seizure.'

'Hold please,' said the female voice.

Seconds later a male voice came on the phone. 'Cass, it's Matt. Where are you and Ollie, and how long has he been convulsing?'

Cass almost sighed as she recognised Matt's soft voice. He had always been Ollie's vet and she hadn't dared hope he would be on duty.

'Home. I don't know how long. I just got home. His teeth are gnashing and his tongue is bleeding a bit. He's wet himself too. He won't respond to my voice. What do I do, Matt?'

He heard her voice, thick with panic and said, 'He hasn't had seizures before has he? I'm at the surgery – I can be with you in about forty minutes or you can bring him straight in?'

'I'll bring him in. Do I need to do anything? Or just pick him up and put him in the car?'

'Just bring him. I'll get the emergency room prepped. Mind yourself when you lift him, he's not in control of his teeth. See you soon, Cass. Try not to panic and drive safe, OK?'

Cass hung up the phone, rammed it into her pocket and picked the dog up carefully, feeling his convulsions ripple as she held him to her chest. A single tear trickled down her cheek and she acknowledged she was petrified.

Ollie was her best friend.

Taking a breath to steady herself, she carefully lifted the dog, and carried him to the car before laying him in the boot, jumping in the driver's seat and quickly driving off.

Not registering her speed, she arrived at the surgery in around twenty minutes.

'This way, Cass,' ushered Matt, bypassing the receptionist and leading Cass to a room at the rear.

Ollie's convulsions had slowed but he was still jittery and twitching. Matt carefully listened to his heart, which was pounding fast, and silently checked his eyes, and breathing.

'It's possibly an isolated incident. His seizure is slowing now, Cass. I'm going to give him some Valium and a little anaesthetic to help it stop and allow his body to recover. We'll then run a scan and see if we can locate the cause. He's going to be here at least overnight, Cass. Get yourself home, and I'll call you as soon as I've finished the exam.'

'What if he wakes and I'm not there?' Cass gulped, the lump in her throat feeling bigger by the second. Her voice sounded small to her, and she for a second she wondered if she needed to repeat herself so Matt could hear.

'Cass, I'll look after him. You need to go home, love. I'll call I promise.'

He placed a hand on her arm, giving her a gentle push towards the door. He always felt bad having to force the owners off but he had work to do and he couldn't do it with her standing there.

Cass nodded, swallowing hard. She didn't remember the journey home but by the time she pushed open the front door, she wasn't able to stop the tears falling. She sat on the couch, pulled her knees to her chest and wept. Ollie had always been there for her, and she knew he was in the best place but she still felt guilty for leaving him and worried he wouldn't be OK.

When the phone finally rang, Cass jumped visibly, still lost in her own little world. She glanced at the screen and took a deep breath before answering.

'Hey, Cass, it's Matt. The seizure's stopped. He's still anaesthetised but I'm hopeful he'll be responsive when he comes round. I'm going to stay with him tonight so you don't need to worry. I'll call if anything else happens, OK?'

'Thanks, Matt,' was all Cass could manage.

'Cass I don't want to scare you but I still need to do an ECG tomorrow. Long seizures like this one can cause brain damage. There is still a chance Ollie won't recover. I can't do that until tomorrow but I will ring you as soon as I'm done. Try not to worry. I'll be looking after him as if he was my Bruno.'

Cass hung up the phone, and sat for a minute, just staring into space.

Eventually the silence of the cottage invaded her thoughts, and she jumped up from the couch. She started by cleaning the kitchen floor, throwing the cold food into the bin and scrubbing the tiles hard before moving onto the surfaces. Within a couple of hours, the cottage was sparkling and Cass needed something else to distract her. The black sky threatened to envelop the woods from above, but she grabbed the hose and began washing her car, quickly progressing to hoovering the interior. One benefit of living in the sticks was you didn't have to watch the noise levels so much.

The exterior light shone on her as she scrubbed the car cleaner than it had been the day it had first sat in the show room. Tiredness was slow in seeping into her bones though, and once she finished on the car she smiled grimly to herself in the dull glow.

Deciding there wasn't a lot more she could do cleaning wise, she wandered into the kitchen and picked up the phone.

'Mama? It's me. Sorry to wake you,'

'Cass, is everything OK? It's two in the morning. Something's happened. Are you OK?'

Cass felt her breath catch as she answered.

'I'm fine, Mum. It's Ollie. He was having a seizure when I got in from work. I've had to leave him at the vets. Matt doesn't know if he's going to pull through. He's going to do some scan or other tomorrow and ring me.'

Her voice dropped to a shaky whisper. 'I'm scared, Mum.'

'Aw sweetie, I'm sure he'll be OK. He's a strong pup. He wouldn't have made it through everything he did when he was tiny just to give up now. And you're strong too, love. No matter what happens, everything will be OK.'

'You're right, Mum. Thank you. I'm sorry I woke you.'

'Anytime, love. Now you won't have eaten tonight, I want you to make a snack, just some toast or something, and get yourself off to bed. Matt's the best there is, you've said so a million times. He will look after Ollie, and you need to look after you. '

'OK, Mum. I'll ring you tomorrow.'

At her mum's acknowledgement, Cass hung up the phone and mindlessly opened the fridge. She knocked up an omelette, and carried it through to the living room. Eating on auto-pilot, she turned the TV on, quickly found the Good Food channel and let the soothing voice of James Martin wash over her.

Sleep soon arrived and feeling the chill, her subconscious prompted her to pull the tattered blanket round her shoulders. Alex had left it on the couch and she hadn't really been home to move it since. She took a deep breath, inhaling his faint scent, with her head on the arm, and then quietly whispered 'Alex,' before her mind left her in slumber.

30th September, 0640 hours – Ryhope Police Station

Cass prepped the fresh coffee maker in the kitchen, putting cups out ready for the team who would be in shortly. She knocked hers up, inhaling that smell that only freshly brewed beans can give, and wandered through to her office.

It was still too early to ring Matt, but her body had pulled her from sleep with a jerk a few hours before by the nightmare returning. This time though she woke alone, with no sloppy kisses from Ollie to dry her tears and let her know everything would be OK. So she had gone for a walk to clear her head, and then headed into work. She had already placed a load of exhibits from the store into the property system, and organised the staff rota for the next month.

Cass sighed a little; she would be glad when Kevin finally came back to work. She missed having him around to talk things over with. She had prescheduled a staff meeting for the three area depots for later that morning, intending to bring up the little things that had been bugging her for some time – the things Kevin normally dealt with. She supposed it was part of management, but it didn't mean she had to like it.

She glanced up as a shadow passed by her door.

'You're in early, Frank. Lots of transports today?'

The handyman stared at her for a second, almost not comprehending.

'Oh, yeah, there sure is. Just trying to get a head start. Gonna be a long day. How come you're here so early Cass? Normally it's only me and the 24:7 boys in at this time, and right now it's about time for their McDonald's run.'

Cass felt her stomach curdle at the thought. McDonald's was bad enough later in the day as an emergency meal, but for breakfast? Not that she had tried their breakfast range but grease first thing on a morning was something she had never been able to face.

'I feel the same way,' said Frank, seeing her grimace as he went to move away from the door. He turned to leave, then almost as an afterthought, he turned back towards Cass.

'How's the murder enquiry coming along? You know who the killer is yet?'

'Evidence is there so fingers crossed, though nothing as yet.' Her response was automated, her attention already turned back to the computer screen.

'Well you have a good day now.'

'You too, Frank.'

She listened to the soft tread of his footsteps as he made his way down the corridor.

The 'to do' pile on her desk now looked a little less intimidating than the 'done' pile. Cass took a long gulp of her now lukewarm coffee, and got up to take the bags of property through to the transit store in the front office.

When she returned she could hear the grumble of the coffee maker as it worked to keep the coffee warm. Popping her head round the door, she saw Deena in the kitchen. 'Hey, Deena, you OK?'

'Thanks for the coffee, Cass. I'm fine thanks, just heard from Faith. She's on her way in and she's bringing us all breakfast. She grabbed one for you too.'

'Great thanks. I'll be in my office.'

When Faith walked in a few minutes later with her arm full of McDonald's bags, Cass almost groaned out loud. What were the odds?

She thought for a moment she might get away with just not eating but Deena and Faith decided invading her office and eating together was the plan for the morning. Deena placed a fresh cup of coffee in front of her, and Faith handed her a small bag.

'Hope you like sausage and egg muffins?'

'Who doesn't?' said Cass, trying not to give away the fact her stomach was threatening to churn.

She pulled open the top of the bag and her stomach, taking her by complete surprise, growled loudly in response to the hot, fried smell coming from the bag. Faith smiled at her, her muffin already in her hand, and took a big bite.

They both groaned their appreciation, chewing as Cass pulled hers from the bag. Tentatively, she took a bite and her mouth exploded, lost in the taste sensation.

'Mmmmm,' she muttered. 'Why have I never tasted this before?'

Deena exchanged a glance with her friend, 'Never?'

Cass shook her head and took another bite, just as the office phone started to ring loudly.

'Cass Hunt,' she answered, swallowing the food down quickly. It changed to a solid lump in her throat as she heard Kevin's voice. 'Cass, it's going to be a couple of weeks before I'm back. Madge passed away in her sleep last night.' His breath caught on the sentence and she could hear how close to tears he was.

Her eyes began to shine as her voice turned gruff with emotion. 'I'm so sorry, Kevin. Take as long as you need. If there's anything I can do please let me know.'

He caught a sob as he said his goodbye, and Cass carefully replaced the receiver, her appetite now well and truly a thing of the past.

Deena and Faith had also put their breakfast down.

'Poor Kev. We'll get a card while we are on the rounds today. I'll email round about a collection. Did he say when the funeral would be?'

'No, not as yet. When I find out I'll let you know. Faith, thank you for the breakfast. I'm sorry I can't finish it.'

Faith nodded as she packed up the wrappers and left over food, and they made their way back into the CSI office.

Cass put her head in her hands, for just a moment as her composure threatened to break. Poor Kevin. She'd got to know him quite well since being promoted to CSM. Madge was his whole world. She could only imagine how he must be feeling.

After a few minutes of thinking about Kevin, her thoughts wandered to Ollie and she decided she'd waited long enough, picked up the phone and called the vet's number.

30th September, 1435 hours – The Denes Park, Sunderland

Sitting on the bench, Albert was lost in thought. He barely registered the shadow of a man passing him, but he noticed the weight change on his bench immediately.

Eyes blazing, he turned to confront the interloper, believing it to be those horrible kids from the bandstand. Surprised, his eyes took in the figure of a man. Registering his dishevelled clothing, Albert realised the man was like him. Homeless. His eyes narrowed suspiciously.

'Wanna drink, old-timer?' asked the man, offering the neck of the open bottle of Bells. Albert wanted to refuse, he really did. But it had been so long since he had had a swig of whisky. He was still pondering when the man added, 'It's alright, mate. I'm just in the mood for company is all. Normally sit over in the Lodge, but the damn kids are running riot. Bloody skateboards and bikes flying everywhere. Can't stand the little shits.'

Tentative friendship sealed, Albert reached for the bottle. He drew in a long gulp, and then coughed as the instant warmth spread down to his belly. 'It's been a while since I had the good stuff,' he said, handing the bottle back.

The man shook his head a little, 'Nah, you keep it, mate. I really need to get back to the Mrs before she blows a gasket. I'm John by the way.'

'Albert.' He nodded slightly, keeping a tight grip on the bottle.

'See you around, Albert. Might start coming here on occasion if you don't mind the company?'

'Not at all, laddo. Thanks for the drink.'

He watched John walk away, before opening the bottle and greedily taking another long drink. He felt his eyes start to droop slightly, and carefully put the bottle under his coat.

Nice lad that. And after that final thought, he drifted off to sleep.

30ᵗʰ September, 1605 hours – Cass's Cottage

'Well if that's what you think then no problem. I'll pick him up tomorrow afternoon. Thank you, Matt.'

Cass put the mobile back in her pocket and pushed open the cottage door. She was immediately hit by the smell of baking, the sweet aroma leading her straight to the kitchen.

'Mama, you're here! I thought you weren't arriving until tomorrow? You should have called me. I would've picked you up from the train station.'

She waited for her mum to put the spoon of butter icing down on the counter, then threw her arms around her mum's ample form. Cass breathed in the smell of her mum's perfume and allowed herself to feel like a child again, just for a minute. Her mum pushed her back and held her at arm's length, looking at her in concern.

'Cassandra Meredith Hunt, you have lost so much weight you're positively skinny! Have you been eating properly? How's the pup?'

'Ma,' groaned Cass with a grin. 'He's OK, coming home tomorrow. Matt says he's still a little weak so not to walk him too far but he's going to be OK. We need to see if he has any more seizures and if he does then he'll be put on epilepsy medication.'

Her voice softened, and she added, 'I'm glad you're here, Mama. I've missed you. How's Roger?'

Her mother blushed slightly, 'Oh he's wonderful. As usual. I still can't believe I managed to find him. After all this time.'

Roger was her mother's school sweetheart. They'd dated all the way through senior school then had attended different colleges and drifted apart. Rose Peters had met Cass's father in college, they had dated and then she had fallen pregnant quite quickly with Cass. Her father had insisted they get married, it was the 'done thing' in those days, and then when Cass was tiny her dad had proceeded to run off with another woman, leaving Rose to raise Cass on her own.

Rose was the first to say how hard it had been, working part-time to make ends meet, and running around after a toddler with no additional family support. But she had done it. Even if Rose couldn't afford a pair of tights she had always made sure Cass never wanted for anything.

Roger had lost his wife in a tragic car accident and was on a downward spiral when he had noticed Rose in the bar a few years earlier. They had talked, and within weeks were living together. Cass had been a very happy maid of honour at their wedding a few years back. The best part for Cass though, was knowing that Roger would always take care of her mum, no matter what happened. He was Managing Director of a large transport company so always had the funds to spoil her and make her feel special. And Rose felt very special; not a day went by when she wasn't grateful for reconnecting with Roger and for all that represented. She acknowledged all the time that she wouldn't care if he had no money, and maintained part-time work in a call centre to keep her independence.

'I'm going to go jump in the shower, Mama, it's been a long day. Have you baked something yum for tea or shall I go pick us up some take out?'

'Home-made corned beef pie, with mash and peas. That OK?'

'Mum. I love you. You're the best.'

Cass was still smiling at her mum cooking her favourite meal as she headed down the hall towards the stairs. She had no sooner put her foot on the first step when she heard a loud knock at the door.

As she pulled the door open, Alex was on the threshold, a tin of shortbread and bunch of flowers in his hand.

'Alex, you're back. How was your trip?'

'Great yeah, Mary and Violet are both doing well and are home now. Mum's rushing about like a very proud blue-arsed fly. How's you? Where's Ollie?' he asked, looking past her for the dog. He pulled out a large bone from behind his back and smiled, 'I had the butcher cut him the best bone.'

Cass swallowed a little, still upset that Ollie was in the vets, and touched by Alex's sweetness of thinking of him.

'He's at the vets – I came home on Sunday and he was having a seizure. He's OK, comes home tomorrow. I'll put the bone in the freezer. You coming in?'

'Yea sure. Something smells good.'

The kitchen door swung open, and Rose popped her head out shouting 'Cass,'

Her voice lowered as she noticed Cass in the hall. 'Oh, you're there. I thought you were going in the shower? I was just going to ask where your masher is.'

She paused and directed her gaze towards Alex. Her eyes narrowed slightly as she quickly assessed him. 'I'm Rose, Cass's mum. And you are?'

'Alex McKay, ma'am. A colleague from work.'

'Ma'am is what they call the Queen. I'm not her. Rose is fine,' she paused then added, 'Cass doesn't have colleagues over. Is something wrong?'

'No, I was just bringing Ollie a bone. Cass told me he was feeling under the weather,' said Alex in what he thought was a smooth response.

'Funny that, didn't realise the dog was allowed shortbread and flowers too.'

Rose paused a moment, watching as Cass's cheeks filled with heat. *Well well, my daughter likes this guy.*

'I'm just messing, Alex. Come on in, I'm about to dish up dinner. I presume you like corned beef pie, mash and peas?'

Alex smiled broadly as Rose retreated back into the kitchen.

'I like your mum.'

'She's great – I'll kill her later though. Teasing you like that.'

'It's fine, she reminds me a little of my mum. Sharp wit. You sure you don't mind me staying for dinner?'

Cass shook her head, took the bone off Alex, and headed into the kitchen.

Chapter Eleven

'Mum, I said I shouldn't be late tonight. Stop fussing over Ollie.' Cass paused, slightly frustrated as her mother rambled on down the phone. She frowned as she took in her next sentence. 'He's not allowed on the couch! He knows he's not allowed, Mum. Please shove him off. You're pandering to him.'

Alex knocked lightly on the door, giving her a smile as she motioned him towards the chair in her office.

'Mum, last time. Don't let the dog on the couch. He has two beds of his own and he sleeps on them quite happily. And stop feeding him chicken! He has his own food; he does not need people food!'

Her mother once again spoke down the earpiece, and Cass sighed as she said, 'Yeah I love you too. I'll see you tonight.'

'Mothers,' she muttered, looking up with a grin at Alex.

'That's what mums do I guess,' his mind wandering to his own mum for a moment. There was nothing she loved more than the house full of her brood and comfort food cooking on the stove.

'Families are strange. I know my mum frustrates me, but we are so close. I can't ever imagine her just not being there.'

'Yeah I know what you mean. I'm the oldest of eight. My mum's the glue that holds us all together. When Dad died, we all leaned on her, and through her grief she managed to support us and hold every one of us as we cried. I can't imagine anything being so bad that we would just walk away.'

'How come you moved away?'

Alex paused, trying to formulate his words. His relationship had ended badly, but he didn't like to badmouth Helen. It wasn't her fault he was so focused on his career. He knew it had ended because of him.

'Helen's family live in Sunderland. Her job was down here, all her friends. We decided here would be the best place to start our lives together. After we split up I guess I always thought I'd go home eventually, but that day just hasn't arrived yet.'

'You moved down here for Helen? Because it made her happy and it was what she wanted? You must miss your family a lot, Alex.'

Alex coughed a little, clearing his throat. He often tried to convince himself he stayed for the job, but he knew deep down the real reason he hadn't moved back to Edinburgh was that he felt like a failure. As much as he loved every member of his family, they were all married with kids, except himself and Ali. Alex had sacrificed any chance of that when he had pushed Helen away by choosing his job over her. And in those rare moments of clarity that suddenly occur when a light bulb goes off, he was ashamed. No woman should ever be second best to a job. His mother had taught him to respect women, and his dad, despite being a police officer until the day he died, had never ceased to make his mum feel special.

Realising suddenly that Cass was looking at him in concern, he smiled a sad smile. 'Yeah, I miss them. I'm actually planning on heading back up there in a week or so, all being well.'

'That's great, Alex, that you visit them so regularly I mean.'

He rose to his feet, using the movement to stretch a little. 'I'd better get back upstairs. The paperwork on my desk is about to take over the office. Thanks for the chat, Cass.'

'Anytime,' said Cass, watching thoughtfully as he walked out of her office. She found herself listening to his footsteps down the corridor and couldn't help thinking they were the steps of a man whose past was weighing heavily on his shoulders. Sighing deeply, sadness suddenly glazing her eyes, Cass knew she recognised the same heavy steps when she walked. She of all people understood how hard it was to let the past go and move forward. Or at the very least the letting the past go bit, she was still working on it after all.

2nd October, 1340 hours – Unit 12b, Enterprise Park, Sunderland

He smiled to himself as he sanded the piece he was working on. Slow smooth strokes along the grain the wood. This coffin was already a masterpiece, the intricate carving on the lid section finally complete. It had been an order for a unique piece, placed through his website with a very specific description.

He had to and fro'd with the buyer on the price, and the intricacy, and eventually they had settled on the design being a section of the lid instead of the whole thing. A piece so elaborate would have taken him a year to complete effectively.

He had started the business when he was in his late twenties, and was now established and had an excellent reputation for delivering the goods as promised.

Not that he was really worried about reputation, but he enjoyed the work. He enjoyed the fact other people would carry out their own morbid fantasies in the items he built, felt a kind of empowerment because of it. No matter what they did, they were always linked to him through the carefully handled wood.

His mother had always loved his woodwork. Not that she had known he made coffins. But when he had portrayed a talent for carpentry, she had pushed the Vicar into letting him repair anything that broke in the church. The Vicar had always complied; free labour was appreciated.

This piece was almost ready for shipping. It had to be at its designated location in six days. The buyer had wittered something about a convention of some sort in Whitby, and wanted it delivering to the convention address, after which time she would be taking it home. The courier was due to pick it up tomorrow.

But it had to be perfect first.

He could not entertain imperfection in any way.

Imperfection like the old man. He was easy to befriend, just coaxing with food and alcohol was enough to gain his trust. Stupid fool.

He was patient though, not rushing him, and didn't question him constantly. Everything he had found out so far had been through the old man running his mouth off when he was drunk.

Not long to go, everything was falling into place. In a week he would be putting on his second show. Just as soon as he found the place the old guy called home. It was one secret he had not yet disclosed.

Perhaps tonight though; he'd already bought a nice cheap bottle of whisky to help things along. The old man was particularly partial to a tot of Scotch. He intended to let him drink more than a tot.

His keen eyes noticed a slight blemish on the side of the coffin. Concentrating, he slowly swept the sandpaper back and forth over the mark until it eventually vanished. Finally, happy it couldn't be any better, he put down the sandpaper and reached for a cloth to wipe the surfaces before he began staining the wood.

Chapter Twelve

Cass sighed deeply as she left the meeting room. Her individual consultation had identified her as one of the at-risk roles, which she had already known but it still stung. And with Kevin being off it had fallen to her and Jason to bolster staff morale. Greg was due back in for a late shift today and had his meeting scheduled for 5 p.m.

Cass had already decided to wait and have a chat with him, but a glance at the clock made her realise he would be delaying his meeting. There were already four jobs in the late shift file on the board, two of which were urgent. Fred, who was supposed to finish at 4 p.m., had taken an additional couple of tasks and headed off to get them done before he went home.

The phrase 'one of those days' popped into her head as she sat down and opened her inbox.

First on the list, and marked urgent, was a mail from someone whose name she didn't recognise.

From: Patrick Kelly
To: Cassandra Hunt
Heading: Advanced notice of release
Miss Hunt,

> *My name is Patrick Kelly and I work for the probation service in Durham. I have been advised to inform you of the impending release of prisoner, Carl Jameson, into the care of the service, with myself being named as Probation Officer. Carl is due for release on 19th October and has been ordered to reside in the Durham area. He has conditions not to enter Sunderland or contact you in any way, and if he makes attempts to speak with you, I would advise you to contact the Police immediately. I understand that this may come as a shock, and that you may have concerns regarding this release but would like to reassure you that Carl has been through some progressive therapy while incarcerated and is not believed to be a threat to himself or others at this time. His early release is due to a successful appeal hearing last week. The appeal panel did not receive any comments from you in relation to his*

unsuitability for release and it was presumed that you believe he has reformed.

I can be contacted in the office on 01918858585 should you wish to discuss this matter. Your contact information was provided to me by Teesside Crown Court as the most accurate and up to date. I have also issued a letter to your home address to confirm.

Yours sincerely
Patrick Kelly, Senior Probation Officer.

Cass felt bile rise in her throat as panic threatened to envelop her. How the hell could he be released? It had only been eight years. He had been sentenced to twelve, the presiding Judge specifying he should serve the full term.

She had sent the letter stating she did not believe he was capable of acting as a normal human being, she was sure she had. She had prepared it at work on the day of the murder and put in the internal mail. Hadn't she? Hyperventilating slightly, she quickly rummaged through the outbox tray on her desk, pulling out the pile and scattering it on her desk. And she stared in numb shock at the pristine envelope addressed to Frankland Prison.

'Shit.' She muttered under her breath, fighting to maintain her composure and not grab her keys and make a run for it. Forcing herself to breathe deeply, she tried to calm herself down. He didn't know where she was, nothing she had was listed publicly. Even her Facebook account had minimal friends on her list.

Tears pricked and she muttered 'Shit,' again.

'You stupid idiot. How could you forget to post the single most important thing you send every year?'

'Talking to yourself is paramount to craziness,' said Alex softly from the doorway. Then, realising how upset she was he entered quickly and closed the door.

'Cass, what's wrong?'

She shook her head at him, unable to speak as her breath caught in her throat.

'Is it Ollie? Cass, come on, love, tell me what's wrong. Maybe I can help?'

'Not Ollie,' she whispered softly. Taking a shaky breath, she looked up at Alex, and in that moment he wanted nothing more than to gather her in his arms and tell her everything would be OK, and make the statement true.

He walked around the desk, and knelt in front of her, placing his hands gently over the top of hers.

'Tell me, Cass.'

Taking a shaky breath, Cass began. 'Eight years ago I was in a relationship with Carl Jameson. He … hurt me, and now he's being released from prison cos I was stupid enough not to send my rejection of appeal letter to the board. How could I forget to send it, Alex? After what he did, how could I be so stupid?'

Alex's anger spiked – this was who had hurt Cass, caused the shadows in her eyes the morning he'd startled her. He paused, letting her take a shaky breath and continue.

'I'd been with him for two years. I was so naïve, Alex. Every time he hit me and apologised I would just hope he wouldn't do it again and he would mean it this time. He had me move away with him, I hardly saw mum, or my friends. And then he came in from work and thought that I had been out with someone he knew. I hadn't, I'd been in the house cleaning all day. He was blind drunk, and I was in bed when he came in. I woke up to him hitting me,' she paused again, trying to stop the tears before they fell, 'He kept hitting me and didn't stop. I've been told that I was unconscious within a couple of minutes but that he kept going. It was a neighbour who reported him, saying she had heard me screaming. I woke up in hospital five days later, with severe concussion, cracked cheek and jaw, broken collar bone, and several broken ribs.'

Cass cracked and a huge sob caught in her throat. She hadn't told him everything, she couldn't. The other stuff was too much. The psychiatrist had told her that the memories were too painful for her to deal with. But faced with it all here, head on, she was on the verge of remembering. Taking a deep, shaky breath, she pushed the thoughts to the back of her mind and steadied herself.

Looking at Alex, she gave an almost imperceptible shake of her head.

'It's OK, you don't need to say any more, Cass. What do you want me to do? I'll phone the prison, speak with probation, whatever you need.'

'He doesn't know where I am. I'll be fine, Alex, honest. It was just such a shock. I still can't believe I forgot to post the letter. I'd prepared it on the day of the Mackintosh murder. It just slipped my mind to put in it in the post.'

'Everything's gonna be OK, Cass. I'll speak with the local DCI and see what's what. Which prison is he at?'

'Frankland. He's due for release on the 19th.'

'OK I'll take care of it, Cass. What're you doing now?'

'I need to speak with Greg but I just want to go home. Mum leaves tomorrow. I need to tell her about this too.'

'I'll go tell Greg you're heading home. Just go, Cass. Helluva day. I'll come up and see you later.'

Cass nodded slowly. She looked into his eyes and then did something completely out of character. She leaned in and kissed him briefly on the lips.

Flushing slightly, she added, 'Thank you.' Then gathered her things, and walked out, leaving Alex staring after her in shock.

7th October, 1005 hours – Ryhope Police Station

'What do mean you're putting me through to someone else? You just told me you were putting me through to the Sergeant who dealt with the case. Please, don't put me on ... dammit,' cursed Alex as the inane, tacky hold music blared in his ear.

He was only on hold a moment when a gruff voice answered.

'DCI Clinton Proffitt speaking. DCI McKay?'

'Yeah, just Alex will do fine.'

'Clint to my friends. I understand you're making enquiries about the Hunt case?'

'Correct. I need to speak to the sergeant who dealt with the case.'

'I ran point on that case. Hell of a thing. Not one I'll forget in my lifetime. Jameson beat her so badly you could barely recognise her.'

'He's due for release next week. Cass, I mean Miss Hunt, failed to send her rejection to appeal letter in due to unforeseen circumstances. What else can you tell me?'

'The neighbour phoned it in. Domestic violence was a regular occurrence at the address, but the neighbour said this sounded different, said it sounded like he was killing her. Our boys were there within five minutes of the call, but Mrs Bradley, that was the neighbour, had delayed calling as she didn't want to be seen as a busy-body. I saw the scene myself after the medics had removed Miss Hunt. It was like a wild animal had been let loose in the bedroom. Sheets were all torn up, there was blood spatter everywhere, and the mirrors were all smashed. It was a damn shame what happened. And what he did to the baby, well that was just incomprehensible.'

Alex felt bile rise up into his throat.

'Baby? Cass had a baby?'

'No, son, you misunderstand me. Miss Hunt was pregnant. Twenty weeks along. Jameson stabbed her at four points to her stomach, not with the intention of killing her, the consultant said, but to kill the child. We couldn't get him on murder of the baby because the law states that murder of a foetus is not murder. The CPS took it under advisory when sentencing for Section 20, and the judge advised he shouldn't be allowed an early release as long as Miss Hunt maintained that he was a danger. When did you say he was being released? I'll need to make sure the beat bobbies are made aware. He's a monster.'

'Next week. The 19th,' said Alex, his tone distracted. He was still trying to process that Cass had been pregnant at the time of the attack. It was bad enough she had stayed and put up with him hitting her for years. But to stay when there was a child involved? Alex was struggling to understand how any woman could stay when she was pregnant. He shook his head in disbelief.

'Is there anything else I can help with, Alex?' asked Clint after a momentary pause.

'No. Thanks for the update, Clint, much appreciated.'

Alex hung up the phone, surprised at the leaden feeling he had in his gut.

How could she stay when she was pregnant?

His phone alarm went off suddenly, making him jump. Pushing the thoughts of Cass to one side, to be pondered over later, he made his way to the Super's office for the management meeting.

Chapter Thirteen

'Mum, I'll be fine honestly. You need to get back to Roger. He'll be missing you like crazy,' said Cass, hugging her mum while trying to push her towards the train standing at the platform.

'Cass, promise me you will invest in an alarm system. I don't want that man to come anywhere near you. After what he did last time, I'm so afraid for you. If I stay and he turns up, I'll wring his bloody neck before he gets his maulers on my daughter again.'

Rose was staring at Cass, unshed tears in her eyes. She had seen her only child in the hospital bed, damaged at the hands of such violence. She had been there when Cass woke up, and held her as the great wracking sobs had forced their way out of her daughter to the point that the doctor had had to sedate her. And she had sat with her every day until her release. Roger had paid the deposit on the cottage, under protest, and Rose had helped Cass move in, helped her get settled. The thought of that man hurting her daughter again had her beside herself with worry.

Cass smiled at her mum a little, 'I know you would, Mum. But he's not going to come anywhere near me. He doesn't know where I am. I will get an alarm system fitted I promise. And I will call you every day, OK?'

Rose sniffed as she nodded. She dropped her bag on the floor and grabbed Cass in a hug so tight she could barely breathe.

'I love you, my daughter,' whispered Rose into her hair.

Pushing back the lump that appeared in her throat, Cass whispered back, 'I loves you too, Mama. Lots and lots …'

'Like jelly tots,' they both added together.

Cass smiled and waved at her mum as the train pulled out of the station, but all she wanted to do was call her back and have her never leave. She hated saying goodbye to her mum; it just made it more real that she would be returning to an empty cottage. And at the minute, that was the last thing she wanted. She felt a shiver of fear as she left the platform.

Maybe Alex would like some company tonight.

9th October, 1450 hours – Ryhope Police Station

Cass pulled her phone from her bag for the umpteenth time that day. Shaking it a little and frowning, she wondered if she had broken it. She'd sent a few texts to Alex and had no response. He hadn't been in work so she hadn't been able to talk to him, about Jameson or anything else. She wondered what she had done wrong, whether he was ignoring her. He hadn't been in contact with her since she had told him about Jameson.

Finally shaking her head in bewilderment, she put the phone back. She'd just have to catch him next time he was in work.

10th October, 1350 hours – Police Gym, Sunderland City Police Station

Alex felt the burn in his thighs and calves as he pounded the running machine, his headset firmly embedded in his ears. He had barely been out of the gym the last two days, exercise was the one thing he could always control and it helped him think clearly.

A frown marred his face as he thought back to the earlier conversation with Ali.

'You're judging her on an incident you know nothing about, bro. She might have had a perfectly good reason to stay with the scumbag. Maybe she didn't have anyone else to turn to. Maybe she thought she could control the situation by staying. Maybe there were other factors influencing her decision. That's something you need to ask her. But stop being so hard on her. After all she's been through, I would've thought you would be the one person who would want all the facts before jumping to conclusions. You're always the level-headed one. What about Cass makes you so damn pig-headed?'

It had been a long-winded speech, one that had culminated in Ali slamming the phone down on Alex in frustration, something his brother never did.

And now as he pounded the treadmill, Ali's words echoed round his mind.

Who *was* he to judge her? He had told her all about Helen and not once had she said he was a jerk for working constantly and pushing his wife away, not once had she said he put the job ahead of her. She had listened to him. That was it. Just listened.

He pressed the buttons hard on the machine, pulled the headset from his ears and made his way back to the changing room.

I'm a complete jerk.

He pulled his phone from his puma gym bag. Noting the missed calls from Cass, and the texts, he sighed again. Texting wasn't something he was fond of, but he couldn't face speaking to her yet.

Hey, Cass. Sorry my phone's been off and I've been manic. Can we talk tomorrow? Alex.

Chapter Fourteen

10ᵗʰ October, 2010 hours – Hidden Cave, Sunderland Coast

His three-week wait had passed quickly and he knew he was ready.

He watched as the old man shifted his position on the park bench, the old, scraggy mutt curled up next to him, and listened as the man swore loudly at a couple of teenagers passing by. A smile curled his lips as he watched him throw an empty lager can at them – the old man had spirit.

It would be interesting to see how long it lasted.

He had it all planned out now. He'd taken the time to 'befriend' the man, plying him with whisky instead of his usual choice of White Lightning. He'd actually taken his mangy dog a sausage one day and it had sealed the friendship.

For him though, it had taken a lot of resolve to drink from the same bottle as the old man. He hated the thought of germs transferring from the yellow teeth and dank mouth of the old man onto the bottle end, and then to himself. But he had endured, taking great care to increase his own cleanliness when he returned home. It was the only way to gain the trust of the old man, to the extent he had found out his name – Albert Grieves. Not that he didn't already know his name, but it was good to have verification before one attacked.

Albert had been easy to manipulate, providing him with all the information he needed and much more that he didn't, but it had paid off in the end. The old man had eventually shown him where he slept most nights; the secret place he never told anyone about. The place with a couple of blankets and a holey, smelly dog bed for the mutt – the place that Albert called home.

He'd followed him one night, just to be sure Albert hadn't been lying to him. The old man was right about one thing, it was perfect.

The perfect place to put an end to a pitiful life.

He left the park, knowing it wouldn't be long until Albert would progress to the shelter for his supper. He would never let a condemned man not have his last supper after all. And after that, Albert would go to his secret place, and *he* would be waiting.

He was there within minutes, and took great care moving the toolbox from its place behind a rock. He had visited the place earlier that day, taking what he needed as props for his show.

The moon was hidden behind a bank of dark clouds, and what little glow it gave barely illuminated the dark entrance to the cave. He felt his feet sink into the soft sand and knew he had his work cut out for himself afterwards, making it seem like he'd never been there. Forensics, after all, were of the utmost importance. He smirked in the darkness as he remembered the little ants running frantically around the crash site. He had already found the perfect point from which to watch them enjoy this masterpiece.

That would all come later however. For now, it was time to get ready.

He removed the hammer from its home in the toolbox and blended back into the dark shadows of the cave, his finger on the switch to the portable light he had also prepared earlier.

10ᵗʰ *October, 2310 hours – Hidden Cave, Sunderland Coast*

Albert's steps were unsteady as he made his way back along the sea front. The meal at the Salvation Army hostel had filled him, and now all he wanted to do was sleep. Sometimes, he kept some cider back for the day after, especially when his dole money was running out, but not today. Today was the anniversary of his son's death, so he had downed the whole bottle and some of the next one. His mind was now almost devoid of emotion, his thoughts hazy as he made his way to the place he called home.

It had been nice though, John sitting next to him and listening to his stories about Tommy. John had left hours before, leaving Albert to wallow for the rest of the day while drinking himself into oblivion.

His feet slipped slightly as he made his way down the small rabbit path that led to the beach. His cave was set back from the sand, hidden by a number of bushes. Hardly anyone knew it was there. Being hard to get to, the beach wasn't the most popular with tourists, which suited Albert down to the ground. The spot was his home.

Reaching the bottom, Albert headed for his favourite bush, undid his flies, and took a leak. He heard the dog kicking his back legs at the sand, and knew he was finished his business too.

'Come on, Scruffpot, let's go to bed.'

As Albert entered the cave, Scruff stood to attention beside him, growling into the darkness.

A light suddenly hit his eyes, and instinctively he blinked, taking a step back.

A burst of anger filled him as the man stepped into the light.

'Get out of my cave!' shouted Albert, stepping forward.

The man took a couple of steps towards him, and slowly recognition arrived.

'John,' gasped Albert, not seeing the hammer until it was too late. It connected with the side of his head with a dull thud, and pain exploded behind Albert's eyes as he staggered.

'Please, John. Stop.' He begged as John swung the hammer again.

10ᵗʰ *October, 2325 hours – Hidden Cave, Sunderland Coast*

Time passed quickly, his anticipation building, and in what seemed like only moments, he heard the gruff voice of the old man as he made his way down to the cave entrance. As Albert entered, he flicked the switch, the compact generator kicking in with a low hum, and flooding the rear of the cave in false light.

He smiled as the dog jumped and let out a yelp of shock and took a step forward as Albert's mouth opened with a wide 'o.' He kept smiling as the flash of rage crossed the old man's face, and Albert yelled, 'Get out of my cave!'

He moved his head from side to side silently, and as Albert took a step forward, he swung the hammer round hard, feeling it connect with the side of the old man's temple. To anyone else the crunch would have been sickening, but he felt the rush flood through him. Impressed by the old man's resolve, he swung again and connected with the same thud, feeling the faint splash of blood spatter on his cheek. Swinging hard once more, he watched with satisfaction as Albert finally dropped to his knees, and fell face down into the sand with a groan.

Albert lay there now, shivering with fear.

He stepped away for a moment, heading towards the old dog which though loyal, was petrified and cowering beside a rock. He vaguely heard Albert scream as the hammer sped down to meet the dog's head, right between the eyes. His death was almost instantaneous. But still he made the old man suffer by raining yet more blows on the furry body.

Albert just lay there, sobbing, begging him to stop.

He turned back towards the old man who was now curled up into the foetal position. 'Please. Please don't kill me. I never did nothin' to you, John. Please.'

He listened as Albert begged, his body heaving with wracking sobs as his tears fell into the dry sand.

Ignoring him, he pulled one wrinkled hand from under the old man and held it in place by pressing a knee into Albert's shoulder. A little belatedly, he stuffed a rag into the old man's mouth, muffling the fear induced hiccups, and swiftly brought the hammer down onto Albert's fingers, smiling into the dull light as they shattered with a resounding crack.

Albert screamed his pain into the dirty rag, his eyes bulging as the tears ran rivers of pain through the wrinkles on his cheeks.

Now the old man understood the severity of his situation.

It took almost an hour for Albert to die, though the light extinguished from his eyes long before his heart finally gave out. He'd found it much harder work than killing the dog, and he was tired. But he carefully placed the metal fragment into the jacket pocket worn by the old man, listening as it jingled slightly with the collection of bottle tops Albert kept.

He smiled again at the confusion he knew the police would endure at the tiny piece of metal, wondering what it was and what it represented. The fact he put it there just to confuse them pleased him.

The old man's battered body lay twisted and broken in the sand, his blood decorating the cave walls like the art of some ancient tribe. Albert's still eyes watched lifelessly as he took the lamp and generator to the car and returned to remove the evidence that he had been to the cave. By the light of his head torch, he took great care in cleaning all evidence of himself from the cave. He used a second rag to clean the blood and tiny bone fragments off the hammer before replacing it into his toolbox. His final actions were to brush a large section of seaweed over his shoeprints, eradicating all tread detail, and dragged it behind him as he made his way up the steep path to his car.

The sun was just starting to appear on the horizon as he threw the seaweed back down to the beach, placed his precious toolbox into the boot, got into the car seat covered with a cut up black bin bag, and drove to the place he had so carefully selected; his own private balcony from which to watch the next act of his great show.

11th October, 1205 hours – Burglary Crime Scene, Sunderland

Cass jabbed the squirrel hair brush through her pony tail in one motion, before gathering up the pots of powder and acetates from her forensic kit and closing the case with a snap. She carefully sealed the evidence bag containing the swabs and placed it, with the lifts, into the pocket of her combat trousers.

It had been a busy day so far; Faith had phoned in sick after getting some bug off Joey who, she had been reliably informed, was still off school. Deena was on annual leave which left Fred Everett working the jobs, until the late-shift came in anyway. It was turning out to be one of those days, so Cass had dutifully picked up several jobs off the log. When it was busy everyone mucked in, at least everyone was supposed to. She frowned as she remembered the conversation with the city centre depot earlier that morning and their complete lack of support relating to the outstanding jobs. She would have to schedule a meeting with them to discuss the benefits of team work and cooperation, and brief Jason on any impending problems. Kevin was still off work, Marge's death hitting him hard, and Cass didn't know when he would return.

Her current job, a bogus official, had been a quickie she had attended on route to another. Grabbing her case, she wandered into the living room to tell the elderly victim what would happen next.

'Martha,' she said, kneeling down in front of the frail woman sat on the sofa. She waited patiently until Martha looked at her, tears glistening in her opaque eyes. 'I've taken some swabs from the mug you said the woman had used. I'm going to send those off to our DNA lab to see if there's anything on them. I've also got a couple of fingerprint lifts off the mug itself which we'll check against known offenders on the computer.' Cass was fully aware of CID listening in from the armchair by the fire, but purposefully kept her attention directed at the frail old lady. Understanding passed over Martha's face, and she nodded at Cass.

'Thank you,' she said, the shock rendering her voice all but a whisper.

As Cass stood and nodded to Sam Walsh, one of the CID Burglary Team, she heard her name mentioned on the radio clipped to the side of her belt.

Taking her leave, she quickly put her gear in the van and jumped in, twisting her radio and pulling it from its clip. Turning the volume up slightly, she depressed the side button to speak. 'LV, this is 7265 Hunt, did I just hear you call for me?'

'Hey, Cass. Sorry to push this on you, I know you guys are busy. But it looks like we have a murder coming in. DCI McKay has requested you attend the rendezvous point as quickly as you can.'

Cass sighed deeply. It never rained but it poured. 'OK, LV, thanks. I'll call in some cover but can you make sure no ETAs are given for any jobs coming in? Also please ring the IPs for any outstanding jobs on the log and advise them of potential delays. I'll update you with staff details as soon as I have them. Where's the RV point?'

She jotted down the location quickly, clipped her radio back on her belt and turned the key in the ignition. She had received Alex's cryptic text yesterday and hadn't said, figuring today would be there soon enough. Now though, she doubted her decision, wondering what he would say when she got to the scene.

As the car radio kicked in, the gruff tones of Nickelback blared from the speakers, singing words about living and dying, and for a moment Cass felt a lump in her throat. Some days she wondered what the world was all about, when old ladies were robbed and people were killed; she took a minute to reflect on her silent question, resting her head on the steering wheel. If it wasn't for the evidence left behind, these people wouldn't get caught. It was why she did the job she did, to help those that couldn't help themselves, and give a voice to those who couldn't speak. Her sense of security rebuilt, she put the van in gear and headed for the scene.

It seemed like hours had passed before she arrived at the car park on top of the cliff, but really it had only been around ten minutes. She parked the van, took a deep swig from the bottle of water she always had to hand, and walked over to the melee of police cars.

Squinting in the bright sun, she stopped as a shiver suddenly passed through her. Cass shaded her eyes with her hand and scanned the area in the distance, feeling the little hairs rise on the back of her neck. She once again acknowledged the lead weight in her stomach. Shrugging in surrender, she knew it would be a bad one – but then she always got that feeling when it came to murder.

She had just given her name and force number to the loggist when she heard Alex's voice.

'Cass, thanks for getting here so quick. I was just about to start. We have a white male, believed homeless from his appearance. Severely beaten to death in a cave on the beach. His dog's also been killed. Containment is proving difficult as the cave entrance overlooks the sea – we've already got media on boats with telephoto lenses. I've got the Media Liaison trying to gain control but you know what that's like. Have also taken the liberty of contacting the coast guard who are en route with some floaters to manage the media. The body was found by two school kids who were bunking off school, they've been taken back to the station.'

Cass nodded, realising belatedly that he wouldn't want to talk at a crime scene. 'Poor kids. We can put up a tunnel tent at the entrance that should help obscure anything the press can see. How many officers have been in the cave?'

'One. The first officer on scene is only just out of probation. I've sent him back to the nick.' Alex sighed, then almost as an afterthought he added, 'The vomit to the exterior of the cave entrance is his.'

'OK. If you don't mind, I'll head down and begin. I'll need a couple of officers to help with the tunnel tent and equipment until my staff arrives. They're travelling from South Shields.'

'Porter, Johnson, you accompany Cass to the beach. Mind the path though, it's steep.' Alex turned slightly, dismissing the officers and Cass silently.

Alex had been right; the cliff path was steep. Cass almost fell a few times, her bulky kit causing more of a hindrance than a help. Porter and Johnson also concentrated on not slipping as they carried the stepping plates, tripod and large bag of other assorted kit between them. They all paused at the inner cordon manned by two more officers, and promptly plonked all the equipment down.

'Wait here while I take a look,' said Cass. She pulled on a white scene suit, and put blue plastic covers over her boots. Already she could feel the perspiration start to flow. It was uncharacteristically warm for the time of year, and the heat made the suits even worse. Snapping on two pairs of purple gloves, she yanked up the hood to the suit, and pulled a face mask over the top. Checking the settings on the camera, she began taking shots of the area leading to the cave.

As she approached the cave entrance, the sudden aroma of vomit filtered through the mask to her nostrils. Catching the gag reflex, she breathed deep and purposefully through her mouth, avoiding looking at the large pool that resembled vegetable soup. Of all the smells she encountered at a crime scene, vomit was always the one that knocked her for six and had, in the past, caused her to throw up in response.

Hugging the edge of the cave, she made her way inside.

'Jesus Christ,' muttered Cass as she took in the image of the blood-painted walls and the horrific injuries to the man and dog. She was surprised to feel bile rise in her throat. In the seven years she'd been doing the job, she had never seen anything quite so gruesome. The blood patterns up the wall showed multiple hits with whatever the killer had used. Grey brain matter was scattered around the old man's head and he was covered in contusions and lacerations. A wave of compassion flooded through her as she took in the torn, dirty blankets and the precious dog bed. Whatever his problems, the old man had tried to make the best for himself that he could. It was clear that this cave had been his home.

Cass finished her photography, before using her own footwear marks as a guide to retrace her steps back to the entrance. The sunlight hit her like a bolt and she fought back another wave of nausea. She pulled the mask off, bent over and put her hands on her knees as she gulped in breaths of air. Shaking her head ruefully, she acknowledged that for once, she was glad she had skipped breakfast.

Telling the officers to stand by, Cass made her way to the top of the cliff to speak to Alex.

'Alex, a word?' she said, motioning Alex to one side with her hand.

'You OK? You look a little green.' said Alex quietly.

Trying to hide how shaken she felt, she said, 'Yeah, hot in here.' She unzipped the front of the suit before continuing, 'We need a Blood Pattern Analyst and the doc down here. It's bad. Worst I've seen to be honest.'

'Nigel Evans will be here in a little over an hour. I'll ask COMMS to get the on-call analyst out. The lounge is here, you should go get a drink and what-not. Get out of your suit.'

Cass felt her cheeks flush at his innocent comment. Normally she was much thicker skinned; working for the police did that. Alex realised the implications and shook his head, rolling his eyes in an effort to diffuse her embarrassment. She felt herself start to smile back, and then feeling somewhat mortified at the thought of flirting at the scene of a murder, she drew back and said, 'It's OK thanks, I'll cool down later. Gonna head back down. Will you show Nigel where I am?'

Alex nodded. 'You want me to send your staff too?'

'No it's OK, tell them to wait in the lounge. The analyst and doc need to have a look first. Am going to put some stepping plates down, get the tent up and start my notes.'

As she turned, Alex slowly moved his hand and swiped at her face softly. Cass felt electricity shoot down her cheek and into her neck at the contact. She pulled back slightly, looking at him, silently asking him what he was doing. He cleared his throat, his cheeks flushing slightly. 'You erm....' clearing his throat he finished his sentence. 'You've got silver powder on your cheek.' Sensing his embarrassment, Cass grinned and said. 'Just call me the tin man. Silver face and no heart, that's me.' For a millisecond, a look of utter sadness crossed her face, but it was gone in an instant and Alex half thought he had imagined it.

By the time he thought to reply, she had turned away and was heading back down the cliff. He watched her figure retreat for a moment, then, pulling his head back in the game, he turned and headed back towards the lounge.

Cass had been on the beach for around an hour when the blood pattern analyst was led down the path. The tunnel tent had been erected at the entrance, and the front flapped slightly in the sea breeze. She put a hand over her eyes, trying to obscure the sun to see the woman that stood before her.

'Moira Phillips, I don't believe we've had the pleasure?' she questioned directly, holding her hand out towards Cass. There was the hint of an Irish accent and the red hair and pale skin backed up the evidence of her descent. With her short, slim frame, she looked almost like a pixie and Cass stretched out her own hand, shaking firmly, a little surprised at the strength of the grip from the unusually short female.

'I'm Cass, thank you for coming so quickly. Have you been briefed?'

Moira nodded in return, her keen eyes taking in Cass's somewhat dishevelled appearance and guarded look. 'Pretty bad is what I've been told but I'm guessing from how you look that it's worse than pretty bad?'

Cass nodded slowly. 'We have a male and a dog inside. The body can't be disturbed as the doc hasn't been yet. There's a lot of spatter and brain matter, and with the heat, he's starting to smell a little. The spatter may have been disturbed by either the offender as he cleaned up, or the boys who found the body.'

'Boys? Jesus. The things people do never cease to amaze me,' Moira muttered under her breath, before visibly steeling herself. 'I'm ready to go in.'

Cass held open the flap entrance to the tent, and allowed Moira to go in first, watching as she stepped carefully on the silver plates that had been strategically placed around the cave. Cass had managed to rig up some lighting, which though relatively dim, helped illuminate the inbuilt delve in the cliff face. There was also a ray of light coming in through a crack in the ceiling above the entrance and Cass heard Moira gasp as it seemed to illuminate the body of the old man.

Moira had been in the cave for around twenty minutes when a shout came from the cave entrance. They both exited quickly and came face to face with Nigel who was pulling on his foot covers.

'Two in a month, Cass? Something you're not telling me?' he joked lightly, smiling to accompany his humour.

Cass smiled back warmly and quickly introduced Moira, before escorting Nigel back into the cave. He frowned, the dim lights of the cave casting shadows over his straight-cut features. 'The PM's going to be a long one,' he said quietly as he pulled out his digital recorder and began making verbal notes.

11th October, 1320 hours – Ryhope Pier, Sunderland

It had taken him a while to get set up. His fishing line hung over the edge of the pier, aimlessly touching the water with no intent of catching fish. The brown fishing hat hung low over his eyes, helping the fake moustache obscure his features. Sometimes disguise was essential, and he took great care to ensure he used different ones for each job. He had invested in the likes of cheek inserts and fake teeth coverings. He currently looked right at home on the pier with the other fishermen.

The reality of course was that it just provided him a good vantage point from which to observe what was happening on the shore opposite. His grin had spread wide as he watched the young police officer bring up his breakfast outside the cave. Keen interest had almost marred his attempt at blending in as he watched *her*, the one who'd dealt with scene of his previous kill, boss some officers into helping her with a long tent at the entrance to the cave. He had already noticed the telephoto lenses on the boats drifting just deep enough not to beach themselves on the virtually still waves of the ocean, and he knew they were recording his show. He would stop at the newsagents on the way home and see what the headlines were saying.

He felt a moment of satisfaction – it was all thanks to him.

Momentarily he wondered who the tiny red-headed woman was, but as she came out of the cave when a male approached and started sketching, he decided she was some kind of scientist, designed to help tell the crime scene manager exactly what had occurred.

He frowned as he tried in vain to see to the top of the cliff where the persistent flashing blue lights proved a large police presence. He wondered if her sex slave was there, whether he had been lucky enough to nab the same team for his second show as for his first.

He was tired now. It felt like he had been up forever, and he knew when he finally crawled into bed, his hard work would be paid in full with the promise of a deep sleep.

His train of thought was suddenly interrupted by a gruff voice. Guardedly, he glanced up, knowing his hat and sun shades were helping hide him well. A young male stood in front of him, his tracksuit bottoms tucked into the tops of his socks and bright white Nike trainers stark against the wood of the pier. His eyes travelled up past the Sunderland football shirt to the lad's spotty, arrogant face. 'I said, can I have some spare change, mister,' spat the lad, scowling at him with a complete lack of fear.

Dislike brewed, and instantly he knew he had just discovered his next work of art. Deciding to begin his preparation work, he smiled at the young man

'Yeah sure.' He fumbled in his pocket and pulled out a few quid, holding his hand out to the lad, but clenching his fist closed before the coins were released, 'What's your name?'

The teenager paused for a moment, his eyes narrowing in suspicion. 'Andy Smith,' he said, holding out his hand.

Letting the coins drop into Andy's hand, he said, 'Sit yourself down, lad. Seems to be something going on over there.'

Shrugging, Andy sat down, cross-legged beside him, not noticing as his new friend's face twisted into a slight grimace.

Making friends was never a problem.

Chapter Fifteen

Cass had let the staff from the Shields office go home, only an hour past their mid-shift end time which wasn't too bad. Fred had long since left for the day and Greg was out processing the backlog of jobs. Cass's office resembled the proverbial bomb site, as the exhibits gathered thus far were strewn all over the floor and spare work desk.

Her own desk was covered in paperwork, thumbnail images and just general stuff. She sighed to herself – it was going to be another long night.

Knowing Alex was still somewhere in the station hadn't helped matters when she first started. She wanted to see him, to talk about what the hell was going on because she didn't have a clue what had changed from one day to the next.

But instead of pondering further, she had got on with the paperwork.

Carol and Frankie, two of the South Shields' CSIs, had already booked the exhibits out of Socard ready for Cass, and she was busy bagging them up and sealing the bags with unique tags. Some would go to HQ for processing and internal examination, and the rest would be handed to the Exhibits Officer who was due in her office at 10.30 p.m.

Deciding she needed a caffeine hit to boost her before starting on the murder box, she jumped up and strode out of the door – and bumped into someone coming the other way.

Impacting hard with a solid force, she stepped backwards instinctively, and grunted with a loud 'Oomph' before looking up into Alex's surprised face. His hands reached out quickly to steady her, his eyes not breaking her gaze.

She watched, fascinated, as they changed to a darker shade of grey and smouldered with sudden desire.

Her lips parted slightly, and she felt her breath grow shallow. *What on earth was going on?*

Alex broke the stare by stepping back from her with a small cough.

Momentarily confused, she blinked at him.

'You OK, Cass?' he asked, his voice a little gruff.

'Yeah, sorry. I ... I was just making coffee. Want one?'

He nodded and stood back to allow her into the main office.

Alex stood for a second in the corridor wondering what had happened. He felt like he'd been hit by a freight train. For the first time since Helen, he had almost kissed a woman. He wondered if Cass knew. He thought he spotted a reaction but he wasn't sure and it had made him step back in confusion. The fact she'd rushed past him to make the coffee, led him to believe she was upset. Realising he had to make it right, he followed her into the office.

'Cass, I'm sorry about that. I don't know what happened. I'll not bother you any more except in a work capacity. I've behaved in a manner that's ... untoward.'

Incredulous and mortified, Cass turned to look at him.

'Untoward? Which part? The part where I pour my heart out and tell you about Jameson and then you don't speak with me for days, or the part where you completely blank me today at the scene? Or possibly the part where you just looked at me like you wanted to kiss me, then pulled back in revulsion?'

She realised her voice had turned high pitched, and her cheeks had flushed a deep red. 'I know what Jameson did has ... damaged me. But I didn't think I was that repulsive.'

She caught the sob before it escaped, breathing deeply to try to push the emotion back as Alex just stood there in shock.

'Cass, what the hell are you on about? I didn't blank you at the scene and I was most definitely *not* repulsed. I thought I'd gone too far. That's why I stepped back – we're at work and I was bang out of order.'

He strode down the office in three large steps, put his fingers under Cass's chin and shook his head.

'You are not repulsive. Jameson has not damaged you. He is a complete prick who I would gladly wring the neck of if he ever comes near you again.'

A glimmer of hope shone in her eyes as she said, 'You're the second person to say that to me. Mum said it too.'

'Then your mum gets more kudos from me,' said Alex softly.

His thumb brushed across Cass's cheek. She hiccuped quietly, and he was lost. His head moved closer, her breath warm against his lips as her eyes shone brightly. He was so close he could almost hear her heartbeat. Their lips were close to touching when footsteps suddenly sounded in the corridor.

'Cass, you in?' said Greg's voice loudly.

Cass coughed, stepping away from Alex and back into the kitchen.

'In here, Greg. Just making a cuppa. You want one?'

'Yes please. Am bloody knackered. Whacked off ten jobs like. Has owt else come in that can't wait until tomorrow?' asked Greg as he dumped a bag of exhibits on the desk, along with his work file.

'No, log's clear, Greg. If you get them put through Socard and I'll sort the mail for tomorrow. Just leave what you need sending on your desk. I'm in the middle of it anyway.'

Greg looked up and realised Alex was there too, 'Oh hey, boss. Didn't see you there.' Redirecting his attention to Cass, he added, 'So what's going on with the murder?'

'Various samples recovered, should hopefully be something there. Will you be OK to attend the PM tomorrow with me and Sue? I need to pop over to the city depot and speak with the staff in the morning, then I'll be attending the forensic strategy meeting with Alex once the PM's done. It's scheduled to start at 10 a.m. at the Sunderland Royal.'

'Yeah sure, boss,' said Greg, popping his ID card into the computer and opening Socard as Cass placed his tea in front of him.

'Strong and black, just how you like it.'

Greg showed his thanks by taking a huge slurp, and Cass turned to get the other two cups but Alex had beaten her to it and was walking towards her.

As they entered her office, Cass shut the door behind them.

'Almost feel as if I'm in the headmaster's office now,' joked Alex as he set the mugs down on the table.

Cass stayed quiet as he turned to look at her. Deciding on honesty, he said, 'I haven't done this in a long time, Cass. I like you, I think you like me, but I'm out of my depth. I don't know how to deal with this.'

Blinking, Cass nodded her agreement.

'There hasn't been anyone since Carl. I never have people to my cottage so you're already closer than most people have ever been. I don't know how to deal with what I'm feeling, Alex. I'm petrified of starting anything with anyone and I'm crap at dealing with emotion. But I do like you too.'

She drew in a shaky breath – it was hard for her to talk to anyone about how she was feeling. It was like he had stripped the parts of her that were linked to emotion, leaving nothing but an empty shell. Only now something burned inside the shell, a glimmer of hope that maybe she would be able to move on.

'So ... we take it slow? Start as friends maybe? And if *this* leads to anything then fair enough, if not we both gain a friend? As clichéd as that sounds?'

'OK,' said Cass thoughtfully, nodding at the same time. Deciding to change the subject she added, 'So are you attending the PM tomorrow?'

'Yeah I will be. 10 a.m. you said, right? You gonna be here much longer tonight?'

'No, I've gotta hand over the exhibits in a bit, and prepare the murder box. I'll be away soon enough – Ollie needs his walk.'

'How is Ollie? All recovered I trust?' Alex heard the false polite tone and cringed inside. He really was bad at this.

'Yeah, good as gold. Matt's checking him over again tomorrow night. But he seems a lot better. No other seizures which is good.'

'OK great. Well I'll let you get on. I'll see you at the Royal tomorrow.'

Cass sighed as he walked out of her office. She still had no clue what was going on. Taking a long gulp of her coffee, she started compiling the file.

11th October, 2205 hours – Pallion, Sunderland

He was sitting on the sofa in the living room when his mind suddenly wandered back to *that* day.

That particular day in June 1980.

He remembered hoping his mother hadn't seen him watching, and he had known it would mean the beating of his life if she had.

Strangely though, he wasn't scared. He just hid in his room, right beside the bed, thinking about what he had seen.

The look of utter surprise on his father's face as his mother had dropped the radio into the water had rapidly changed to one of horror as his body had convulsed with the current running through the water and into his veins. Now, he couldn't help but see his father's face, twisted in a grimace with his eyes bulging as he twitched.

And then the twitching had stopped – and his father's eyes had vacantly stared right at him.

Back then he hadn't quite understood the things he had felt. To him, it was kind of like the time he had killed the dog in the garden, the satisfaction he had felt as its life force had left the limp body, the pleasure he had felt inflicting pain on another living thing. It was almost the same feeling, but not quite.

He supposed he should have felt sad, shocked and maybe a little afraid; most children would be. But then, he hadn't been most children. He'd always known that.

Still, he had hoped she hadn't seen him watching. He still had the yellowing bruises from the last time. If she beat him again, it would be bruises on bruises, and that always hurt a little more.

He had listened to her footsteps as she walked down the landing, and sighed as she had stopped outside of his door. There was no point putting off the inevitable so he'd stood as she had strode inside.

Any flicker of emotion had drained from his eyes as she silently bent him over the bed, pulled the cane-handled feather duster from her waistband, and raised her hand, counting the time with each stroke.

He hadn't yelled or cried; he'd learnt years before that crying out just made it last longer. He had become adept at staying silent, travelling to the place in his mind where he wasn't there and it didn't hurt as much.

When she was done, she'd turned him around, pulled him into her bony, flat chest, and whispered, 'You're such a good boy. Mummy knows you will never tell. You're cleansed now, no more sins. The Vicar will be very pleased on Sunday. My good boy.'

He had barely heard the words, staring past her towards the bathroom instead. And he had wondered if it hurt to be electrocuted, and how he could find out for sure.

As his mind drifted back from the past, a soft smile curled his lips as a plan began to form. He knew exactly what kill method he would use this time. It was effective, easy to plan, and he had experience with it. This would be the best show yet.

Chapter Sixteen

'Hey, Nigel,' said Cass, clattering her way into the mortuary with Greg and Sue trailing behind.

'Everything but the kitchen sink as usual, Cass?' asked Nigel, taking in the two boxes being carried.

'Yeah the mortuary boxes needed restocking. Figured since we were here we might as well get it all done. Is Alex here yet?'

Sue and Greg made their way through to the back of the building, leaving Cass with Nigel.

'No. He rang to say he's been held up in a briefing with the Critical Incident Manager. He said to start without him and he would land shortly. Are you about ready? I've a feeling this is gonna be a long one.'

'Yeah I sure am. Let's get started.'

Cass followed Nigel into the morgue. She inhaled deeply, knowing how strange she was. She had found comfort in the clean smell of the morgue ever since she started working for the police. It always portrayed a place of calm for her, a sense of peace.

She left Nigel as he entered the male changing room, and quickly got changed into the sterile white suit, covering her work boots with blue covers. Immediately her temperature rose a couple of notches and for a second she remembered that warm July day last year when, to raise money for charity, she had done a sponsored day in her crime scene suit. By the end of the afternoon she had been so warm her hair had looked like an afro, and the suit had stuck to every inch of her exposed skin. She had literally had to peel herself out of it. She grinned to herself in the dim light of the female changing room.

The morgue itself was set out as usual, Gordon being the ultimate professional. The metal table in the centre sat over the top of the oversized plug hole, the small trolley holding various tools was standing beside the body and Nigel stood next to it pulling his gloves on with a snap.

The only thing that looked out of place was the second trolley carrying the mangled body of the dog. Cass stared for a moment, and stopped herself getting upset as she thought about everything the scraggly dog had represented to the old man.

'Been a while since I've seen you,' said Gordon as he bustled about finishing his prep.

'Yeah, I've been tied up in the office unfortunately,' said Cass, pulling her mind from the dog and onto the rest of the post-mortem.

'OK, I'm going to begin,' said Nigel softly, his strong finger pressing the record button on his recorder.

'Victim is a white male, approximately 60-65 years of age. Presents as somewhat dishevelled, with clothing dirty and well worn. Grey, neck length hair and a thick, unkempt beard. Hands show visible defensive wounds with evidence of four obvious breakages to the right digits and ...'

At the end of the five-hour examination, Nigel glanced around the morgue before making a decision.

'Before we progress to the examination of the dog, I suggest we take a half hour break. Is that OK with everyone?'

Cass looked at him in surprise, her head taking a moment to comprehend and allow her attention to detail to kick in. Sue looked exhausted, the well-used camera hanging limply round her neck as she helped Greg fill in the multitude of exhibit bags. Greg looked pale, sweat beading his forehead. For all the cool temperature in the morgue, the white suits were as warm as thermal jackets when it came to holding in body heat. Gordon looked a little frayed around the edges.

'A break sounds like a good plan. Don't know about you guys but I'd kill for a cuppa right about now.'

She watched as Sue and Greg laid their pens down and left the room.

'Thanks for that, Nigel. I was in the zone. I should've noticed how tired they were.'

'It's OK, Cass, we all get that way. It shouldn't take too much longer after the break. I've got a Forensic Veterinarian on standby to walk me through the PM on the dog. Unfortunately, she's otherwise engaged or she would have travelled up to perform it herself. I'm not ashamed to admit I'd rather she was here but we work with what we have right? Gordon's gonna set up the webcam in the morgue for a direct consult.'

'I wondered whether you would be doing the exam, different physiology and all that. Who's the vet?'

'Sally Goodwyn. She's always had a penchant for investigating animal crime. I was glad I pulled her name out of the National Crime Faculty hat.'

'Isn't she the vet who produced the paper on matching canine DNA and paw prints? I read it a while back. We'll take some samples just in case.'

'Yeah that's her. Let's get some coffee. I noticed Alex arrive as we worked. He's probably waiting in the kitchen.'

'Hey, Cass,' said Alex, handing her a steaming cup of coffee as she walked into the kitchen. 'I got here a while ago but I didn't want to disturb you guys. Nigel, your Earl Grey is on the side.'

Nigel nodded his thanks and wandered over to the kettle.

All too soon the break was over and the team were back in the exam room. With the webcam set up, the post-mortem of the dog was much quicker than that of his owner. Cass efficiently took plaster casts of the paw impressions after Nigel had finished taking his samples. He and Sally concluded that the dog had been killed prior to the old man, meaning he had been forced to watch his beloved pet slaughtered. She could only imagine what had been going through the old guy's head as he had watched. Had he tried to save his dog? Had this resulted in more viciousness in the attack? She felt her eyes tear up slightly and had to stop her train of thought. It was hard though, she felt an affinity with the man, couldn't help but let the emotion show.

Steadying her voice with a slight cough, she said, 'You guys OK to take the exhibits back? I'll book them through Socard if you pop them in my office. Just do your scene notes then get yourselves off home. I need to have a quick chat with Alex and I'll see you back there.'

'Yeah no probs,' said Sue, casting a quick glance of acceptance at Greg who nodded back.

'Give me a sec to get out of my suit before my skin melts off and I'll grab a lift back with you if that's OK?'

She watched as Alex nodded, then rushed off to get changed.

'That was a long one. Twenty-seven blows with the hammer? That's excessive. It tells us a lot about the offender. He's motivated, physically fit and more than likely has no disabilities. He appears to be very controlled, however it's possible he has devolved towards the end and the attack became more frenzied. Obviously John Doe knew the attacker. I don't know one homeless person who would show a stranger where he lives, assuming of course that the killer didn't just find him on the off chance. The killer is also sadistic by nature, forcing the old man to watch as he killed the dog just exudes his power, makes him stronger. The old guy never had a chance. With the limited evidence found at the scene, I would say the killer is forensically aware too,' said Alex as they settled into the car.

'Yeah I agree,' she sidled a glance at him, 'Someone's been reading psychology books? It's been a busy month. One murder is bad enough but two in the same month in the same area. Must be a full moon or something,'

'Nah not the books, just stuff I've picked up over the years. Am tempted to call in a profiler to be honest, I don't want this to turn into a trend and violence breeds violence. We'll see how it goes. And you're right on the full moon.'

A comfortable silence fell between them as Alex drove back to the station.

12th October, 1820 hours – Ryhope Police Station

Alex glanced at his mobile as it started vibrating loudly against the desk. He felt the grin spread across his tired face as his brother's smiling features flashed at him.

'Hey, bro. You OK?' As Ali's voice travelled down the line, he felt a sense of calm overtake him, then suddenly realised that something might be wrong.

Sitting up straight, he said, 'Hey, Ali, what is it? Is Mary OK?'

'Nothing wrong, bro, I just thought you'd want to know that Mary and the bairn are home. Just took them there from mums. Now she's out of the hospital your niece looks cute as a button.'

'That's brill, Ali. Thought they'd keep her in a while yet. Sorry I've not rung; we've had another murder. A bad one.'

Alistair of all people knew what it was like. 'Is there such a thing as a good one? I'll message you a photo. If you need a sounding board, just ring me, bro. Sometimes clarity is just a phone call away.'

'Thanks. How's mum?'

'She's OK. Misses you as usual. She was chuffed to bits with your visit, hasn't stopped telling everyone and sundry how you came home. You'll not leave it so long between visits next time I hope?'

'Definitely not. Listen I'd better crack on, I'm just compiling the statements so they can be loaded onto Holmes.'

Alex hung up the phone and sighed deeply, knowing that Alistair had no idea how close he was to his mum really. Alex phoned her nearly every day. When she had got into financial difficulty after he had moved in with Helen, it was him she had come to. Alex had paid the mortgage so she could keep their family home as a base for them all. But none of his siblings knew this. With his dad gone, he was the man of the house. He had never had any doubt that it was his responsibility – it had become ingrained into him as he had grown up. He also knew if Ali and the others knew about it, they'd have all got themselves into trouble trying to raise the funds to keep their mum in the family home. It was just one of those things best kept between him and his mum.

The central door to the office clicked open suddenly, the noise loud in the silence of the office.

His breath caught in his throat as Cass entered. Her hair was tied up messily and tendrils hung down around her face and neck. He almost smiled as he saw the pens stuck through the pony tail at the back. Tiredness marred her eyes and he knew she'd had a tough day too.

He frowned slightly, remembering the image of the old man in the cave before he had been taken to the morgue. It was imprinted on his brain, and he knew he would revisit it later both before and after sleep came. He shook off the thought and smiled at Cass as she approached his desk.

'Hey. I just wanted to pass you the preliminary disk of photos from the PM. I've sorted through and put the most relevant on there. The exhibits are all on Socard and have been handed over to the exhibits officer.'

Alex nodded slowly. 'Brill thanks. You off home?'

'Yeah, everything's pretty much tied up for now. Time to take Ollie for a walk.'

Alex allowed a millisecond of thought before asking, 'Would you like some company?'

Cass stared at him, surprised after their earlier conversation that he wanted to spend time together. Then she came to a decision, 'Yeah, sure. It's a nice night out. Meet you in the car park?'

Alex nodded. If he'd thought about it, he probably wouldn't have asked her at all, let alone expected her to say yes. She flashed him a grin and left.

'What the hell are you doing?' he muttered to himself as he quickly organised the paperwork into a pile, grabbed his mobile, keys and wallet before following Cass.

Within what seemed like minutes, they were clipping the leash to Ollie's black and silver collar and leading him out of the back door to the cottage.

'How come you live so far from town?' asked Alex.

Cass paused a moment, considering her answer before replying. 'The area is brilliant for Ollie. He gets in and out as he wants with the electronic key in his neck, and he just loves to chase the bunnies. I like the solitude, when I come home from work there's no traffic sounds, no people, just this.' She indicated 'this' with a wide sweep of her arm, towards the shadowy woods at the bottom of the garden.

'I guess some people are just suited to country living. I like working in town, but I love coming home to peace and quiet. What about you? You live in town, right?'

'Yeah, just a little apartment. Helen got the house when we divorced a few years ago. It's enough for just me.' It was lonely, however. Despite talking about his ex, he kept the bitterness out of his voice.

'Do you get on?' asked Cass, curious to find out more.

Alex shook his head and then remembered they were walking in the middle of a dark copse and that she probably couldn't see him.

'Not so much. It didn't end very well. It wasn't her fault; she was looking for something I couldn't give her at the time. I was always working, trying to give the force my all to progress and get us the life I thought she wanted. I sometimes spent nights and days at a time at work. It got so we barely saw each other – and before I knew it she had moved her stuff out, saying she couldn't cope with being a cop's wife. I guess it was just one of those things that aren't meant to be.'

Cass heard the emotion and pain in his voice, and didn't know what to say. She bent and unhooked Ollie's leash, smiling into the moonlight as he bounded off to chase invisible prey. As she glanced up at Alex, he caught her gaze with his, his eyes piercing in the dim glow of the moon.

'I'm sorry,' she said simply.

Alex paused a moment, contemplating how to respond.

Eventually he settled on 'Me too,' and carried on walking alongside Cass.

Suddenly she left his side at a dead run, the oversized dog lolloping along with her. He stared for a moment, not quite understanding. Swiftly, he followed at a jog.

'You OK?' he asked as he caught up to her with ease.

Smiling a little ruefully, she slowed her pace down to a walk.

'Sorry, Alex. Sometimes I just like to run with Ollie, I forgot you didn't already know that if that makes sense. Besides I have cobwebs at the moment that need clearing.'

They jogged together for a couple of minutes, then Cass slowed and turned to face him. Under the light of the moon, he could see the concern on her face.

He stopped too, waiting patiently and allowing her the time to gather her thoughts and continue.

'I have a little trouble trusting people, and more trouble opening up. Since Carl hurt me, I've never really spoken to another guy. It makes me a little nervous that you're here with me, and more nervous because I feel like I can talk to you.'

'You can tell me anything, Cass. Though I should probably tell you I already know about the baby. I spoke with DCI Proffitt at Durham.'

Alex watched as Cass's face went deathly pale. Shit – he'd been nowhere near her train of thought. The silence stretched and suddenly Cass turned and ran full pelt back along the path towards the cottage.

Running behind her, Alex said, 'Cass, wait. Please.'

Dammit, you're a bloody idiot McKay.

He pushed open the back door, and paused, listening for her. Faint sobs were coming from the bedroom, and he took the stairs two at a time, his stomach in his mouth as he approached her. Ollie glared at him from the bedside, asking with his doggy eyes how he could be so stupid as to upset his mum.

She was face down on the bed, crying quietly into the pillow.

'Cass,' he said softly, placing a hand on her back. 'I'm sorry. I didn't mean to upset you. Cass, please.'

Slowly she turned to her side, her eyes glassy. She had a look of desperation, and for a moment he was lost for words.

Without speaking, he gathered her into his arms, and started stroking her hair. She tensed, then slowly collapsed into him, letting her emotion loose and shuddering with each heartfelt sob.

Eventually her shoulders stopped shaking, and she pulled back, wiping the tears from her face.

'Sorry,' she whispered, 'It's just so hard to think about losing…'

'I shouldn't have brought it up, Cass, I'm so sorry. I didn't mean to hurt you.'

'You didn't, Alex. I should've told you already.'

'Why did you stay, Cass? Why did you stay with him if you were pregnant?' His voice was raw and he felt like a tool for asking, but he needed to know. It had bugged him since he found out, and the more time he spent with Cass, the more he wanted to know about her, to understand how someone so amazing could put up with something so horrible.

He heard her inhale deeply, preparing herself to speak.

'You need to understand something. Back then I wasn't the person I am now. I was so shy, I had no self-confidence and my self-esteem was low. I didn't know what I wanted out of life. When I met Carl, he was charming, good looking and way above my league. I was flattered he showed an interest. When we moved away together I genuinely thought I was going to spend my life with him. I was happy.'

She paused, struggling to keep her emotion in check. For the first time, she actually wanted to talk about it with someone other than her counsellor.

'The first time he hit me, he was drunk. He'd been out with the boys from work and his tea was in the microwave. He'd decided he didn't want sausage and threw the plate at the wall in a temper, and then hit me for not knowing that he didn't want sausage. Afterwards he was so apologetic, he cried, and I thought it was a one-off. By the time I realised it wasn't, I barely spoke to my mum, had no friends, no job and I was a wreck. I didn't know who to turn to, and Carl had told me so many times that the police would agree with him, that I was useless and a crap girlfriend who didn't take care of him, that I believed it.'

She stopped again, glancing at Alex. His face was passive and she couldn't read what he was feeling, but she continued.

'I was a slow bloomer. I didn't know I was pregnant 'til I was nearly four months gone. That was about two weeks before Carl …'

Cass coughed a little, trying to control her emotion. Alex held her hand, silently encouraging her to go on.

'Carl was over the moon, he thought I would have a boy and he could bring his boy up to be just like him. And I was terrified that he would do just that. He stopped hitting me, didn't lay a hand on me once for weeks. I said before he thought I had been with someone he knew? That someone was his best friend, Tony. Tony was always nice to me, he knew something was wrong, knew Carl hit me. Tony did come round that night, he came to ask me if I was OK, he told me he would help me leave, gave me money. But I was so terrified Carl would find out, I wouldn't let Tony in the house. He left about half an hour before Carl came home. He was steaming drunk – I'd packed a case but I knew I wouldn't make it before he got home. I kept thinking just one more night.'

Tears filled her eyes again, spilling over onto her cheeks.

'Carl came in the bedroom full of hell. He thought I'd been sleeping with Tony, that I'd been having an affair for months. He dragged me out of bed, and starting punching me, screaming that the baby was Tony's and that when he was done with me he was going to go and teach him what it meant to be a best friend. I don't remember a great deal about what happened. When I woke up in the hospital with my mum next to me, I just knew I wasn't pregnant any more.'

A huge sob escaped, and Alex pulled her into his arms, kissing the top of her head. He whispered softly, understanding now, 'It's OK. Shhh, you're OK.'

'I killed my baby, Alex, I should have left. I should have left,' she sobbed against his chest.

Alex felt tears prick his own eyes, and he was angry that Cass had been in the situation in the first place. All too often the police know what's happening but their hands are tied unless the victim says something, agrees to press charges. For Cass, they had never had chance to help, all because she was so afraid. He felt a knot settle in his stomach. If Jameson ever came near her again, he would wring his neck. Pigs would fly before he let that bastard hurt her again.

All the shit he'd had with Helen suddenly paled in comparison. Yes, she had never seen him, and he loved his job more than her, but he had never once hit her or thought about hitting her. Not when she slapped him, not when she screamed at him an inch from his face, and most definitely not when she had left him. He couldn't imagine a time when he would ever raise his fist to a woman. He hoped Cass knew that too.

Alex shifted position slightly to lean back on the headboard and pulled Cass close, until her sobs finally ebbed and he felt her breathing eventually slow into slumber. He lay there for a while, pressing his lips to her head, and eventually dropped off himself.

Chapter Seventeen

13th October, 0840 hours – Cass's Cottage

Cass stirred as the sun's rays shone through the window and onto her eyelids. She moved against her pillow, thinking how warm and cosy it was. When her pillow moved in response, she lifted her head and opened her eyes.

She was greeted with Alex's grey eyes staring back. He smiled sleepily, and whispered, 'Hey,' as he kissed her on the head.

Suddenly shy, she felt her cheeks flush as she smiled back.

What on earth is the matter with me? She felt like a giddy school kid with her first crush.

Noting her silence, and that it wasn't awkward, Alex let her process for a moment. When she looked up at him the second time, the shyness had gone to be replaced with some other emotion in her eyes. It took a minute for him to recognise the look as need, but when he did he was lost. He bent his head towards her slowly, his lips pausing millimetres from hers as he felt her breath quicken against him. He was surprised when she leaned forward, pressing her lips to his softly.

A bolt of electricity shot through his veins as he deepened the kiss, tasting the sweet tang of her tongue as she brushed it swiftly against his. Groaning slightly, he pulled her closer, increasing the pressure slightly as she ran her hand up his chest and onto the top of his arm. His skin prickled as he felt her breasts harden against his chest, and his senses went into over drive.

A sudden thought invaded his mind that they had agreed to take it slow, and forcing himself not to rush her, he pulled back slightly, breaking the kiss and opening his eyes.

Cass whimpered her disappointment, her eyes opening, filled with desire as she stared back at him. She allowed herself to let her feelings envelop her, recognised that she felt safe in his arms, and wondered for a split second whether she could be imagining it.

His voice gruff, Alex said, 'I don't want to rush you Cass. We agreed we would take it slow and...' his voice cut off as Cass leaned in, catching his lips with hers once more.

He felt his arousal rise, and not breaking the kiss, he moved position so he was over her side. Their mouths ground together hungrily, her arms round his back, her nails gently scraping at his T-shirt. Torn between not wanting to stop, and feeling responsible, he pulled back again.

'Cass, wait, I don't want to force you into something you might not be ready for.'

'You're not forcing Alex,' pausing slightly, she stared into his eyes, and made the decision to be completely honest. 'I want you. I need you.'

It was all the affirmation he needed. Moaning into her mouth, he enveloped her, their movements much more frenzied now. Cass arched her back into him as he gently cupped one breast, gasping as he moved his mouth to her neck. She dragged her nails down his back, grabbing the bottom of his shirt and lifting it, sliding her hands underneath. He moaned into her neck, suddenly needing to feel her skin on his. Sitting back onto his side, he pulled her slightly into a sitting position.

He lifted her shirt as she raised her arms. The delicate lace of her bra did nothing to hide her arousal as he reached behind and unclipped the clasp, allowing the scrap of material to fall off the bed. Cass undressed Alex, both of them silent.

He drew in a shuddering breath, her closeness almost too much to bear. They quickly threw off their trousers, and Cass shyly pulled the top throw over herself. Alex responded by pinning her to the bed gently as he pulled the cover away. He kissed her again, the skin on skin contact almost too much. Within moments they were both panting, wanting.

He rose above her, and thrust forward slowly, controlling his speed and entry until Cass couldn't take any more and pushed forward onto him. Their mouths connected once more as they moved together. Groaning simultaneously, the world exploded, stars flew and Alex collapsed onto Cass.

'Wow,' whispered Cass against his neck. 'That never happened before.'

Alex lifted his head, kissed her tenderly, and whispered back, 'to me either.'

'So, taking it slow is out of the window I guess,' grinned Cass, pushing him so he shifted his weight off her. 'I'm gonna go jump in the shower – you can join me if you like.'

He grinned back, her mischievousness was infectious, 'Lead the way.'

14ᵗʰ *October, 1400 hours – Ryhope Pier, Sunderland*

He glanced down the pier towards the cave one last time. Today was his last visit to watch the goings on. The news crews had got bored, their little boats no longer bobbing out on the steady waves. And for all he understood the basics of forensics, he didn't know why the police held the scene for so long. It surely couldn't take this amount of time to determine that the old guy had been beaten to death with a hammer.

It had served a dual purpose though.

The young man was now well and truly established as show stopper number three. He knew Andy saw him as an easy mark. He gave him money when he asked, bought him alcohol and cigarettes, and was generally playing the part of being the lonely middle aged man with a new friend.

His dislike of the young man was growing in intensity, and he wasn't convinced he'd be able to keep up the pretence much longer. Andy was growing ever more demanding and somewhat threatening. He also knew he was being drip-fed false information. The boy thought he could lie to him and get away with it. He pushed the sudden wave of anger back with difficulty. Why not just kill him now and be done with it? He was convinced Andy was going to try and rob him at some point and knew the teenager was offering a fake story to ward off any unwanted police attention.

It had taken him until that morning to figure out why Andy was so familiar.

He had seen Andy and his girlfriend in the park harassing Albert on several occasions. Andy had probably seen him too, but he was confident that his disguise in the park had been different enough for the teenager not to realise. The he was a homeless man; now he looked like a fisherman, shaggy beard, flat cap and a gum shield.

He knew where Andy lived and that he worked in the local McDonalds with a bunch of other spotty, arrogant teenagers, and he also knew Andy was actually called Scott Anderson. He knew Scott's girlfriend was called Kourtney with a K, and generally sported large gold loops in her ears and a velour tracksuit that was around two sizes too small for her chubby middle. It was just too easy nowadays to find out information.

It was Scott's attitude that was proving hard to bear.

He gritted his teeth. It was never good to be pressured into doing something sooner than planned.

But try as he might to stay calm, his patience was growing thin. He liked the routine of a three-week wait between shows, the time to plan every last move. It was the perfect amount of time to allow things to die down before his next masterpiece.

But this one wasn't progressing as well as he had hoped.

Suddenly his mind flashed back to those Sunday mornings. His mother would wake him at 5 a.m. on the dot. His father was always allowed to stay in bed. He was not a religious man, much to his mother's exasperation. Quietly, so as not to wake the man that was her husband, she would put her son into a scalding bath and scrub his skin until it was red raw, telling him softly that she was scrubbing out his sins. When he was little he would cry, the tiny spots of blood scaring him. Startled by the noise, she had started pushing the flannel into his mouth, muffling the sobs. He soon learned that if he stayed quiet she would stop quicker, and he wouldn't be subjected to the flannel. And then it would be off to church, to show the world what a wonderful son she had.

Right up until the day she had died, he had detested Sunday mornings. He still did.

But a Sunday would be a good day for the show. The 'day of rest' in the working week meant fewer people in the town centre and more on the beach. People would certainly remember this show, especially if the scene was placed in plain view, ready for their attention as they scurried like rats fitting everything into their day off. It would prove a little more intricate to plan, but he still had over a fortnight left. He knew he could do it.

Chapter Eighteen

15th October, 1200 hours – Sunderland Outreach Centre

Brian sat in his office, Gill standing beside him as they both stared in consternation at one of the local beat officers, PC Rob Watson, who was sitting in front of them.

'Are you sure it was Scott? He couldn't have been coerced by another boy?'

Brian frowned as the man shook his head.

'Brian, I'm sorry. I wanted it not to be Scott too – I personally looked at the footage for the shop and also picked some up from over the road. There was no one with Scott except Kourtney. He left her on watch outside, entered the shop, punched the shop owner and made off with the money from the till. Mr Ahmed, the owner, doesn't want to press charges, he just wants Scott warned off. Says this happens all the time. But with the CCTV evidence I don't really have a choice, Brian. I need to arrest Scott, which means he will be in direct breach of his probation order. There isn't anything I can do. I actually thought Scott might have tried to turn his life around with the chances you guys have given him.'

Frustrated, Brian swore softly. Running his hands through his hair, worry lines deepening into wrinkles on his too young brow, he sighed.

'You know what, Rob, it's not your fault. Scott had every chance to improve himself. I don't like washing my hands of any kid, especially one I'm sure is inherently good at heart, but he made the decision to go into the shop, he chose to take the money and hit the owner. You need to do what you need to do. It's nobody's fault but Scott's that this is happening. If the judge decides to be lenient I'll happily keep him in the programme – but if not, then there's not really a lot I can do.'

'Sucks though, Brian. How're you holding up anyway? Didn't expect to see you back at work so soon.'

'I'm OK, getting through one day at a time. I was going a little nuts in the house to be honest. Maureen's great, but she's practically moved in since Susan ...' he paused taking a breath, steadying the wave of emotion that threatened his composure. 'I can't complain though. She's great with the kids, they need her at the minute. And I had to come back to work sometime.'

'Yeah I guess. You've got my number, right, in case anything happens here? What time's Scott due in today?'

Brian glanced at his watch, 'He should be here anytime now. His session's booked in from 12.30 p.m. for the afternoon. Gill, can you arrange for Stan to give you a hand with the session – the other kids will need motivating if Rob here is going to arrest Scott in view.'

'Sorry, Brian, I'll be as discreet as I can. Know the uniform makes the kids uncomfortable.'

Brian nodded, acknowledging without reply. It didn't take a genius to know that kids with problems had an aversion to the police. Most of them had encountered the wrong side of the law at some point. It was a big part of why they had to attend the centre.

'Actually, Rob, would you mind staying in the office? I'll bring Scott to you – less disturbance that way.'

'Sure thing. As long as this pretty young lady wouldn't mind making me a coffee while I wait?'

He batted his eyelids at Gill, who smiled widely, laid her hand on his arm and said, 'I'm way too old for a youngster like you, and I don't *make* coffee, sugar, but I will show you where the kettle is. Come on.'

Grinning at Brian, Rob got to his feet and followed Gill as she sashayed her way out of the corridor in the general direction of the staff kitchen.

Scott turned up about half an hour later, and Brian dutifully herded him into the office, where Rob was waiting. Scott's scowl turned to hatred when he saw Rob waiting.

'You grassed me up? You twat,' he spat, in Brian's direction as Rob quickly cuffed him.

'Enough, Scott, he didn't grass you up. CCTV did. The whole thing was caught on camera. Scott Anderson, you're under arrest. You do not have to say anything, but it may harm your defence if you do not mention, when questioned, something you later rely on in court. Anything you do say may be given in evidence.'

He walked Scott out of the office, leaving Brian looking on, shaking his head in disappointment. He hated being wrong.

15ᵗʰ *October, 1305 hours – Sunderland Outreach Centre*

He had watched as Scott entered the centre. He'd noticed the police car parked round the corner when he arrived, and he had wondered if it was for the kid.

Five minutes later, he watched as Scott was marched out of the centre in cuffs and walked to the car.

Damn it, the kid couldn't keep his nose clean for a second. It would be a gift to society getting rid of the little shit. Provided of course he wasn't kept in custody, or remanded when he attended court, which would no doubt be soon.

He scowled at the officer as he placed Scott into the backseat of the panda, and jumped into the driver's seat.

Damn police had the worst timing.

He glanced at his watch, it was almost time for work. Grumbling to himself he wandered back to his car, and wondered what he would do if Scott was remanded – it would most definitely scupper his plans. Perhaps he should have a back-up.

A cold smile flittered across his lips as he decided this was a good option. There was one person he already knew a great deal about, it wouldn't be too hard to alter the plan for Scott to the beloved Kourtney instead. Or he could do the meddlesome CSM or her slave. He knew enough about both of them now, where they lived, worked, and shopped. Though he would admit their routines were somewhat irregular.

Not one of the three would expect it.

'Choices, choices,' he thought, as he turned the key once, turned it back to the off position, then started the engine and drove home to get ready.

Content now, he grinned. Every good plan should have a backup.

15ᵗʰ *October, 1330 hours – Sunderland City Police Station*

Alex made his way down to custody, unlocked the door and entered the waiting area. It was only seconds before he was buzzed through to the booking desk.

It was busy today; the stench of warm sweat and chemical cleansers mixed with the faint undertone of fresh paint and assaulted his nostrils as he glanced around the recently refurbished suite.

Walter Saunders, or Wally as he was called, to his face at least, was seated behind the main desk, his puckered face reddening in the central heated cluster of rooms. Behind his back though, the officers were far less kind. Wally was less affectionately known as Nar Nar, so named for his response when being asked to do something by anyone *not* holding rank. *'Wally, could you do me a favour?'* a colleague would ask and Wally would respond with his force wide known reply, *'Nar Nar, not my job, mate.'*

For people like Alex though, the response was always more akin to the TV character off the old TV show Roots, when Nar Nar would quickly become *'yes, boss.'* Alex didn't like the man, but he respected his position. Custody Sergeant wasn't a role suited to everyone, and despite his attitude, he was in the right place.

There was a queue of officers waiting to book prisoners in, all of whom looked sullen and miserable as Wally slowly allocated them their cells for their time in the criminal version of the Holiday Inn. The prisoners were given the basics only; toilet breaks if they were in the small holding cells without a toilet, food, water and a thin, plastic coated mattress to lay their weary heads. The Ritz however, it was most definitely not. Frequently, the offenders showed their displeasure at the room allocation by smearing their own faeces and blood all over the walls. The cells were not a pleasant part of the station.

Alex leaned against the wall and sighed, it would be a while before he would get the file he wanted. But for once, he had time to wait, and he quite liked watching how people acted in environments that weren't his own. He'd had his fair share of run-ins in custody though, a faint smile passed over his lips as he remembered one particularly colourful incident from his days as a beat bobby where he had assisted in a strip search of a male who turned out to be wearing women's lacy knickers and stockings under his masculine clothes. That gave the whole nick something to talk about for weeks.

He straightened as he watched one of the male offenders, approaching the front of the queue. There was something about his body language that was virtually screaming 'watch me blow.' His fists were clenched in his cuffs, his legs slightly askew and apart, his stance solid, and his pupils were pin pricks: he was obviously high on something. The officer at his side was still young, possibly a probationer, and his colleague had gone to escort a second prisoner to the cells.

Alex barely had time to blink as the man acted, throwing himself at the young officer and sending him into the wall with force. Wally hit the alarm behind the counter quickly, bellowing at the prisoner to stop. Frantic now, the lad looked for an escape but was blocked on every side by other offenders and officers.

Alex stepped forward, grabbing his attention.

'Easy,' he said softly, holding his hands out in an effort to placate the man, who snorted like a wild animal, spit spraying from his mouth as he gasped his breath. Alex knew there would be no way to talk him down, he was flying higher than the Angel of the North, and probably didn't know where he was. Alex moved slowly to the side, watching out of the corner of his eye as the officers started closing in.

Seeing a gap, the man decided his best option was to run for the door, and he bolted, crashing into another offender and sending him flying to the floor. Alex stuck his foot out, tripping the runaway and causing him to stumble. He then grabbed the man's arms, and put his knee into his back.

'Easy, stop struggling. You'll make it worse for yourself.'

The wailing that came from the man was primal, but it was quickly silenced to a whimper as three more officers quickly helped Alex restrain him. The other waiting prisoners set up a chant to encourage the offender on the floor into further rebellion but it was rapidly extinguished by harsh stare of warning from Wally.

Within a couple of minutes, the man had been placed into additional restraints and moved into a cell to await a visit from the duty FME.

Alex stood slowly, brushing his trousers down, his cheeks a little pink. He took note of the officers watching him, and nodded in acknowledgement.

He walked over to talk to the probationer, who was sitting on the bench to one side looking ashen.

'You get 'em like that every now and then. Trick is to watch their hands. If they're relaxed, then they're not likely to kick off like that. If they're tense, then just be on your guard. Are you hurt?'

'No, Sir, my ego's a little bruised but that's it.'

'It's just Alex, no need for Sir. And bruised egos mend, you'll be more aware next time.'

The lad nodded slowly, and Alex turned back towards the desk where Wally was back to his old self and swiftly booking people in.

'What is it I can help you with today, boss?' he asked, glancing up as he signed his name on a custody record.

'I just need to see the custody file for Rob McNally, SRN 984442. I'm not in a rush though, just give me a shout when you've sorted it out?'

'Yeah sure, I'll sort it out as soon as this lot are settled in and have one of the guys bring it up for you.'

Alex nodded, and turned to leave as the side door opened and Rob, one of the beat officers, ushered in a sulky looking teenager.

He grinned at Alex, and said to the teen, 'Well Scott, looks like you'll have a bit of a wait looking at the queue here. Hope you didn't have plans for the afternoon.'

'I'm not staying in here all day. Get me done first,' said Scott, scowling at Rob who remained passive. 'For fuck's sake, I need to take a leak,'

'Well you'll just have to hold it in. You'll get to the front soon enough,'

Scott slammed his back against the wall in temper, wincing slightly as the cuffs chafed at his wrists with the impact.

Alex manoeuvred past the two and made his way back out to the corridor. He found himself wandering along to the CSI office, despite knowing Cass wasn't there. She'd told him she was at the central depot all day, in and out of meetings and sorting through some evidence.

He grinned to himself as he remembered her shyness after their shower; she had drowned herself in the oversized bath sheet, hiding her body as she got dressed beneath it. He had teased her a little, and it had been comfortable. It was a long time since he had felt comfortable with anyone. The more he got to know her, the more his feelings about what had happened with Helen faded, and he was starting to believe he wasn't a bad person. When he thought about their relationship honestly, and looked past the blame, he could remember the constant bickering and nit-picking. The way Helen had constantly hidden her mobile phone from his view, and spent ages in the bathroom. As he looked back now, he wondered if she had been having an affair – not that it mattered, he was sure never having him around had given her every right, but now he was starting to wonder whether the split had been as mutual as he initially thought, or whether it had been orchestrated by her so she had an excuse to leave.

When it had finally broken down completely, he had felt a sense of relief. For him, and her. Overwhelming guilt but also an ultimate sense of relief.

He paused outside the CSI office, wondering where this sudden rush of emotion had come from, and listened for a moment as he steadied his thoughts. A burst of laughter emanated from within. Whatever the joke was, it was obviously funny as more giggles came from inside.

On impulse, Alex grabbed his phone and sent Cass a text asking if she fancied dinner that night – they'd both left the cottage in their respective vehicles without discussing when they'd see each other next. And he wanted to hear her laugh like that.

Finally deciding he was now guilty of just wasting time, he headed back up to the MIT office to have another look at the files piling high on his desk.

Chapter Nineteen

15th October, 2320 hours – Cass's Cottage

He stood in the shadows, his form completely obscured by the trees around the cottage. Pulling his jacket close as a shiver rippled through him, he acknowledged that winter was on its way. He'd been stood in the wood now for an hour, and the cold was starting to seep into his core.

Cass's beat up Peugeot was parked up but the cottage was in darkness. He hadn't seen them leave, but he knew she would be with *him*. He'd seen them up close, practically canoodling in full view. Yes, they were definitely screwing each other.

In his opinion it was a crying shame the UK police forces didn't employ similar policies as their US counterparts when it came to inter-office liaison. Over there, this kind of behaviour would have meant disciplinary action.

He heard the car approach before its headlights lit up the driveway. Shrinking back into the shadows, he watched as Alex pulled up, the white Audi stark in the flood lights around the cottage.

Scowling to himself in the pitch black of the wood, he watched Alex open the car door for Cass and guide her to the front door, his hand at her back.

He didn't like Alex. Cass was OK he figured, she'd been nice to him once or twice, but Alex barely knew he was there – had actually blanked him earlier that day to his face.

He didn't know yet whether Scott had been released from custody yet to take up his role as the fake, spotty, arrogant Andy. His plan was still focused on Scott, but he did like being prepared. This was the perfect location to start on Cass if he needed to. She would be easier than her slave to get rid of. And there was just something about her. He'd already seen the huge mutt that kept guard; a good dose of steak laced with a hefty dose of poison would soon get rid of that problem. As much as he enjoyed a good torture, there was no need to get close enough to let that monster bite him.

The woods provided an ideal backdrop, secluded, no neighbours, no one to hear her scream. Yes, this would definitely do as a backup.

Now he only had to decide how.

It was only another seventeen days to his three-week deadline after all.

He froze as he heard soft voices to the rear of the cottage and realised they were taking the dog out. Worried it would pick up his scent, he left his hiding place and made his way back to the car.

He would look at Google Earth when he got home, see if he couldn't find a better vantage point to keep watch from. If she was going to be his back up, then he would do it properly. He might get rid of Alex too as a bonus, after forcing her to watch him endure a slow painful death of course. Might as well enjoy it.

Without the backup plan, Alex would have eventually paid for blanking him. No one did that, not any more.

He got to the car and slipped the key in the ignition, listening to the engine roar to life, turned the heating on full, and set off home. He had taken a risk coming in his own car that evening, but he had just finished work and he didn't really have time to pick up his mum's car. He was confident he hadn't been spotted though. The old logging track hadn't been used in a long while.

Tomorrow would come soon enough, and he would continue with his planning.

16th October, 1105 hours – Ryhope Police Station

Cass pulled at the collar of her polo top. It had been a cold morning, the first frost of the impending winter leaving fairy dust sparkles on every surface. In response the station's heating had been cranked up the max, which was fine for all the warm blooded folk who ran for duvets and duffel coats at the first sign of a chill. Not for Cass though. The heat in the conference room was almost unbearable.

The forensic strategy meeting had already been going on for an hour. She had heard the gist of the search team's findings from Danny, a lot of generic evidence recovery from the cave and the surrounding beach which wasn't surprising from a public area. Even Danny had admitted the likelihood of anything being of any substantial value was limited.

Alex had already gone through the PM findings. Nigel's report had come through that morning, verifying what he'd said at the time about cause of death, and she'd already been over the forensic evidence her team had found. It was limited but she was hopeful about the partial footwear marks recovered, and one section of bloodied rag which the lab had said they would examine for DNA other than belonging to the victim. Separating DNA profiles was difficult but not impossible, with new techniques being developed all the time.

Cass figured it wouldn't be much longer before the meeting would be wound up, and tugged at her collar again as Charlie took the floor to go into Albert's history. She had just opened her mouth to speak, when there was a loud rap at the door.

Everyone looked round expectantly as the door opened and the Chief Constable strode inside, quickly followed by the Assistant Chief and one of the Chief Superintendents. Cass watched as everyone's mouth dropped open in shock. Plainly no one had known this visit would be taking place. She hadn't heard the CC was in the nick today.

'Morning everyone, I was in the area and just wanted to pop my head in and provide some reassurance regarding the money-saving initiatives we are all facing. I want you all to know that my priority is not to lose staff, I am aiming as much as possible for people to be deployed into alternate roles, however, you're all aware that a lot of departments have been identified as being at risk. I trust everyone here has at least had their initial department meeting at this stage?'

At the cautious array of nods, he continued, 'Good. I've set up an email suggestion and comments filter. I want you all to know that your ideas matter, so send over any suggestions you have, or comments about the process, to Money Suggestions Mailbox. I know how hard this is on everyone, you all need to know that I am here and approachable. All emails will be answered. OK, so that said I'll leave you to your meeting, I'm busy working my way round all the depots at the present time.'

And as quickly as he had entered they left, leaving everyone a little shell shocked.

Danny was the first to speak, 'Our opinion counts huh? So I guess he'll be taking a wage drop to save money then? A few less tens of thousands on his yearly wage? What a prick.'

Several of the officers murmured their agreement, and Alex, sensing that things could potentially get out of hand, had to interrupt. 'OK guys, odd time for the CC to visit but we need to crack on with the meeting 'cos the room's booked out for another one starting in forty minutes. Charlie, can you start again on Albert's history please?'

Chapter Twenty

He was really annoyed; so annoyed he could actually see white spots dancing in front of his eyes.

They thought *he* was dispensable; that they could just get rid of him; throw him out like a bag of rubbish on trash day?

He felt his blood boil, who did they think they were? He would make every one of them pay; if he couldn't work there he'd make damn sure no one else could. If it took him ten years to make that thought a reality, he would do it.

Inhaling a deep breath, he tried to calm down. He still needed to ring Scott and find out what had happened at the police station. He'd tried to contact him yesterday but got no answer. He needed to know which plan he would be following. Confusion was not good.

He punched the redial button and held the receiver to his ear. He was almost at the point of hanging up when Scott's sullen voice answered.

'Lo,'

'Andy, it's John. Haven't heard from you in a couple of days, just checking you're OK.'

'I need some money. Pigs are chasing me. Need to get away, me and Kourt.'

'I don't know whether I can get anything together. When are you leaving?' He asked carefully, knowing Scott would think he was stalling.

'Tomorrow. I'm not staying in this stinking town a day longer than I need to.'

He felt panic rise like bile from his stomach – how would he complete his plan if Scott left? Yes, he had a backup, but Scott was and would remain his first choice. He wanted to see the jumped up little squirt beg for his miserable life. Thinking he could play him. Just like *they* thought they could play him. He knew he was being irrational, lumping Scott with them like they were one. They weren't, but they were rapidly becoming intertwining acts in this great show of his. Scott couldn't just leave. He needed him to stay.

'How much do you need?'

The question hung as Scott contemplated his answer.

'I had this mate once, made friends with an older guy like you. This mate wanted like a grand, and the old guy had to give it to him cos he threatened to go to the police, tell 'em this bloke had been touching him and stuff. See, the bloke didn't have a choice really. He gave me mate the money, and me mate got the bike he wanted. He did it a few times after that. Not me though, I don't need to go to the police. 'Cos you're my real mate aren't you, John? You'll help me out.'

He almost fell over in shock, the jumped up little prick was trying to blackmail him. For the first time that day, he felt his anger dissipate and a feeling of control took over.

'Yes I'm your friend, Andy. I'll do what I can to get you some money. I can spare maybe £30 until payday. Will that be enough?'

'£30 measly quid? Come on, John. I know you can do better than that. I need more than £30.'

'Well if you can wait 'til the first of the month I can spare £500. Will that be enough of a loan to get you and Kourt started wherever you end up? You can just pay me back whenever,' he purposely kept his voice neutral, knowing that Scott had no intention of paying him back. Would his offer would be enough of a carrot to make Scott stay?

'I'm due back at the nick on the 2nd to answer bail. You get me the money by then, yeah?'

He bit his own cheek, hard, needing to sound a little naive and weak. 'OK, Andy, no problem. What's mine is yours. I trust you'll let me know your location so I get the money back? When you're sorted of course.'

'Yea you'll know. I'm going to the park tonight. You wanna meet us and have a few smokes?'

'I'm working tonight, but I'll see you soon, Andy, OK? We'll have a catch up. I'll bring the beer.'

He hung up the phone thoughtfully. Shame *they* couldn't be manipulated as easily as Scott. He shook his head and pushed back the wave of anger threatening his composure. The anger peaked again as he suddenly realised what he'd done. He'd gone and called Scott's mobile number from the work phone, not his mobile.

He grabbed the van keys, left the office and jumped in the van, pulling in at the service station round the corner to refuel. If ever he was questioned he could just say he had been out of the office – the CCTV at the services would put him there. Not that he thought for one second it would happen, he was brighter than they were. He knew how evidence got missed and misplaced within the police, how easy it was.

He ought to after all. He worked for them.

17th October, 2350 hours – Cass's Cottage

Cass had had a busy day. She never understood why they were defined as 'rest days' when not one person she knew ever used them for resting. She had seen Alex off that morning as he left for work. They had become more comfortable in each other's company in the past few days and he'd stayed at the cottage every night since that first night. It made her feel special, and a little naughty, because nobody at work knew what was happening. It was like they were two different people at work. No one had guessed they were dating.

Is that what this was called? She wasn't sure.

Smiling to herself for the millionth time that day, she acknowledged she was falling for him. Since he had left that morning she'd tackled the daunting task of pruning the trees surrounding the garden and cottage ready for the autumn. She'd done all the boring household tasks like her washing and ironing, sorted out the bills, walked Ollie twice and had made dinner.

It had been 8 p.m. when Alex had finally arrived from work, only to sit down at the table to eat and promptly be called back to the nick to deal with an armed robbery.

Her head now firmly back in 'work-mode', she sat at the table thinking. The proposed job cuts affected everyone; Cass had heard the day before they were cutting the handymen, the cleaners, even the front office staff were at risk. A lot of the stations were going from 24:7 opening to daytime only, which meant money saving in not having to run the station round the clock, and also from other things such as shift allowance. It was all just happening too fast. Cass could already see the implications if the cuts went ahead after the consultation period.

She knew of several people jumping ship before it sank; Greg had opted to take his redundancy a few years before his thirty years of service was up. It saddened her. Greg was one of the best CSIs in the whole force, let alone in her area command. When she had been promoted to CSM and asked to manage the Ryhope depot, she'd heard rumours from the other supervisors about Greg. He was reported to be gobby and unpredictable, and didn't like women. Cass had held her reservations in check and found it all to be complete bollocks. Greg was a hard worker, he liked being treated with respect and would say when he didn't agree with something. But she'd never had a problem with him.

She often wished some of the other CSIs would take his lead, be a little more headstrong and say what they were thinking.

Deena wasn't too bad on that front. Years of experience had taught her when she could say no effectively, but she was still a bit of a follower. Faith was wrapped up in her own problems and was an emotional person. Cass liked her a lot and had respect for how well she did the job, but often found herself a little out of her depth when Faith got upset at over something her police colleagues had said or done. She also had a habit of bringing her personal life to work. For all Cass needed to learn to handle Faith's emotional outbursts a little better, she couldn't help but think Faith needed to develop a thicker skin. Thick like Fred's would be good; Fred had been in the department almost as long as Greg. He was confident and has no qualms about saying no to anyone of any rank if what they were asking was outside of the CSI remit.

Productively though, all the CSIs who worked from Ryhope were marked among the highest in the area command. Certain statistics were monitored – primarily identifications from fingerprints, DNA and footwear. It would be hard for anyone trying to make a case to cut the number of CSIs, but she knew it would happen.

Pulling her thoughts away from work matters, Cass decided it was time to take Ollie for another walk. She had a week off scheduled and was intending to work on her latest paper for the Forensic Journal, on the implications of using technology at crime scenes, as well as meeting her mum at Rockliffe Hall for an overnight spa break starting the next day.

It was cold outside, and she shivered, pulling her jacket closer as she and Ollie navigated the stile at the bottom of the garden. She'd invested years before in a head torch, and she adjusted the angle slightly before heading off at steady pace, her breath leaving wisps in the night air as she walked. She loved nights like this, when it was cold and fresh and the woods came alive. It hadn't taken her long to realise that the night-time sounds in the woods were completely different to the day time ones. She listened carefully as she walked, with Ollie bounding ahead scrabbling for rabbits. She heard the trees whisper to each other in the breeze, the hoot of a barn owl in the distance, and ducked as moths danced towards the beam of light on her forehead. She had never found the woods scary though she knew a lot of people would. It was alive with wildlife and it never failed to amaze her.

She paused as her light picked up a small roe deer, frozen in momentary fear at the approaching beam. And she smiled as it turned on its heels and gracefully bounded away. Ollie had his head down a rabbit hole and didn't notice it. Normally he would woof in surprise and look at Cass as the deer ran off. He'd never been one for giving chase, and Cass was grateful. He really was a pleasure to walk.

They walked another fifteen minutes down the faint path, then turned back towards the cottage. Ollie was tired now, his tongue lolling out the side of his mouth as he walked beside Cass.

Suddenly he stopped and stared intently into the darkness of the wood. Surprised as he growled softly, Cass paused too, feeling the hairs stand to attention on the back of her neck. She instinctively put her hand on Ollie's collar, slowly moving her head from side to side to illuminate the path ahead and get her bearings. They were still about ten minutes from the cottage. Cass didn't know what had startled the dog, and wasn't used to feeling fear in her woods. She let Ollie's collar go and said, 'Home, Ollie. Go,' and followed at a fast pace.

It was probably nothing more than some animal Ollie had perceived as a threat, but Cass wasn't taking any chances. Both she and Ollie made their way back to the cottage at a hasty speed and, once inside, Cass bolted the back door.

'You OK?' came Alex's voice from behind her.

Cass jumped and turned, her hand clutched to her chest.

'Jesus, Alex, you scared me. I thought you were still at work. We were in the woods and Ollie just stopped and growled but I couldn't see what it was and I panicked and we both ran...'

'Whoa, slow down, Cass. It's OK, you're safe. Come here,' interrupted Alex, pulling her into his arms.

Kissing her gently on the forehead, he whispered, 'It's OK. Now tell me what happened.'

Cass looked up at him.

'I don't know, Alex,' she sighed. 'Ollie never growls at anything. He scared me. I thought, I dunno. I guess I thought someone was out there. I'm probably just being jumpy.'

'I'd have jumped too. Shall I make us a hot chocolate? Nothing like a bit of chocolate to sooth fear so I hear?'

Cass smiled at him and nodded.

'How'd the robbery go?'

'We got two arrests. They entered the garage and threatened the cashier with a knife. Nicked maybe £60 out of the till and a crate of Fosters. CCTV showed them leaving the forecourt and one of the officers recognised one of the lads. We found them both in his flat, both onto their second can with a takeaway on their plates.'

'Quick result. Nice one.'

'What day did you say you were going to Rockliffe? I'm off for four days from tomorrow but was thinking of going up and seeing Mum and co. You don't mind do you?' Cass heard the hint of vulnerability in his voice as he asked.

'Mind? Why would I mind, Alex? I think it's great you're going up to see your family.'

Alex smiled at her, and then slowly took her cup from her hand and placed it on the table.

'Let's skip the chocolate,' he said quietly, 'I can think of something better to ease fear,' and took her hand and pulled her to her feet.

He leaned in and placed his lips on hers, filling her with the promise of things to come, before leading her off to the bedroom.

18ᵗʰ October, 0025 hours – Woods, Cass's Cottage

He froze as he heard the dog growl. Realising he had got too close and the mutt had picked up his scent, he stood still, hidden behind the tree.

He saw the glow of her torch move quickly over his position and held his breath in anticipation. Acting right now was not on his agenda. He would if he had to, but he hoped that if he stayed still she wouldn't see him.

As she bounded off along the path with the dog, he sighed with relief.

He would have to be more careful next time.

He was confused. It wasn't something he had felt before, and it worried him. He had picked Scott as show stopper number three. He knew he should be paying attention to Scott, but something about this woman kept grabbing his attention. He had done some surveillance on Scott earlier that day, and bought a greasy McDonald's to see if his presence aroused suspicion, but it hadn't. He wasn't recognised in his normal day to day attire. He should have continued after work, but he didn't. He'd found himself driving down to her cottage.

He had been watching as she had left the house with the dog, and had taken the opportunity to go inside while she was out. He hadn't stayed long, not knowing how long she would be out walking the monster. But it was long enough to ascertain that whatever relationship she had with the slave, he didn't live there.

He had pressed the back door key into the moulded plasticine in his pocket, knowing his own copy would come in handy one day, and had left the cottage, following the thin footpath through the woods to his current location.

It had been a risk.

One that had almost got him caught.

It wouldn't happen again.

Chapter Twenty One

'Cass, are you OK? You've been really quiet today. I'm worried about you,' said her mum, as they sat by the pool in their dressing gowns.

Cass looked over, seeing the deepening wrinkles around her mum's eyes as if for the first time. 'Sorry, Mama, I guess I'm a little distracted. Jameson gets released tomorrow. I'm not scared he'll find me or anything, it's just weird, you know? Knowing he'll not be behind bars any more, that he gets to live his life as though nothing happened.'

'I get it, sweetheart. I would be worried he would find me, but you're stronger than me. You always were. Everything you've been through and you just keep fighting. I love you very much, my daughter, and I am so proud of you,' tears glistened in Rose's eyes as she got up from her pool bed and sat beside Cass, pulling her into her arms and holding her tight.

'Please just promise me you will be careful. I couldn't bear it if anything happened to you.'

Cass hugged her mum just as hard, 'I don't feel strong, Mama. I am scared, but I can't dwell on what happened. I have to try not to think about it. He won't come near me but I will be ultra-careful. The alarm guy's coming on Friday. I've started my self-defence classes again. It'll be OK, Mama.'

Rose pulled back and gave Cass a shrewd look. 'I bet Alex wouldn't let him anywhere near you anyway.'

Cass smiled back and nodded.

'You're right,' she admitted, 'Alex scares me too. I've never been with anyone since Carl. But I'm really comfortable with him, we talk, you know? What if I'm reading more into it than there is though, Mum? What if he's just after something light hearted and I'm after something more long term? I'm not that great at reading man-signals.'

'Nobody is, but judging him on my first and only meeting with the man so far, I think it's a safe guess he's pretty smitten. Men don't think to buy gifts for nothing you know,' said Rose, patting her hand knowingly.

'It was just a tin of shortbread and some flowers, Mum,' groaned Cass with a grimace. 'But you think he's smitten? Really?'

'I most definitely do. Now, shall we go have our mani and pedi done? I'm getting peckish so if we get our nails done we can head up and get ready for an early dinner? It's Roger's treat and he said not to argue,' said Rose with a grin.

'Sounds good to me. Let's go. I need to ring the kennel and check on Ollie on the way though, OK?'

At her mum's nod, they both jumped up and made their way into the changing area.

19th October, 1800 hours – The Dene's Park, Sunderland

He watched as Scott dragged Kourtney behind him. They had been drinking in the park since goodness only knew what time, and she was verging on hysteria. She had managed to piss Scott off somehow and he had yelled at her, then slapped her across the face saying he was taking her home. She was crying and trying to pull away from him.

If he didn't intervene, Scott would be getting arrested all over again.

Straightening his wig, he turned the corner and came into their direct view.

'Andy. Hi. Is everything OK? I was just heading to the shop.'

He paused, waiting for Scott to reply. Kourtney had calmed slightly and although she was still sobbing, she now gripped Scott's arm tightly.

'Is she OK?' he asked.

'Yea she's fine. Was kicking off for a while but she's OK now right, Kourt?' At her slow nod, he continued. 'You get me some smokes from the shop, mate? Am out.'

'Sure, no problem. Do you want anything Kourtney?'

The girl shook her head silently, gripping Scott's arm so tightly he could see the white marks appearing beneath. He walked past them and into the nearby corner shop.

'I don't like him. He really creeps me out. His smile doesn't reach his eyes,' she slurred at Scott, pouting at him.

'Kourt, don't speak until he's gone, OK? He's going to give us money to piss off and live our lives. Do not mess this up, OK?' Scott's tone had turned quiet, and Kourtney was still reeling from the slap he had given her in the park. She nodded silently, abruptly releasing his arm from her death grip. She swiped at the tears streaking her face, swiping wet mascara across her cheeks without realising.

Scott just shook his head. Maybe he should just ditch her and get with someone else. That Tonia lass she hung around with was pretty fit and he'd never seen her with a guy. But he did have feelings for Kourtney. He let the thought pass, he had a feeling she would learn from the slap. His mother had never learnt from his dad, was always getting beaten, but then she had always pissed him off. Kourt didn't *always* piss him off, only sometimes. Tonight had just been one of those times was all. He was sure it wouldn't happen again, he hadn't liked the feeling of his hand connecting with her face, the look of terror in her eyes as she had stared at him in shock and her tears had bubbled over.

John came out of the shop and Scott grabbed the cigarette packet from his outstretched palm. 'Thanks, mate, much appreciated.'

Lighting one up, he watched as John handed Kourtney a small handy-sized bag of wipes and a bar of Dairy Milk.

'Chocolate solves all problems, and the wipes are for your face. Your makeup is streaked.' He turned back towards Scott, and added, 'I'll see you around, Andy. You guys need some cab money?'

Scott nodded silently, watching as he unfurled a ten pound note and handed it over.

They both wandered off down the street in the direction of the string of takeaways that littered the main drag through the town. He didn't particularly care whether they got a cab or not. What he cared about was his plan still being on course. If Scott had been arrested again, then there was a possibility he would have been remanded until his court appearance in November. And that was something he could not allow.

When he'd told Scott his name was John, it had been the most boringly common, random name that had popped into his head. He was glad of that now. Kourtney had met him, seen him, had potential to identify him. But he was confident in the disguise. Scott didn't recognise him when he wasn't made up. Stage make-up and dental inserts made a big difference. Add a false moustache, eyebrows and a wig, and he was unrecognisable.

He had always enjoyed that side of what he did. As a child he kept a dress up box in the garage, and his mother had always raved about what a good actor he was. He played a few parts in school productions. He learned early that showing emotion was a bad thing, where his mother was concerned, but the acting gave him more time away from home.

He liked being someone else. And he did it well.

20th October, 1600 hours – Ryhope Police Station

Cass picked Ollie up from the kennel, dropped her mum at the station and had just decided to call into the nick to get some evidence for a case file example for her paper. She parked up, grabbed Ollie from the boot for a visit and wandered in through the front office. She nodded at Ben through the glass and slowly the staff door opened at Ben's silent command.

As soon as they were through the connecting door Ollie pulled at his leash, and it slid from Cass's grasp. He scratched at the door to the front office, wanting to be in. Humouring him, she grinned and opened the door.

'Ben, I think Ollie wants to say hi,' Cass called out, before opening the second door and allowing the dog access. Ben was already on her knees at the base of the supply cupboard when he bounded over to her with his tail wagging hard, and his tongue hanging out of the side of his mouth. A huge smile lit up Ben's face, and it was all the invitation he needed. Planting himself in front of her, he greeted her with a sloppy kiss to the cheek, then promptly rolled onto his back, legs in the air, inviting her to stroke his tummy.

'Aw he's gorgeous, Cass,' said Ben, obliging him by rubbing her hand along his tummy. He almost groaned with pleasure – there was nothing he loved more than getting attention. Deciding this office was new, he jumped to his feet and sniffed contentedly around the floor.

'I'd better take him through to see Faith or she'll never forgive me. Busy night?'

'No, steady away but not too many peeps coming through the doors tonight. I'm just stock taking so I can put the order in tomorrow. I don't know what our lot do with the pens they take but I order hundreds every month! The Sergeant will be telling them to bring their own in before long I reckon.'

'Glad it's quiet, hope it stays that way and you get it all sorted. Come on Ollie.'

Cass flashed a quick smile at Ben as she left the office and made her way down the corridor, waited for the door to close behind her, and let Ollie off his leash. He'd visited the station with her enough times to know where he was going and quickly bounded into the CSI office, knowing someone in there would feed him treats.

Cass smiled as she heard Faith squeal his name enthusiastically.

'Hey. Am just popping in, forgot to take my file with me when I left the other day. Everything OK?'

'Yeah it's all fine, Cass, been steady away today. Greg's just picked up a couple of jobs, and Fred left a couple of minutes ago. Jason's said I can get a flyer so am just finishing up then gonna head off home.'

Faith handed Ollie a large piece of the sandwich from her desk, and smiled as he gently took hold. She ruffled his ears, and grinned as he pushed his head into her hand.

'Can I leave him with you for a sec? Just need to grab the file from my office. Is Kevin back? Jason said he was coming back in today?'

'Yeah he's over at central. Spoke with him earlier. He seems a little quiet but kinda happy to be back I think? Must be hard rattling around the house without Madge there.'

'Definitely,' acknowledged Cass, 'I'll give him a quick ring while I'm here.'

Leaving Ollie with Faith, she made her way into her office and paused at her desk, something bothering her momentarily. 'Where's my address book?' She muttered under her breath – her desk was testament to her mild OCD and everything always had its place. She found the address book on the floor under the desk and frowned. How had it got there? She carefully placed it back down beside her pen pot, and decided one of the team had probably been in her office. She gave her head a shake, and sat down to phone Kevin.

'Johnny, it's Cass. Is Kevin around?'

Seconds later Kevin was on the line. 'Cass, you're supposed to be on leave for the next couple of days or did you forget?'

Smiling down the phone at him, she said, 'You know me, Kev, can't stay away from the place. How you holding up?'

'Can't complain. No one would listen anyway. I'm glad to be working again if I'm honest. The house just feels too big without Madge there.' His voice broke a little on the mention of his wife's name. Pulling himself together, he added, 'Enough of all that anyway, get what you need and get on with your leave, Cass. I don't want to hear from you 'til you're back OK?'

'OK, Kev, I'll just grab Ollie from the office, if Faith will let him go, then I'm heading home. Gunna try and get my paper finished for the submission deadline this month. You know where I am if you need me though, right?'

At his assent, she hung up the phone, grabbed the file and wandered back into the office. Ollie was lying at Faith's feet, his tongue lolling out happily, and Cass couldn't help but notice the absence of the rest of Faith's sandwich. 'Hope he didn't woo you with those puppy dog eyes?'

'Nah, I'd had enough anyway. You getting off now?'

'Yeah. Tell Greg I said hi. And bye.'

'OK. Enjoy the rest of your leave, Cass.'

20th October, 1840 hours – Cass's Cottage

Cass pulled up in front of the cottage, opened the boot to let Ollie out and grabbed the kebab box off the back seat. She really should have just cooked something, but she was on holiday so why not indulge? She wandered to the front door, unlocked it and went inside. Her eyes took a moment to adjust to the darker interior, and widened as she registered the scene. The drawers from the unit in the hall were upturned and the contents strewn all over the place. She stood still for a moment, head cocked as she listened. Quietly she placed the takeaway on the cabinet and opened the door to the living room. It was in complete disarray, all her belongings and ornaments spread all over and the sofa cushions lying on the floor.

She began to shake as shock set in.

She had been burgled.

Tears filled her eyes. *Thank god Ollie was with me.*

She dreaded to think what burglars would have done to him if he had been there. Sensing something was up, Ollie stayed by her side as she made her way into the kitchen. The cupboard doors hung open, even the fridge contents were on the floor.

She took in a shaky breath and dialled the non-emergency number for the police.

'North East Police, this is Laura speaking. How can I help.'

'Laura, this is 7295 Hunt. I need to report that I've been broken into.'

Things were always dealt with a little differently when it was an officer or civilian involved. In her mind, Cass could see the log being created and switched over to the Duty Inspector for information. It was only twenty minutes later that the panda pulled up on her drive, quickly followed by Greg in his van.

Cass stood at the door as he jumped from the van, left his kit and ran over to her.

'Are you OK?' He asked.

'Yeah I'm fine, just a little shaken up.' Forgetting herself for a moment, she added, 'Wish Alex was here.' Realising what she had said as soon as the words left her mouth, she glanced at Greg who was grinning widely.

'You think we didn't know? We all had bets on – I thought you and he would've got together months ago.'

For a moment Cass was shocked, then she remembered she worked for the police managing a team of trained observers. If they hadn't noticed, then she should have been worried. She smiled back at Greg, turning as Harry Green approached her.

'I'm just going to head inside and have a quick look around – is the kitchen area OK to take the crime details, Cass?'

'Sure, Harry. I'll be in in a moment.'

Cass had already phoned Alex, who was going to travel straight back down, but Edinburgh was a good few hours away. She had promised to ring him as soon as Harry had taken her statement.

Harry completed the paperwork and left, leaving Greg processing the scene. It turned out to be quite a big job, and he moved from room to room efficiently, leaving Cass following behind – she would tidy once he was done. Ollie lay in the hall, perturbed by the strangers in his home. Greg was just completing the bedroom when Alex burst through the living room door.

Striding quickly inside, he grabbed Cass and pulled her into his arms.

Ignoring Greg for the moment, he kissed her head gently, and held her for a moment, almost a little too tightly. He sighed softly as he held her at arm's length, looking at her intently.

'You OK? I got here as quickly as I could.'

'Am fine, was a bit shaky when I first realised but I'm alright now. Honest.'

Cass pulled back slightly, her cheeks reddening a little as Greg approached. In the space of a few hours her work mates now knew where she lived and who she was dating. Being open would definitely take some getting used to, she acknowledged to herself.

'Several fingerprints and footwear marks, Cass. Also got some fibres from the point of entry. Reckon you'll need a new back door, though I've managed to jimmy it securely for now. Offender tried to gain access using Ollie's flap first like, think that thing must've been designed by the makers of Fort Knox 'cos he couldn't manage it. Oh, and I've swabbed something that looks suspiciously like spit from the back door step. Might be something, might be nothing, but I'll get it sent off if there's no idents off the prints.'

Cass nodded as he spoke, and watched as he got his stuff together and departed, leaving her alone with Alex and a whole lot of mess to clean up. The trouble with being the victim of a crime, was more often than not the CSIs didn't have time to clean up after themselves.

'Let me help, Cass,' said Alex softly. He knew she would probably get upset later, but for the moment she was focused on the task at hand.

She smiled at him, full of false bravado. 'It's just stuff, Alex. Would you mind putting things away? If it's wrecked just bin it. I'll grab some wipes from the kitchen and start cleaning the surfaces. Ali powder's a bitch.'

It took a good couple of hours to get the house back in some semblance of order; and Cass, who couldn't bear the thought that someone had been in her fridge, had ditched the contents with everything else. Alex had just left to take the last bin bag out of the kitchen when suddenly it hit her.

Someone had been in her home.

She felt tears prick at her eyes, and Ollie, who hadn't moved from her side, cocked his head and whined. She smiled a sad smile at him, bending to stroke the fluffy fur behind his ears, and dropped to her knees, grabbing his scruffy neck and pulling him to her.

'Am so glad you weren't here pup, what that man would've done to you I don't know but I'm glad he didn't get the chance. What are we going to do now?'

Cass hadn't heard Alex approach and only turned when he spoke.

'Now you and Ollie will come and stay at mine. At least until your door is fixed and you feel safer coming home. Or I stay here with you until your door is fixed and you feel safe here again.'

'Those are my options? OK, maybe you could stay here? You live in a flat and Ollie needs his walks. I'll phone a joiner tomorrow. Thanks, Alex.'

He walked over and held his hand out, 'Come on, you threw the food out and I've binned the cold kebab, so we are going to go get takeout. Ollie too, I think he deserves something nice.'

He took hold of Cass's hand, and led the way to the front door.

As they drove out of the drive, neither noticed the shadowy figure hidden behind one of the trees.

Chapter Twenty Two

21st October, 1110 hours – Pallion, Sunderland

He wasn't sure how much longer he could continue with this charade.

He'd been doing his best to avoid Scott, meticulously planning the way he would put the detestable youngster into the carefully prepared, makeshift coffin, and choosing his final resting place.

But Scott wasn't so keen on leaving him alone. He had been ringing and texting constantly, getting more and more aggressive about the money he had sneakily 'demanded'. He could hear the desperation creeping in each time they spoke. The kid was actually scared about going to court, not that he'd ever admit it of course.

'He's no more getting that money than he's going to see his next birthday,' he muttered to himself.

It just wouldn't do. He wanted to wait three weeks, but with eleven days until that deadline, he was out of time. It needed to be done soon, or he risked Scott going to the police with his lies and then his window of opportunity would be lost.

His face was grim, his fine jaw line sagging slightly as he struggled to keep his anger under wraps. He hated being rushed into things. But he also learned from his mistakes.

Never again would he choose an unpredictable teenager as a victim – Scott had proved much too hard work and had become adept at backing him into a corner.

He'd have to do the job sooner, despite his schedule now being all to pot and everything else off kilter.

He pulled the curved hunting knife from the top shelf of the toolbox. Maybe he would use it on Scott. It wouldn't end his life, but it would help him be compliant. After a couple of minutes though, he shook his head. He had much bigger plans for Scott.

There would be just enough time to add Scott's name and death date onto the top of the plywood coffin before leaving his unit for the day. It was early, yes, but he would be ready. The following Sunday would be 'D-day.'

He chuckled at his humour, D for death.

His eyes glazed as he placed the knife back onto the shelf in the box. He loved that knife. It had cut through the flesh of many animals since he bought it years before. Without registering, he ran his thumb over the slight scar on his left hand, and for a moment the memory of the cat incident filled his mind.

The cat was the fourth animal he had killed. The first was the old man's dog, the second and third were the pet rabbits belonging to two permanently squabbling children who lived down the road. They had been no challenge at all, he barely remembered the knife sliding through their flesh, but the cat, now that was a different story.

He had learnt very quickly that cats had claws, and they used them. In its panic, the ginger tabby had objected to being picked up off the street and carried to his shed in the garden. It had lashed out viciously, catching him off guard and causing a deep gouge in the soft padding on the outside of his thumb. He had responded by grabbing the cat round the neck, stifling its angry screeches. And then he took his time to make it pay for drawing his blood using the knife to cut the sharp claws from the cat's paws. Whimpering the cat had tried to run, putting bloody paw prints all over his work bench, but it didn't get very far, and before long the knife had removed the head from the body. It had been messy; taking him a good few hours to clean the surfaces down, and he still remembered the sting of the bleach in his cut. He buried the cat under the tree at the end of the garden and it was still there. Along with the bones of many more of his conquests.

He smiled to himself again, before getting into his mother's car and heading back over to the unit to finish Scott's box.

A shiver of anticipation rippled down his spine. Let Scott try *his* claws out and see what would happen.

21st October, 1245 hours – Cass's Cottage

Cass and Alex had spent the morning shopping, and had just returned. A frown passed over her face as her hand hovered on the edge of the fridge door. She felt very comfortable in Alex's presence, more comfortable than she ever had in fact. Since Carl she had naturally been wary, but even before him she had not been intimate with many men. As great as things were just now, it seemed to be happening very fast and she found that scary. She shook her head.

Some people are never happy. Besides I've got to move on from Carl at some point. Why shouldn't it be with Alex?

She turned to fill the kettle at the sink, and paused as something caught her eye in the garden. She couldn't quite put her finger on what it was but something looked out of place. She unlocked the newly installed back door, courtesy of the joinery firm used by the police who had attended first thing that morning and went outside.

It was overcast and threatening to rain, giving a greyish hue to the greenery. Cass glanced around, unsure what she was looking for. Then her eyes picked up something small next to the rear gate. She went to investigate, senses on high alert and couldn't stop her hands flying to her chest as she realised what it was.

A mutilated dog carcass lay there. It wasn't a dog she recognised, but she could tell from the wounds the animal had been tortured. She spotted a piece of paper partially obscured by one paw and bent slowly to pick it up. Her eyes widened as the scrawled message travelled the synapses to her brain. The paper fluttered to the floor as she turned and ran inside.

'Ollie, where are you?' She yelled as she entered the kitchen.

She pushed open the door to the hall and ran smack into Alex. He grabbed her arms, 'What's wrong, Cass?'

'Outside,' she stammered, eyes wild in fear. 'Where's Ollie? I need to find Ollie.'

Hearing his soft paws pad on the tiles in the hall, she dropped to her knees and pulled the dog close.

'He's OK, he's safe. Now tell me what's outside, Cass?' said Alex, as he helped Cass back to her feet.

'A dead dog. It's by the back gate. There was a note saying Ollie was next. God Alex, what the hell is going on? Do you think this could be Carl? Has he found me?'

'Even if it is, he will not hurt you or Ollie, I give you my word, Cass. Go pack a bag, you're both coming with me. I'll not have any arguments. I'll call one of my team to come and clear up the dog and we'll have uniform do drive-bys here. Whoever this is, it's personal. We will find them.'

Alex pulled her into a quick, tight hug, then released her, giving her a gentle push towards the stairs. 'Go pack your bag, I'll get Ollie's stuff sorted.'

Leaving Ollie in the kitchen, he made his way to the back of the garden to have a look. He felt bile rise in his throat as the dog came into view. If there was one thing he was a sucker for, it was animals. Bending to pick up the note, by the edge to preserve potential fingerprints, he placed it into a plastic bag he had grabbed from the drawer on his way past. He used stones to secure a bin bag over the carcass, and made his way back to the house. In his mind he was already sifting through the evidence. Whoever had killed the dog was disorganised, and sloppy. It was a message aimed at Cass and he frowned deeply as he registered the implications. It was too much of a coincidence that Jameson had been released a couple of days earlier. He knew in his gut it was him, and though he was trained not to rely solely on his gut, this time it was too strong to ignore. Pulling up the number he had painstakingly added when Cass had told him about Jameson, he dialled the probation office.

'DCI Alex McKay. I need to speak with Patrick Kelly as a matter of urgency.'

'DCI McKay, this is Patrick. How can I help?'

'You have a man called Carl Jameson on your books, correct?'

'I'll need to ring your station to confirm you're an officer before I can disclose any information DCI McKay, which force do you work for?'

'North East Police. If you ring the control room, they'll put you through to my mobile.'

A couple of minutes later, Alex answered the call with a quick hello.

'Apologies DCI McKay, you understand why though, I'm sure. Yes, Jameson is managed by me. But he failed to attend his scheduled appointment this morning. You should also be aware that my office was broken into in the early hours of the 20th, the offender is believed to be Jameson. The only thing he took was his file, which contained contact information for the witness in the assault case against him, Cassandra Hunt. Do you know her?'

'Yes, I know her. Has she been made aware of this?' Alex kept his tone purposely neutral. Kelly should have reported the incident to the local police, who should have also made Cass aware for her own safety, and he knew that hadn't happened.

'I don't believe she has as yet, I was going to ring her this afternoon. I've was waiting for the forensics team to finish with the office, then it became too late to ring last night.'

'I'll inform her. Thanks for your time, Mr Kelly.'

When he finished with Kelly, he phoned Charlie and asked her to meet them at his place in an hour. There was definitely too much coincidence for his liking and the more resources he used the better. He was banking on Jameson not knowing where he lived or there was no way he'd be taking Cass there.

As an afterthought he decided to put in a quick call to Ali. At the time of Cass's call, which now seemed like an eternity ago, he'd been with his brother. He knew Ali would be worried. He sighed as the call connected; Ali was going to be pissed.

'McKay,' his brother answered.

'Hey, bro. It's me,' he paused, waiting for the chewing to begin. It never came.

'Hey, Alex. Gonna have to call you back. In the middle of something. Ring you later.'

It sounded as though Ali was driving, so Alex said his goodbyes and hung up.

By the time he got back into the house, Cass was in the kitchen, with her bag and a carrier filled with Ollie's food and toys. She looked scared, and he acknowledged that he was too, though his fear was more for Cass than himself. All he wanted to do was get her away, put her somewhere safe and catch the bastard that had hurt her. But he knew she wouldn't let him. With fear shining in her eyes, there was an underlying look of determination. She wouldn't let Jameson break her again.

Within half an hour he was pulling the Audi into his private parking space outside the small block of flats.

Grabbing the bags, he said, 'There's a park over the road. We can walk Ollie there. I don't want you going alone though, OK?'

At her nod, he took her hand in his and led her inside.

Cass glanced around. Not that there was a whole lot to see. Sparse walls showed whatever pictures had been up when he moved in, and the furniture was functional. The only part of the living room that made it appear homely was the collection of family photos on the mantle. Slowly she studied them. At the centre was a large photo of an older man, with slightly greying hair but with similar features to Alex. He was in full police blues, and the crow's feet at the corners of his eyes were clear evidence of a happy man who smiled a lot. Despite pride of place on the mantle, she realised Alex had never mentioned him.

'Your dad?' She asked, glancing over at him.

He nodded slowly, placed her bags on the floor and walked over.

'Yeah that's Dad. He died sixteen years ago. In the line of duty.'

'Sorry, Alex,' said Cass, placing her arm on his.

'It's OK. Wasn't easy, Mum was devastated and everyone except Ali and me were so young. Mum lost her way a little, she's OK now but it was a tough time. He was her whole world, and she was his.'

'Understandable. I didn't know my real dad, he left mum when I was born. We never saw him again. I never needed him so didn't bother looking. Then mum met Roger and he became a father figure. He's great and she loves him to bits.' Cass's tone was matter of fact, but her eyes filled with love talking about her family. She was so close to them.

She looked up at Alex, and saw his eyes burning with a sudden rush of desire. He bent and captured her mouth with his, turning her round and pulling her into his chest. Forgetting for the moment, they kissed hungrily.

A sudden knock at the door caused them to pull apart like naughty teenagers caught behind the bike sheds. Alex gazed at her for a moment, then placed a gentle kiss on her reddened lips.

'We'll pick this up later,' he promised, giving her a smouldering look before turning to answer the door.

'Hey Charlie, that was quick, I.......' He started as he tugged the door inwards. His sentence tailed off as he realised it wasn't Charlie.

'Hey, bro. You gonna invite me in or stand there gawping at me all day?' Ali's voice held a hint of humour as he raised his eyebrows at Alex.

Alex moved to one side, then grabbed Ali and hugged him hard. 'What're you doing here, bro? I thought you were tied up?'

'I was. Tied up driving here,' he smirked back. 'You left like a bat out of hell, scared Mum half to death and I was given strict orders to come make sure you and Cass were OK. Mum really wants to meet the girl who has stolen your heart, bro.'

Alex felt his cheeks redden as he stepped aside. His family's mouths were way too big at times.

Cass was already smiling as Ali walked in.

Glancing at Alex and smirking again, Ali crossed the small room in three steps and enveloped Cass in an unexpected bear hug. Surprising herself, she hugged back.

'Pleased to meet you. Alex talks a lot about you, about all of you.'

'Back at you. He said you were beautiful, but he didn't mention how beautiful. It's a good job he's staked his claim or I'd be in line,' he grinned, liking her already. The wide grin she shot back made the banter worthwhile.

'So does a guy have to die of thirst here before he's offered basic hospitality? I'd kill for a cup of tea.'

Alex turned towards the kitchen shaking his head, still somewhat bewildered. As he put the kettle on, he heard the front door go again. *I really need more furniture if people are going to keep coming round!*

Chapter Twenty Three

He stood in the woods to the front of the cottage.

It was cold, and the darkness was spread all round him like a blanket, the moon and stars acting like a reading lamp illuminating the picture page of a book.

He was wrapped up warm though, and barely noticed as his breath turned to icy mist in front of him.

He frowned.

Her car hadn't moved. She could still be inside since he checked last night, but nothing else had moved either. The lights were still off, there was no sign of life from inside, and for a moment he wondered if she had gone away or something. His concern turned to annoyance as he realised she was probably with *him* at his flat in the town.

As he watched, he saw a slight movement to the west. He focused in, giving his eyes a few seconds to adjust, and saw the shadowy figure of a man.

'Now what have we here?' he whispered, watching intently.

The figure approached the front door, and tried the handle silently. When this failed to yield, he walked to the rear.

Not wanting to give his location away, but needing to see what was going on, he followed, virtually silent footsteps not disturbing the morning peace.

He stayed within the tree line.

And he watched.

He saw the figure try the back door, and use his shoulder to try and force it open. He heard him grunt in surprise as the door held fast. It was as if the figure had been in before and expected the door lock to be weaker than it was.

Suddenly a deer jumped from the trees to the south, startling both him and the shadowy form. They both froze, staring at the deer momentarily.

He heard the man curse under his breath, and saw him pull something from his pocket. He heard metal on metal and envisioned him putting the key in the lock and turning it.

Now his anger rose.

Whoever this was, he was after his prize. He had made the decision the day before that when he was finished with Scott he would focus on her; there was no way someone else was going to beat him to the punch.

He pulled back into the trees, melting into the darkness and made his way to his car. Time to check the sex slave's address, and then time for work.

Later he would find out who was trying to get at her.

And he would deal with it.

22nd October, 0745 hours – Alex's Flat

The journey hadn't taken long and now he sat in his car outside Alex's flat, watching for anything that would indicate to him that Cass was there.

He was confused, which was not an emotion he felt often. He couldn't fathom why he couldn't get her out of his head. It was almost like an obsession, but why was he obsessed with her?

He shook his head in the hope of dispelling the confusion and led his thoughts elsewhere. He had finished Scott's coffin last night. The cheap plywood box now had his real name and death date etched on the outside. Craftily, he had also embedded the small triangle of metal in a heated swirl below Scott's name. It looked different; out of place. There was no way the dimwit officers could miss it this time, but they would never find out what the triangle meant. After all, if he didn't know, how could they? He smirked as he ran his hand over the top of the triangle. Nice, smooth and set properly into the wood, he knew he'd done a good job.

On the off chance, he had checked the duty roster at the station. He knew Alex and Cass were both on duty on the date he had designated as Andy's death date. He could only hope they would be allocated to deal with the job. If they didn't link the scenes this time then maybe it would be time to provide further evidence of the link, but he would cross that bridge when he came to it.

Momentarily he wondered whether they had respect for his work. His intricately designed plans and executions should impress a person who deals with crime daily. He supposed he had expected them to be better than they were. Not as good as he was obviously, but better none the less.

He hunched down into his seat as the main door to the flat block opened and watched as Cass and Alex left the building. He was about to sit back up when another man followed them out with the monster on its leash.

Curiouser and curiouser.

The stranger walked under a street lamp which illuminated his features just enough for him to recognise him from the photo on Alex's desk. He'd seen it when he was snooping for background information. They had similar features, and he was confident if he hadn't remembered the photo he would still have realised he was a relative.

What had happened to make Alex phone in reinforcements?

Still pondering his silent question, he resolved it must have something to do with the shadowy figure he had seen at Cass's cottage. It was time to find out who the interloper was.

He set his mouth in a grim, determined line, started the engine, and pulled out onto the road.

Chapter Twenty Four

Scott gingerly touched the discoloured swelling under his left eye and hissed a loud 'ouch.' The motion jarred the bruising to his ribs, at least he thought it was only bruising. There was a weird crunching noise if he bent over so it might be broken. Unshed tears glistened in his eyes, and he swiped at them angrily.

He tried to pretend to himself that it didn't matter, that last time had hurt worse, but he failed miserably.

He stared in the mirror and the bruising to his eye and nose appeared to darken. Was this really it? Was this all he had to look forward to in life? A mother who'd left him, a father who beat him, a police officer who arrested him and a girlfriend who was now petrified of him?

The stab of guilt pierced into his soul.

He'd vowed he would never turn out like his dad, promised himself he would never hurt his girlfriend and force her to leave. And now he had done that very thing. He could still see the shock and pain on Kourt's face as his palm had connected with her cheek, still hear the resounding slap. He felt the awful thoughts he'd had in his head at the time, and he still didn't know how to deal with them.

He sighed at the mirror. Life sucked.

John-Joe had already told him that despite him passing the initiation and robbing the shop, they didn't want him in their gang. Didn't like 'wife-beaters', they said. Kourtney had hung her head at that. She had obviously told John-Joe's girlfriend, who had dutifully passed the information on.

Yet another failure notched on the belt of the learned fifteen-year-old. Or should it be sixteen now? He supposed it should be. His dad hadn't said a measly happy birthday before he'd punched him to kingdom come. All he'd done was smirk as he wiped the blood off his hand and onto Scott's T-shirt.

Scott knew this beating was his own fault. Normally it was drink fuelled, but not today. He had pushed his old man's buttons on purpose. The way he was feeling, he had deserved every damn punch and more.

He pulled open the door to the grimy bathroom cabinet and stared at the array of pill bottles inside. He didn't know what most of them were. Perhaps he should just end it all; Kourt would move on, find someone new. And his dad? Well he wouldn't notice if Scott wasn't there.

Sighing once more, he pushed the door closed.

Frankly, he was tired of taking the easy way out, hiding behind the mask that everyone else saw. One person didn't see the mask though. One person saw the person he was, at least Scott thought he did. He didn't know if he could change the person he was becoming, but he knew he wouldn't be able to do it alone.

He left the house and hopped on the next bus, getting off two streets from Brian's home. For the first time in a long time, he felt like the scared kid he was.

22nd October, 2340 hours – Ryhope Police Station

He leaned back in his office chair, and stared at the screen.

It had been surprisingly easy to find out who the shadow was. A Google search on Cass's name uncovered the news that she had been the victim of a horrific domestic assault years before. Further digging had yielded the name of the person who had done the deed and where he had been sentenced.

A simple phone call to the prison, stating the force he worked for and dropping Alex's name and rank confirmed that Jameson had been released.

He felt anger rise inside him. Not because Cass had been assaulted but that someone had got there before he could.

His eyes glinted in the dim office light; he wouldn't let Jameson hurt her again. That was *his* job.

24th October, 1340 hours – Ryhope Police Station

Ben walked into Cass's office, standing to one side to allow Dave, the cleaner, space to enter too.

'Hey, Dave, how's things?' asked Cass with a smile.

'Not bad, can't complain. How's you lovely ladies?' said Dave, a hint of a Yorkshire drawl in his voice.

Ben grinned at him, 'Can't complain either.'

'You could complain but what would be the point. No one listens to a moaner. Right, Dave?' piped in Cass, exchanging a conspiratorial wink with Ben.

They'd had this conversation many times before.

'So that's where I go wrong with the ladies!' said Dave, placing his hand on his head in mock horror. He gave them a wink, tied a knot in his bin bag and left the room.

'What a card,' said Cass smiling at Ben. 'What's up?'

'There's a kid in reception for injury photos but there's no one in the other office. Can you deal please?'

Cass nodded, stood and followed Ben through to the front desk. She opened the interior door to reception and glanced around. A young lad sat in the waiting area looking as though this were the last place on earth he wanted to be.

'Injury photos?' she asked.

He nodded curtly and stood as she motioned him forward.

She stepped back to let him pass. Self-defence 101 – never let your opponent behind you if you can help it. Not that she expected trouble, but you could never be too careful.

'Turn left here, then it's the first door on the right,' she said to his back.

He hunched his shoulders in response and followed her directions, ending up in the studio.

The room had been adapted for taking photos. The walls were painted bland grey, and there was a curtained area in one corner where people could get changed if needed, though usually this was filled with various camera-related items that required storage. There were several ceiling lamps mounted on moveable brackets which the CSI could angle to get the best photos, and a small desk containing magnifying equipment and further lighting for photographing small items needing additional enhancement or lighting techniques.

As the young lad turned towards her, Cass took in his features. He looked to be no more than sixteen.

'What's your name?' she asked, grabbing a pen from her hair to fill in his details on the notes form. Taking contemporaneous notes was something Cass did without thinking. Officially the stance was that they should be completed 'at the time or as soon as was practicable' which some CSIs and CSMs took to mean filling in later. But she had always believed that the simplest defence was honesty. Meaning if she was asked about it in court, there was no reason to explain why she hadn't done her notes at the time. Several defence solicitors had now taken to ask the CSIs when they had done their notes in an effort to try and discredit their memory of events.

She took his name and date of birth, and paused, turning to look at him.

'Scott, you're only sixteen which means you should have a responsible adult present when I take photos. Do you want me to call your mum or dad, or would you be happy with an officer coming down?'

His sad eyes answered her, and she knew instantly he would prefer a police officer. Shutters of pain had slammed down over his eyes at the very mention of his parents. *Poor kid.*

'Just give me a sec and I'll get someone down,' she said, pulling her radio from her belt clip.

Within a couple of minutes Rob Watson entered the studio.

'What's been happening to you?' he asked Scott as he settled his lean behind onto a tall stool.

'My Dad,' muttered Scott in reply, his tough guy demeanour slipping another notch.

'Who's dealing with the report?' asked Rob. He had always agreed with Brian that Scott wasn't a bad kid; he was just troubled and his bad attitude was his way of venting.

'I dunno, think his name was White, told me to come in now and get photos done. Didn't say I'd have to tell it all to someone else though,' said Scott sullenly.

He looked ready to bolt and Cass interrupted, knowing the importance of having the photos as evidence.

'Scott, we can get started now. I don't need to know what happened, but I will need to know your injuries. Would you mind listing them for me?'

The youth took a deep breath, determination in his eyes. Brian had said he would help only if Scott was willing to cooperate fully.

'Face and ribs. I took a kicking,' he said.

'OK no problems, sweetheart. Do me a favour and stand on the X in front of the grey wall and face me. We'll start with your face and move on to your ribs.'

Scott did as she asked and within a few minutes Cass had covered the general shots of the recent injuries, as well as older scarring. It would all mount up as evidence towards a case of child abuse as well as assault. She exchanged a covert glance with Rob who nodded a little, acknowledging he had seen the scarring.

'Give me a hand with the scale?' she said to Rob, and at his nod handed the small two-sided plastic scale to him.

When Cass had finished, Rob escorted Scott back to the front office as Cass finished scribbling down her notes.

It never ceased to amaze her what people did to their children, and she made a starred annotation to email the OIC to let him know of the older scarring. Likelihood was that Rob would pass the information along, but she didn't want it to get missed.

24th October, 1355 hours – Ryhope Police Station

He felt his heart leap into his throat as he turned the corner and came face to face with Scott.

He had to stop himself speaking, nodding at the officer as he passed with the youth in tow.

Scott was all bruised up, and for a moment he wondered whether Kourtney had hit back. Not that he could ask, not yet at any rate. He would contact him later though, maybe arrange to meet and then find out what had happened.

He could check the force systems, but he'd been doing an awful lot of that lately and if Professional Standards were to investigate he would surely be questioned.

He needed to be more careful.

Chapter Twenty Five

24th October, 2005 hours – Alex's Flat

'Are you sure you want to go home? I can go get anything you need,' asked Alex in a worried tone.

'I'm sure, Alex,' said Cass firmly. 'I can't let whoever this is dictate my life. The cottage is my home, and while your flat is lovely, it's not home. I need to go back.'

Ali watched the exchange from the sidelines. He could understand where Cass was coming from but he also understood Alex's concern. Alex couldn't be with her 24/7, but he could. Making the decision, he silently left the room and called his boss, asking for extended leave which was immediately granted.

When he went back into the living room, the pair looked no closer to an amicable resolve.

'I understand that, Alex, but why should I put my life on hold for someone who may or may not attempt to hurt me? Especially when we don't know for sure who it is.'

'It's pretty obvious it's Jameson. He broke into the probation office, got your details and came here with the intention of finishing what he started all those years ago.'

Cass blanched slightly as his words but her body language spoke volumes. Through gritted teeth she said, 'Maybe it is. And I'm not saying I'm not scared, Alex, but at the same time I won't let him destroy everything I have again. I've worked my arse off in therapy and life in general not to hide away like I want to at times. I can't let him do that to me. Not again.'

Her eyes shone with unshod tears, and a large dose of stubbornness.

'Maybe I can help here,' interrupted Ali. 'I've spoken to my Inspector. He's given me compassionate leave for as long as I need it. I can be with Cass 24/7, Alex, whenever you're not there I will be. Work or home, I will not let her out of my sight until Jameson is caught.'

They both stared at him, mouths agape. He sounded more like a body guard than a police officer.

Alex slowly nodded his head. 'That might work.'

Cass shot him a venomous look. 'I'm quite capable of looking after myself, Alex. I do not need or want a babysitter. Mum's coming tomorrow to pick Ollie up so nothing will happen to him. No offence, Ali, but I don't want or need you with me all the time. You have a job in Edinburgh, Alex has a job here, as do I. Jameson or no Jameson, that is still the case. I will not be turning up to crime scenes with a damn body guard in tow!'

'For Christ's sake, Cass, don't you get it? I care about you. I don't want anything to happen to you. I know I can't be with you all the time, it doesn't make sense with the jobs we do, but I trust my brother with anything. He can look after you. Please, Cass?'

Cass could see the desperation in Alex's eyes. They hadn't been dating long but in a strange way she was glad to see him show he felt the same for her as she did for him. Her expression softened a little.

'I can't have Ali with me all the time, but I guess it'd be OK if he stays at the cottage with us. That way when you're not there he is, and when I'm not there the cottage won't be left empty. So far this person has focused all his efforts on the cottage, I've not had any threat directed at me. Logic dictates that if he tries again, it will be at the cottage.'

Alex exchanged a quick glance with Ali, who nodded in a barely discernible movement.

'Guess we should go pack your stuff then,' said Alex. He watched her head back into the bedroom and raised his eyebrows at Ali.

Women!

25th October, 0920 hours – Ryhope Police Station

Not for the first time that morning, Cass sighed. She was stoically working her way through a mountain of paperwork that had amassed while she was off, but she was bored. She wanted to be out and about, not stuck in the office.

She grinned as an idea struck her. Grabbing her jacket, she locked the door and went into the CSI office where Deena was getting ready to go out.

'Mind if I tag along? Part of the new development plans involve me going out on two jobs a month per person. I'm not there to interfere or tell you what to do, I'll just be observing.' Cass's held her breath, half expecting an objection, but Deena smiled widely and nodded.

She grinned back, glad her staff thought enough of her to know she wouldn't interfere.

It only seemed like a few minutes later that they pulled up outside of a dilapidated, vacant house that had been burgled. The investigating officer was still on scene and Deena got out to speak with him.

'Typical boiler job, Deena,' he said. 'They've kicked the back door in but I doubt you'll get anything, the condition the place is in. There's no electrics inside and you'll need to be careful 'cos they've ripped up the floor boards. Have already radioed for Eastway Housing to attend to board. They should be about three quarters of an hour.'

'Great. Thanks, Craig,' said Deena with a smile.

Cass watched them share a glance. *Go Deena. He seems like a nice guy.* Craig had been with the force for several years and had more forensic awareness than most. Momentarily, Cass wondered whether that was because of Deena, then, flashing him a quick grin, she followed Deena into the property.

The first thing she noticed was the smell. Stagnant water and mould – when offenders ripped out the copper piping and the boiler, whatever water was inside the pipes flooded out. It seeped into the floorboards and with vacant properties it could be some time before the theft was picked up. Offenders had a habit of leaving mucky footwear marks everywhere which provided valuable evidence.

This time though, it looked as if the water had been off a while. There was minimal seepage around the radiator areas and no sign of any footwear marks, the bare floorboards too grainy to hold sufficient tread-mark detail.

Cass followed Deena from room to room as she took photos and performed her visual exam. Cass was pleased to note how methodical she was.

The only evidence, other than the photos, that Deena recovered was a plastic carrier bag. Chemical treatment of the bag might yield potential fingerprints, though she couldn't know if the offenders had dropped it, or if the previous tenant had left it behind.

Moments later they were en route to the next job on Deena's list.

Cass scanned the log as Deena drove to the location.

Anon male cllr reporting burglary to garage in garage block. Sts the door has been forced. Doesn't know owner. Sts it is second garage on left. No further info avail.

The lack of information on the log was normal, the call takers at headquarters could only obtain as much as the caller was willing to give. They all worked to the same standard of short hand, most of the time. Garage break-ins were a regular occurrence and were a current area command priority, meaning that the CSIs had to attend them all on special request from the Duty Inspector. The forensic evidence was usually limited, but a definitive presence was required to ensure peace of mind in the area, and to encourage information flow between the beat officers and CSIs. Often the CSI would note details relating to the *Modus Operandi* and be able to link this to other similar scenes the officer might not know about.

Feeling a strange sense of foreboding, Cass radioed in to control and put them both at scene as they pulled up.

On first glance, the garage subjected to the break in wasn't obvious. Whoever had called it in had seen fit to pull the up-and-over door back down. They approached the second door on the left and Deena began her exam, noting the small striation marks about a foot from the bottom of the door.

'I'll get the tool cast kit while you photo,' offered Cass as Deena loaded a fresh memory card into her SLR camera.

Cass opened the rear van doors, found the right drawer and grabbed two tubes from inside, one blue and one red. She grabbed the door and pulled it shut and jumped as she saw the figure appear.

She felt the colour drain from her face as she came face to face with Jameson.

'You always were predictable,' he sneered at her. 'One phone call and here you come running.'

Deena's voice came from beside the van, 'Cass? Is everything OK? I know where it is if ...' Her voice trailed off as she rounded the van corner and stopped behind Cass. Jameson didn't notice as Deena silently pressed the orange emergency button on the top of her radio.

'What do you want, Jameson?' asked Cass, trying to stay calm. She could feel her heartbeat pounding in her ears and her body was screaming at her to run, but she was doing her best to convince herself that she wasn't that scared kid any more.

Fighting the flight instinct was hard, but she stayed where she was.

Both girls took a step back as Jameson pulled a knife from his pocket, the blade glinting as he moved it from hand to hand.

A sudden burst of static on the radio made him jump, his eyes narrowing in suspicion. When it remained silent, he said slowly, 'Jameson? Since when do you call me by my last name? I'm gonna finish what I started. But this time you won't survive to send in the stupid appeal letters. You won't be able to deny me anything. And as for your friend, she's hot, it's been a while since I was with a woman.'

He took a step towards them.

'Carl, please, put the knife down. I'll do what you say, you don't need the knife.' Cass felt her voice falter, as she stepped between him and Deena. *Please God, let Deena have hit the emergency button.*

Suddenly a siren wailed in the distance, rapidly approaching, and Carl glared at her.

'Don't know what you did, but I'm not going back. They'll have to kill me first,' his eyes widened as the siren came closer. 'I'll see you around, Cass,' he sneered as he leaned in and placed the knife to her cheek. Cass inhaled sharply, smelling his sickly aftershave as he drew the knife downwards slowly causing a thin line of blood to appear. The cut wasn't deep, and the knife was sharp. She barely registered the movement. As suddenly has he had appeared, Jameson ran to the other side of the van and down a nearby cut.

'No way! No way is he getting away. Not this time,' muttered Cass, her fear replaced with a rush of anger and adrenaline. Taking off at a dead run, she gave chase.

Deena stood for a second, comprehension slow in dawning on her. 'Shit! Cass, stop!' Grabbing her radio, she started shouting directions as she followed them.

25th October, 1105 hours – Silksworth, Sunderland

It took him a moment to comprehend what was happening.

The emergency beep had sounded on his radio, opening the airwaves and allowing every officer on that operating channel to hear the exchange. He listened carefully, waiting for Comms to give the location.

Anger bubbled inside him when he heard the name Jameson and realised it was Cass in trouble. This wouldn't do. It was no one else's job but his to deal with Cass. He needed to see how she dealt with Scott's murder, needed to know if she would be the one to link it all together. It had almost become a necessity. If she figured it out, maybe he would let her live. Maybe.

But not if Jameson got his filthy paws on her.

There was a burst of speech as Comms gave the last known location as the cut on Grey Street. He felt a smile widen. He was just round the corner.

He felt a stab of uncertainty – he was in the work van. But, pushing the thought to one side, he pulled away from the kerb. He could hear sirens converging on the area. Officer needs assistance was an urgent call and everyone from community officers to inspectors would be in the area shortly. He needed to find Jameson – and fast.

He tried to decide what Jameson would do. The man wasn't familiar with the area, but he was. Setting his mouth to a grim line, he swung the van around and headed towards the park.

His heart leapt as he saw Cass and Deena, looking around in bewilderment, but averted his gaze and drove by.

He drove up alongside the park, slowing to a crawl as he scanned the tree line. The sirens grew louder and that's when he saw him. A man was sloping towards the next exit, his eyes glancing around furtively.

He felt excitement in his gut. It had to be him.

He pulled up alongside, offering silent thanks to the powers that be for providing staff with unmarked vans.

Leaning to the left, he flung open the passenger door.

'Unless you want to be caught, get in.' His voice was soft, and any sane person would have noticed the menacing undertone, but Jameson was desperate. Quickly he obeyed and ducked down. He'd already ditched the knife, knowing that evidence would incriminate him.

'Thanks, mate,' he said, glancing over. Slowly realisation dawned as he took in the police badge on the jacket thrown over the back of the driver's seat. Jameson's face paled, 'Fuck.'

'Don't worry about the badge, I'm just like you.' He said soothingly, doing his best not to choke on the words. They were nothing alike. Jameson had just proved that by getting into a car with a stranger. *He* would never have made such a rookie mistake.

'Where are we going?' asked Jameson, distrust obvious on his pasty face.

'Somewhere safe,' was the ominous reply. How had this guy managed to beat up Cass? He looked like he could barely fight his way out of a brown paper bag. He felt a quiet surge of adrenaline – this was unexpected. It almost felt like a treat.

It was risky, taking Jameson to his unit. He knew there was no CCTV covering that section of the estate. But he also knew that people are nosy busy bodies. And it was broad daylight. He had to keep Jameson calm so they didn't look suspicious.

He pulled the van up in the car park, and jumped out.

'There's money inside, and keys to an old car if you need it,' he said quietly, dangling the carrot.

'Why would you do that for me, man? You don't know me.' Jameson sounded suspicious and looked ready to bolt.

He though on his feet and decided partial honesty was the best bet.

'But I know Cass. That bitch deserved the beating you gave her. The same as the one she had off me.'

Jameson relaxed. He was in the company of a brother in arms, a comrade.

'Would've done more this time like. Bitch put me away. Just lost eight years of my life rotting in a cell. I'll pay you back the money, mate. What do I call you anyway?'

He couldn't believe it had been that easy. Some people were so gullible. With a half smile, he said, 'John.' Might as well stick to his cover.

He unlocked the door to the unit and motioned Jameson through ahead of him. His eyes adjusted quickly to the low light, and silently he grabbed the heavy Stihl saw off the side.

Jameson didn't see it coming. The tool connected with his head with a dull thud, and he fell face-down onto the floor.

Now he had to make sure Jameson wouldn't get up. He felt deep satisfaction as he raised the saw high above his head once more. The second crunch was louder, and when he looked down, Jameson's eyes were open, directed straight at the front door, and blood was seeping from the wreckage that was his head. A spreading pool was working its way through the sawdust on the floor. He grabbed a latex glove from his pocket, pulled it on and placed a finger against Jameson's neck.

There was nothing there. No faint flutter of a heart trying to survive. Just emptiness.

Jameson would be fine until he returned later. It was by no means his most elegantly designed kill or disposal, but he was glad it was over. He scattered more sawdust around his victim's head, watching it absorb the red liquid. Later he would have to clean, but now it was time to get back to work. He would think about what to do with the body after darkness fell.

25th October, 1425 hours – Ryhope Police Station

'Are you sure you don't need to see a doc? Shock can come on later, Cass, you know that.' The cautious tone of Alex's voice betrayed the worry he was trying to hide.

'Alex I'm fine. Honestly. I've done my statement, it's just a scratch. Truthfully I was more afraid he would hurt Deena.' Cass sighed loudly, 'I can't believe I was stupid enough to run after him though.'

'Dunno if I'd call it stupid, I mean it *was* stupid, but also pretty brave. You faced your demons head on. And your demon had a knife. How many of us can say that?'

Cass just shook her head silently. Jameson could have killed her. She hadn't thought to press the orange button. Thank god Deena had her head screwed on. She was telling Alex the truth though, she *had* been more scared for Deena. Maybe she really was starting to move past the scars left by Jameson, and not just the physical ones either.

'The Super's given me permission to take you home and make sure you rest up. As I say, shocks a funny thing. It can come on later when your adrenaline settles down. You about ready to go?'

Cass nodded, double checked with Fred that he and Johnny could cope with the jobs, and pulled her ID card out of the computer. Deena had already left, under strict instructions to ensure she had someone with her overnight. She had Cass's number in case she needed to talk.

It was all sorted, so why did Cass feel like she was missing something? She knew the officers hadn't found Jameson but there were country wide alerts out for him, he wasn't going to get far. She felt like there was something just outside of her peripheral vision. Something she had seen but couldn't put her finger on. But she'd been over events several times now, and couldn't for the life of her fathom what it was.

Sighing to herself, she grabbed her coat and followed Alex down the stairs.

Chapter Twenty Six

26th October, 0425 hours –
Unit 14b, Enterprise Park, Sunderland

It had been pretty straightforward so far. He'd rolled Jameson's body onto plastic wrapping. It was the kind you could get at any hardware store and he always had a stock of it for wrapping the coffins before they were dispatched. He was wearing a full crime scene suit with the hood up, boot covers and gloves.

One of the joys of being the handyman was that he had a key to every room in the station, including the CSI Store. He didn't intend to leave any trace evidence on Jameson's body. Granted there would be flecks of sawdust, but that could have come from anywhere.

He grunted as he heaved the body onto the trailer behind the car. Rigor Mortis had set in, and was only just starting to loosen, making the body less pliable. He wanted the body to be found by a police officer and knew a small police station, a few miles from his own, which was not manned overnight. He also knew the CCTV there had been broken for months. They would call off the man hunt then and Cass would see what he had done. Maybe she would process the body or attend the post-mortem.

He placed a large blue tarp over the body to hide it from curious eyes and set off.

The journey was uneventful and in no time he had pulled in at the side of the station, his car now obscured by overhanging trees.

He huffed as he hefted the dead weight off the trailer as if it were nothing more than a slab of meat, positioned it at the back door and pulled the plastic away from Jameson's face. Then came the note, cleverly (he thought) printed at the local library, which he pinned to the plastic. It contained just two words.

'You're welcome.'

Stepping away from the body, he pulled off the protective clothing and wrapped them together in a ball. He drove out of the station, whistling eerily, and stopped a couple of miles from his home, to throw the wadded suit into a litter bin.

Time for a cup of tea, he decided. He had worked hard, he deserved it. Besides, it was almost time to get ready for his last shift of the week.

26th October, 0740 hours – Cass's Cottage

Alex took a sip of coffee and swallowed with a soft sigh. He knew coffee was almost as clichéd as the police and donuts, but he loved the caffeine enriched brew, black, steaming and strong. Cass wasn't due at work until 11 a.m. and she was still sound asleep in bed. Ali had been up since goodness knew when and had gone for a run. So Alex got to enjoy his coffee in peace; a peace that was rudely shattered by the shrill ringtone of his mobile.

He grumbled to himself as pressed the answer key.

'McKay,'

His head cocked to one side as he listened intently.

'You're sure?' He asked into the receiver, 'OK, tell the Super we're on our way.'

He felt the coffee rise from his stomach as bile. Someone had seen fit to kill Jameson. He knew what that meant, and why the Super had demanded they come straight in. He was a little surprised a squad of pandas hadn't turned up at Cass's to cart them off in cuffs. As of the time the body had been identified, they were all officially suspects in a murder investigation.

26th October, 1855 hours – Ryhope Police Station

Cass was fed up. She'd been in and out of interviews with Professional Standards all day, rehashing her whole life to anyone who had asked. She had complied and answered all questions honestly, but she felt as if the whole station now knew everything about her. And that was far more than she had wanted them to know.

Alex and Ali had been through the same ordeal, and they'd only just been told they could leave. She knew it was necessary. She had motive, as did Alex, and indirectly Ali. It was all about crossing t's and dotting i's.

The Super had pretty much told them that from the outset, none of the police family believed they were involved, but there were procedures to follow. All in all, they'd been pretty lucky.

They weren't suspended, at this stage they weren't getting notes in their personnel files.

All she wanted to do now was have a hot bath and forget the day had happened. She knew Alex would be feeling the same. She hadn't seen him since that morning, and she wondered whether had finished yet.

Officially, Kevin who had handled the scene was not allowed to tell her anything about the case. But she had heard through the grapevine that Jameson had suffered two blows to the head with a heavy object. The police station had merely been the dump site, and the forensic evidence consisted of photos only, plus the plastic sheeting which had been sent for chemical analysis. The post-mortem was scheduled for the next day, with CSIs from the central depot running point. She was sure she would have an update by the end of tomorrow, even if she didn't ask.

Jameson's death would be handled like any other murder, but Cass had to admit to feeling a little relief. He was dead. There was no way he could hurt her or anyone else now. And though she disagreed with the punishment inflicted on him by the killer, she was glad she didn't have to worry about him any more.

Chapter Twenty Seven

26th October, 1930 hours – Cass's Cottage

He blended into the background of the tree line to the west of the cottage. It wasn't quite pitch black yet and he didn't want to be seen. He watched Cass's car pull up in front of the house. She didn't seem very happy. She should be happy. He had taken care of the problem for her. And this was her gratitude? Her complacent 'I don't give a shit' attitude?

The ball of anger grew in his stomach. That just wasn't on, she should be pleased he'd killed Jameson. His fists clenched tightly, his nails cutting in his palms as he tried to steady his emotion.

He'd done her a damn favour.

He felt his anger unfurling, tendrils reaching into his soul as he struggled to keep control. He would make her pay.

First though, he had neglected Scott over the last few days. It was time to build bridges. Pulling back from the tree line, he tugged the mobile from his pocket and sent a quick text. Moments later the reply buzzed in his hand, and he felt his anger simmer once more.

Don't need the money now. Gonna try and straighten my life out. Can't do dis crap no more. C U around.

Oh, you'll definitely see me around. You think you get to dictate to me when this is over? I don't think so.

He puzzled over his growing anger as he drove to the unit.

He needed to get a grip. Anger caused mistakes.

27th October, 0800 hours – Ryhope Police Station

Alex pulled into the car park at the station and sighed. The day before had been long; after the challenging interviews both on the record and off the record he had finally got back to his flat. Ali had packed his stuff up, now that Jameson was no longer a problem there was no need for him to hang around. Alex had said his goodbyes that morning before hitting the gym after promising he would bring Cass on a visit soon to meet the rest of the clan.

But something wasn't sitting right. The timing was off for Jameson getting killed. It seemed awfully convenient for him to be murdered mere days after being released. Granted if he'd hurt Cass he may have ended up that way anyway. But it was almost too neat that he'd been killed so soon after threatening her. It was as if the killer had known the location and picked him up. He possibly had someone with him, but Alex didn't think this was plausible. Jameson hadn't been out that long, and there was nothing in his history to show he knew Sunderland at all.

He stepped through the rear door, his feet heavy with the lack of sleep.

'Whoa easy there, boss,' said a voice as he trundled inside, not noticing the cart until he almost walked into it.

Alex smiled at Dave. 'Sorry, am away with the fairies.'

'Fairies have a lot to answer for if you ask me,' said Dave with a grin.

Alex held the door open as the cleaner passed through, whistling a jaunty tune. He closed the door, listening as the latch caught, and made his way up the stairs to the office.

He paused at the door and took a breath. Saturdays were always busy, with overnight packages involving drunken souls acting out the night before, not to mention the murder files that were forming a growing pile on his desk. He used the moment to focus his thoughts, then walked to his desk. The keyboard was already scattered with four call-back messages, and there were several new files needing a look over.

'Coffee. I need coffee,' he muttered to himself. He turned to go to the kitchen when Cass appeared, two takeout cups in hand.

'Thought you could use a cuppa. Gonna be a busy day. I'm heading out shortly – there's like eighteen outstanding jobs already.' she coughed, suddenly shy at asking her next question though she couldn't fathom why. 'Are you coming over tonight? Mum and Roger are bringing Ollie back. I think Roger wants to take us out to dinner? They're staying at one of the fancy hotels near the town centre.'

Alex grinned at her. 'Sounds great. What time shall I come over?'

'Mum said they're hitting the hotel for about 4 p.m. then they'll have to get ready and what not. I think they're dropping Ollie off first. Say about 6 p.m.?'

'I'll make sure I'm there on time. Have meetings all day so I'll be in and out of the office. Have my mobile though if you need anything.'

Cass smiled, turned and left.

Charlie made her way over. 'I've put a couple of files on your desk to glance at. Doesn't look like anything and I'll take care of them once you've had a read. You also had a message to ring Emily Grieves. She's the daughter of the old guy from the cave. Local officers have done the death inform but she's asking to speak with whoever is heading up the investigation.'

'No problems. Thanks, Charlie,' said Alex, grabbing the Post-it with her info on. 'I'll call her now.'

He had a quick glance over the file before he punched in her number. It listed Emily as estranged from her father.

The call finally cut to voicemail and he left her a message.

First job done, he turned his attention to the files and it wasn't long before he was returning them to Charlie.

'Consider them looked at and delegated,' he said with a grin as he handed them over. He took in her healthy glow, the look of contentment.

'Everything OK, boss?' She asked, a little uncomfortable under his scrutinising gaze.

'I'm fine. Are you?' He gave her a pointed look.

Her cheeks flushed as she said, 'I'm pregnant. Was going to tell you later today after the morning rush.'

Alex flashed her a wide smile, ignoring the sudden pang of something he didn't quite grasp. 'That's great. Congratulations. I'm between meetings from about 1 p.m. We'll have a sit down then – that OK with you?'

She nodded and turned back to the files as Alex walked back to his desk just as his mobile started ringing.

'McKay,'

'DCI McKay? This is Emily Grieves.'

By the time Alex hung up the phone with Emily, he felt he knew much more about the old man. Albert had turned to drink after losing his son in a motorcycle accident – yet another reason to sell the old Triumph from his garage. In time Albert's wife, Jean, Emily's mum, had lost patience and ordered him out and he had eventually become homeless. Emily had received intermittent phone calls through the years, and she always helped out because he was her father after all. She hadn't heard from her father in eighteen months and had sounded resigned to the fact he would end up dead.

Her final words to him were, 'Please find whoever killed my father, DCI McKay. Whatever his faults, he didn't deserve to die like that.' Alex had promised to do everything in his power to do just that.

There was only once he had made an actual promise to find the person responsible. And that hadn't gone well. Now he only ever promised to do his best.

27th October, 1805 hours – Vacant Lot, Seaburn, Sunderland

He watched Scott walk into McDonald's for his late shift. For a moment he almost felt for him – working a Saturday night was never fun. Especially somewhere like McDonalds – the local kids loved nothing better than to torment the staff when they'd had a skinful of whatever cheap cider they had coerced a well-meaning stranger to buy for them.

But then Scott wouldn't really see Sunday so that wouldn't be fun either.

Everything was in place. It would happen ahead of schedule, but he was ready. Nothing would stop the show tonight. He knew Scott was scheduled to be at work until 1 a.m. He turned the car around and left the car park.

It was time to get everything prepared.

He stopped at his unit to pick up the plywood box and his toolbox. He'd been out the night before and laid white plastic across the fence facing the promenade.

The electrics to the arcade next door had been bypassed and were ready to go. The ketamine was on stand-by – the needle prepped with a mild dose. He didn't really want to knock Scott out, but it would make him much more manageable, so for now, it was a necessity.

He smiled grimly to himself. Doing what he did for the police made it easy for him to gain access to all the restricted areas. Taking a few vials from the kennels years before when access had been easier was simple. They had been in his kit ever since.

The only thing left to do was to lure the unsuspecting youth to the promenade when he finished his shift.

His smile faded. This would be tricky. He knew the offer of money wouldn't lure Scott, not now he had seen the error of his ways. He had to at least get him in the car.

Maybe Kourtney could help with that. A different sedative would be needed if he wanted the effects to last long enough, but it would be interesting to see her reaction when she woke and saw her beloved, dead in front of her.

He nodded – he'd made his decision. He headed to the alley at the rear of the arcades, unlocked the new padlock he put on the old gate, and drove inside.

The rear gates were solid wood, albeit somewhat faded but still intact and able to obscure view. With the front covered too the only thing he had to worry about was making too much noise.

He didn't want to bring attention to himself, not when he had been so careful.

Quietly he set the box in the centre of the vacant lot, checked and double checked the wire bypass, and removed a syringe and vial from his toolbox. He carefully measured the small dose of ketamine, replaced the vial, and took out the Phenobarbital. He knew this had longer lasting, deeper sedative effects and would ensure Kourtney wouldn't wake until he wanted her to. Careful not to mix up the syringes, he capped them both and placed one in each pocket.

He felt the excitement settle in the base of his stomach. This would be the one. The one he had been searching for. This would give him the satisfaction he sought.

Chapter Twenty Eight

28th October, 0220 hours – Vacant Lot, Seaburn, Sunderland

Scott couldn't move.

He remembered being picked up by John. He remembered seeing Kourtney unconscious in the back of the car, and feeling a sense of dread as he felt a prick in the back of his neck. He'd stumbled against the car as his muscles decided they didn't want to work with whatever was running through his blood stream.

He felt like his head was floating outside of his body, looking down on him. He hardly registered the tear rolling from his swollen eye and down his cheek as John had bundled him into the car. And now here he was. His hands and feet bound and tape across his mouth, inside some kind of box.

Scott was scared. More afraid that he had ever been. He could taste the fear in his mouth, and almost gagged from the sensation. He tried to scream but the tape allowed a muffled grunt to escape. He could smell the sea. But it was pitch black and he couldn't see anything except the dull glow of street lights ahead. He listened, and heard the soft whooshing noise of waves hitting the sand, and the sounds of scuffling behind him.

Where's Kourt? I bet he has her. What does he want? I want my dad.

Another tear crept out of the corner of his eye as John appeared in front of him.

'It's time,' said John quietly.

Scott felt his breath catch in his throat, his virtually silent screams going unheard in the still of the night as John calmly applied the crocodile clips to Scott's bare skin and stepped back, smiling eerily at him in the dull glow of the moon.

28th October, 0221 hours - Vacant Lot, Seaburn, Sunderland

He stood back from the coffin, shaking his head at Scott as he tried to struggle against the bonds that held him immobile.

He felt adrenaline surge through his veins. This feeling, he acknowledged to himself, was what he was searching for. This one would be as good as the first time. It had to be.

The seafront was silent – people all tucked up in their beds away from the chill, fast asleep in preparation for work the next day. And if they weren't, they couldn't see through the heavy-duty plastic at the front gates.

He'd felt a rush as he stared into Scott's terrified eyes and clipped the jagged-edged clips to the exposed skin on the youth's chest.

Then he frowned to himself. He couldn't see Scott's expression if he was by the electric box flicking the switch on the current. And he so wanted to see the boy's eyes in his final moment.

He shook his head and took the clips from Scott's chest before setting them down on the floor. With a growing sense of anticipation, he attached the other ends to the electric box.

Scott was crying now, muffled sobs and bubbles of snot escaping through his nostrils, and his eyes widening in terror.

He finally understood what was happening.

He stood before Scott, cocking his head and watching for a moment, allowing the feelings of control to wash over him.

Scott was still trying to struggle, minimal movement allowed inside the box even without the effects of the ketamine and the ropes holding him fast.

Now it was time.

Taking care to ensure he was holding the rubber ended sections of the clips, he applied one to Scott's chest. As he leaned in he smiled, applied the second and stood back to watch as Scott's body writhed and convulsed inside the box. The smell of charring wood and burnt flesh filled the air, and he watched Scott's eyes turn glassy as his body succumbed to the volts coursing through his veins.

It hadn't taken long.

He let the electricity surge for a few minutes longer, a deep frown now marring his features.

It wasn't the same. Why wasn't it the same?

Slowly he swallowed the bubble of anger. He would think about it later. Right now he had Kourtney to remove from his car and a clean-up to do.

28th October, 0720 hours - Vacant Lot, Seaburn, Sunderland

Kourtney felt her head pound as she struggled to open her eyes. Stones were digging into her face, and for a moment she wondered just how drunk she would have to be to fall asleep on a pavement. She groaned loudly as she opened her eyes, blinking to clear her vision.

Everything was blurred and her mouth felt like it was full of cotton wool. She lifted her head, swallowing hard as a wave of dizziness hit her. As bile rose into her throat, she swallowed again, but it proved too much, and as she pulled herself up onto her hands, her stomach emptied the remnants of her last meal on the floor in front of her.

The smell didn't help. It was like someone had overdone the BBQ meat and she wrinkled her nose in distaste. Who on earth had a BBQ in October? Her blurred thoughts were jumbling together, and she was confused.

She could see the sea through a set of wrought iron gates and she shivered as her body registered the cold. How had she got there? The last thing she remembered was, something in her memory, just out of reach. Her hand flew to her neck as she recalled a sharp pain and the sensation of being lifted. Her neck felt tender and she breathed deeply, trying not to panic.

As her senses returned the smell got stronger. What the hell was it?

Pulling herself to her knees, she fought the second wave of nausea and turned to glance behind her.

Her eyes widened as she struggled to understand what was in front of her.

The wooden box was charred in places, and it looked kind of like a coffin. Her eyes moved upwards, pausing to read the inscription below a hole that had been cut in the door.

'Here lies Scott Anderson. He deserved to die. 28th October.'

She felt her throat constrict. This was some kind of sick joke. Her eyes settled on what was visible through the hole.

The smell grew stronger still as she registered Scott's face, his features distorted and mottled, and a small dribble of blood drying underneath his mouth and nose. Kourtney felt a scream rise in her throat, quickly blocked by bile as she threw up again, her body heaving hard through her mangled sobs.

When the dry heaving stopped, she looked up again, tears streaking her face.

She fell forward on her hands, her body collapsing under her, and she screamed.

Chapter Twenty Nine

'Another one, Alex? Is it a full moon or something?' said Cass as they headed for their respective vehicles.

The call had come in seconds before, the first officer on scene almost choking on his words as he made the request for assistance.

The promenade was only minutes from the station, and when they arrived it looked like everyone and their dog was out for a bit of rubbernecking. Alex took charge, giving orders to extend the outer cordon and push people back. It wouldn't be long before the press arrived, and they needed the scene secured.

Fred arrived next, grabbed some tarps from his van, and silently tied them onto the fence at the front of the lot. He and Cass pulled on white suits and boot covers, snapped on double pairs of purple gloves, grabbed their kits and went through the gate.

Cass spotted a kid climbing the gate at the back and yelled a warning. 'Oi, get down from there. You're contaminating a crime scene.'

The youngster dropped out of view, and Fred went to warn Alex to cordon the alley at the back also. He grabbed the tent from his van, and carried it into the lot, with Alex close behind.

Cass had halted in front of the coffin, and as Alex and Fred joined her they too were stopped in their tracks by the gruesome sight.

'What on earth possesses someone to do this to another human being?' whispered Cass.

'I don't know,' said Alex. 'His girlfriend was a witness; it looks like she was drugged and woke up to this sight. She's been taken to hospital by one of my team. Probably be a while before she can tell us anything though. She's in shock. Can I leave you to process the scene? I need to contact the pathologist and speak with the guys outside.'

Cass looked up at him and nodded her agreement.

'You photographing? I'll put the markers down,' said Fred from beside her.

'Yeah, just let me ring Jason though and let him know. Think he might want to come down for this one.'

Cass made the call quickly, then began her visual examination. She immediately noted a partial footwear mark in the soil below the tampered electric box. Carefully studying the ground below her feet as she walked, she made her way over to the coffin. It looked surprisingly well made, and obviously by someone familiar with woodwork.

The inscription had been carved into the wood with something like a hot poker, and though it was plain text with no embellishment, it was smooth and flowed easily into the next letter. She paused for a moment, staring at the words, then focused on the young lad.

From the jagged marks on his chest, it was plain to see where the charge had entered the body. Fred approached from behind her and asked if she wanted him to erect the tent.

She shook her head silently, lost in thought. *I know this kid. He was in for injury photos the other day.* Cass left Fred for a moment to update Alex on what she'd remembered.

Then, after adjusting the settings on the camera, she began taking shots.

Cass and Fred had worked together for years. They were comfortable with each other and could instinctively work the scene without getting in each other's way. She focused on photographing the scene, while Fred placed the yellow numbered markers. The tent was put up to hide the scene from the eyes of the public who despite Alex's warnings, had congregated as close to the cordon as they could, intent on seeing the gruesome sight.

As Cass and Fred progressed through the examination, the footwear mark wasn't the only thing they noticed.

A tiny piece of blue latex was stuck between two wires on the electric box, the edges rough and torn. Cass photographed it with long, medium and short shots, and Fred carefully pulled it out with sterile tweezers, placed it into a small pot and bagged and tagged it.

The possibility of DNA from a murder scene was always a good start.

Cass left Fred casting the shoeprint, and went to the van for a crow bar. They had already been there over an hour and despite the cold morning, she was starting to feel the heat inside the suit.

Striding over to her, Alex said, 'We landed Nigel again. He should be here in about twenty minutes. Tell me what we have so far.'

Cass filled him in and added that she would need several officers to help with holding the coffin once Nigel arrived. First, she wanted it moving onto a plastic sheet to prevent any evidence being lost when they opened the lid.

It took four strong men and some major manoeuvring to get the coffin safely onto the wrap and they had only just finished when Nigel strode through the tent opening.

'Three, Cass? You doing this just to keep me busy? I've barely got all the results back from the old guy.'

'Tell me about it,' groaned Cass. 'Oh how I long for a quiet shift. This one's pretty awful Nigel. Poor kid was put in a coffin and electrocuted. Hell of a way to go.'

'You're not wrong. A current strong enough to kill takes a little time. First the muscles contract, causing severe pain and sometimes breaking bones. This causes the blood pressure to skyrocket, which can cause the heart and other organs to rupture. Even the brain can haemorrhage. Definitely not a nice way to go. Who found the body?'

'His girlfriend. She's at the hospital. Shock.'

Nigel nodded thoughtfully. 'Understandable. She'll need some form of counselling I would imagine.'

'We moved the coffin onto a plastic sheet and laid it down, so it's all ready just to open and begin.'

28th October, 1005 hours – Seaburn Seafront, Sunderland

He was sitting on a bench on the promenade not far from the vacant lot, his hands curled round a now cold cup of tea as he watched the police activity, the now regular frown on his face. He had to be careful – there was a slim chance one of his colleagues would recognise him, through his old-man-inspired disguise.

But he had to watch.

For some reason, Scott's death hadn't given him the satisfaction he craved. He had felt calm when he set the current off, ready for the wave of adrenaline and the same sensation he'd felt when he had killed the first time. It hadn't happened when he killed the old man but he'd been *so* sure he would get it this time.

He shook his head, asking himself why. For a moment he felt rage burn in his belly, he was angry that the feeling had been kept from him, angry that it wasn't the same and he had to fight against the emotion before it overwhelmed him.

His eyes widened as he spotted Cass coming out of the lot. His mind suddenly shifted and he realised something with utmost clarity.

It wasn't his fault. It was hers.

If she hadn't distracted him, made him follow her around and scout her cottage out, then the feeling would have come. He would have been satisfied. Where did she get off doing that to him, taking *that* from him?

He simmered silently, watching as she pulled Alex to one side, no doubt to whisper sweet nothings in his ear, and a new plan began to form. One he was certain would give him the satisfaction he craved. One that would be more spectacular than a body in a coffin by the beach.

His face cracked into a small smile, tiny wrinkles showing in the glue holding his fake whiskers in place.

She would definitely be the one. She had to be.

28th October, 2020 hours – Ryhope Police Station

It had been another long day.

Cass had just finished putting everything through on the system and completing the staff reviews for another year.

The evidence from the murder had already been bagged and tagged, and the tiny fragment of latex forwarded to the DNA lab for examination. Normally Cass had to fight with the submissions department for a sample to go off for a standard exam, let alone an urgent one, but Alex had already phoned ahead so by the time she spoke to them they were happy to authorise sending it off.

She still had the niggling feeling that she'd missed something, even after she had read and reread her notes about ten times. She had gone over and over the crime scene in her mind, and still couldn't put her finger on it.

She sighed deeply, rolling her aching shoulders and flexing her neck. When she opened her eyes, Alex was stood in the doorway watching her. He didn't speak as he entered the room, closed the door, and crossed the office to stand behind her desk. Slowly he knelt in front of her, cupping her face in his hands and gently pressed his lips to hers.

Cass wrapped her arms round his neck, deepening the kiss further as a sudden rush of desire passed through her.

As it ended they both stared at each other, their breaths short and pupils dilated.

'Time to go home?' asked Alex hopefully.

Cass sighed and shook her head slowly.

'Can't yet, love. Need to get all this stuff to the exhibits officer over at central, then Greg wanted a word when he gets back from the job he's at and I said I'd wait. You can head to mine and I'll see you there shortly if you like? I'll give you the spare key.'

He grinned at her as she blushed slightly.

'Ooo aye,' he sniggered jokingly, 'Something in mind, Miss Hunt?'

Responding to his playfulness, she smiled back. 'Most definitely, Mr McKay – I was thinking roast chicken, maybe some mash and Yorkshires.'

He looked startled for a moment, then recovered himself. Bowing into her neck he whispered, 'Your wish is my command.'

She tingled as she felt his breath and pulled him in tightly to a hug.

He grinned as he pulled away and got back to his feet.

'See you soon,' he said, taking the key she offered as he turned.

Cass was still grinning twenty minutes later when Greg walked in. They had a quick discussion about his redundancy application, before she grabbed the evidence bags and headed to her car, figuring she would drop the evidence off on her way home.

Chapter Thirty

29th October, 0120 hours – Pallion, Sunderland

Pure rage was running through his veins.

He was having trouble controlling the urge to scream and break anything breakable in the house. He took deep breaths, trying to calm a shaking that just wouldn't stop.

He had pulled out the white suit and other clothing he had worn to kill Scott and realised there was a small hole in one of the blue nitrile gloves. He had no idea if Cass had found it but he had to presume she had.

This again was her fault. If he hadn't been tied up running round after her and killing that fool Jameson, then he would have had more time to prep. He wouldn't have made such a schoolboy error.

His DNA was on file; everyone joining the police force handling anything to do with evidence had it taken as a matter of course. If she had found the tiny fragment, then it would just be a matter of time before they knew it was him.

He couldn't risk going back to the station now. He'd have to lay low and work from his back up plan.

Working quickly now, he grabbed a bag and began packing. He set off on foot with the bag over his shoulder and his trusty toolbox in his hand, walked a few streets over and called a cab.

The cab dropped him at a block of flats on the other side of Ryhope, one of the rougher estates. He made his way up the stone stairs, past the discarded rubbish and used needles. The place had an almost derelict feel. This was somewhere even the scum didn't want to live.

But it would serve his purpose. He had been renting the flat now for months. Had gone in twice weekly ever since. It was dark, dingy and smelled mouldy, but it was his plan B. It was rented in a fictitious name, the landlord happy for no references in exchange for an additional bond. He had an old runabout parked nearby that he had picked up for next to nothing and had never bothered changing the owner information on.

Yes, plan B was all good as a back-up. He could lay low here, and make the plans he needed to kill Cass.

She would pay. She had ruined everything.

29th October, 0310 hours – Cass's Cottage

The triangles were being thrown at her from every angle, and she was ducking, screaming, trying not to let their sharp edges hit her. Everywhere she turned there were dead bodies, blood everywhere. The smell was nauseating, but she couldn't escape. She knew he was following her, was behind her throwing the triangles, trying to get them to pierce her very soul. She knew in her heart if he caught her she would be dead. Just like all the others. Just like the boy in front of her now, the one in the coffin, the one with the bruises. She stared at him as his dead eyes blinked, and he whispered 'Help me.' She turned away and suddenly came face to face with a monstrous shadow. She felt the scream rise from the bottom of her boots as his cold hands tried to grab her arm.

Alex leapt out of bed, eyes wide as Cass's scream ripped around the room. She was still thrashing and whimpering in her sleep. His heart pounding, he moved to her side. Kneeling, he grabbed her arms to stop her thrashing and quietly repeated that it was OK, it was just a dream.

He watched as she slowly pulled herself from the realm of the nightmare and stared at him, her eyes glazed with panic and fear. They narrowed slightly as she registered what she had been dreaming about. And suddenly comprehension dawned.

'The triangles Alex. The triangles. That's the link,' she gabbled, jumping out of bed and reaching for her joggers from the nearby chair.

'What? Slow down, Cass, what do you mean the triangles?'

'The murder from the car, the old guy and now this kid, Scott. It's the triangles.'

Confusion showed on Alex's face as he struggled to link what she was talking about. Triangles?

In a flash he understood; they had pulled a triangle from the throat of Susan, the old guy had had bits of metal and bottle tops in his pocket and now there was a triangle on the coffin from yesterday's murder.

'They're linked. We've had three murders by the same person. We have a serial killer.' His softly spoken words made it a reality, and they both paused for a moment.

'A serial killer? In Ryhope? That's insane,' but Cass was nodding as she said it. Now it was beginning to make sense.

By the time they were dressed, Alex had called his team in as well as the Chief Super – it was going to be another long day.

29th October, 1000 hours – Ryhope Police Station

'This is DCI McKay from Ryhope Police Station, I need to speak with whoever is dealing with emergency submissions from yesterday afternoon.'

Alex tapped his fingers on the desk, frustrated by the annoying hold music sounding in his ears. Seconds later a female came on the line, her voice soft with a hint of a Birmingham accent.

'Marie Smithson speaking. How can I help?'

'Marie, I need the DNA submission we sent over yesterday examined urgently. It would have arrived first thing this morning by courier – it's vital evidence in a series of murders,' said Alex.

'Well I understand that, DCI McKay, however, as I'm sure you will appreciate, we are the main lab dealing with all DNA submissions from the North East, Midlands and Cumbria. We have several outstanding samples requiring urgent examination. I will do my best to get your sample examined today and entered into the database, but I can't guarantee an immediate result. Give me the details and I'll see what I can do.'

Alex passed over the information and hung up. Glancing at the clock, he grabbed a set of car keys from the wallboard and headed down the stairs. This wasn't a meeting he was looking forward to, but he needed to know more about the latest victim.

Starting the engine, he made his way to the Outreach Centre.

'So, Scott had problems at home?' asked Alex, curling his fingers round the hot cup provided by the bubbly blonde who worked in the centre.

'Yeah. From what I understand his dad is an alcoholic. Mum left when Scott was young and hasn't been in contact since. His dad beat him whenever he was drunk, which was often. It amazes me how Scott was still in his care after all this, how social services hadn't swooped in and taken him out of the situation years ago. Scott's attitude problems have always stemmed from things happening at home, and more recently peer pressure. He was hanging around with a group of older lads. Is it possible they could have done this?' asked Brian, his face still pale from seeing

Alex walk in. For half a second, he had thought they'd caught his wife's killer.

When Alex had explained he was there about Scott, it had almost been like a knife to his chest. It had taken him more than a couple of moments to recover sufficiently to speak.

Alex paused, wondering how much to tell the man sitting in front of him. The revelation that a serial killer was on the loose was bad enough, but that person had killed two people linked to Brian. Despite his alibi for the night of his wife's murder, he could still be a suspect for the murders. Deciding to take the bull by the horns, he watched for reactions as he told Brian they now believed that both Scott and Susan had been killed by the same person.

Brian's eyes widened with confusion as he struggled to make the link.

'How is that possible? Susan never met Scott.'

Brian sounded disbelieving and desperate, and Alex kept his voice neutral as he explained further. He didn't mention the silver triangles – that was one piece of information that wouldn't be released, either to Brian, or to the press when they were finally informed.

By the time Alex had finished talking to Brian an hour had passed. He'd learned plenty about Scott, but he didn't feel any closer to *knowing* the boy who had been killed. He said his goodbyes and made his way to the hospital to speak with Kourtney. Charlie had already taken her scant statement. The girl hadn't remembered a great deal prior to waking up on the tarmac, thanks to the drugs she had been dosed with. But, Kourtney knew Scott. And Alex needed to understand why the boy had been chosen by the killer.

Scott was a troubled teenager, whose attitude left a lot to be desired but it must have been something other than his attitude that had got him killed. Alex was certain Kourtney would have some idea.

29th October, 1705 hours – Ryhope Police Station

Alex was finally back at his desk. He had been in and out of interviews and meetings all day. The powers that be had decided to keep the news of a serial killer under wraps for now and very little had been released to the press.

Kourtney had revealed that Scott had been blackmailing someone, trying to wheedle money out of him by making threats to report him for inappropriate behaviour. She knew the victim only as John, and had said that the man was 'creepy'. That provided Alex with motive, though he was yet to work out how it linked to Susan and the old man from the cave. He'd arranged a sketch artist to sit with Kourtney at her parent's house later the next day. Hopefully that would give them something to work with.

Alex sighed and ran his hands through his hair. His head was pounding, his eyes felt like they were filled with sand, and the day wasn't over yet.

He hadn't heard from Cass since they'd left the cottage that morning. Scott's post-mortem had been scheduled for 2 p.m. and Alex hadn't been able to attend – the meeting with the Chief Super had taken precedence. He vaguely remembered Cass mentioning that Jason Knowles was heading up the examination and he made a mental note to ring him before he left the office.

Sighing again, Alex rubbed his eyes and checked his messages. One stood out from Marie Smithson and he grabbed the phone and punched in her number, hoping he hadn't missed her.

'DCI McKay. I need to speak with Marie Smithson please,'

'Detective, hello. Thank you for calling me back. I have some urgent news but I thought it best to tell you rather than anyone else. It is rather sensitive,'

'Sensitive?' asked Alex, 'Do we have an ident?'

'Yes we do. The DNA profile we pulled from the piece of blue nitrile has been looked at by two separate employees to ensure there's no confusion. I have personally run it through the database several times. My statement and those of my colleagues have already been mailed to you with the full profile information,' she paused again. 'Detective, the profile is for a member of Police staff, working for North East Police. Is it possible that the section of glove was left by one of the Forensics team in error and then recovered by someone else as a sample?'

'I would say that's extremely unlikely,' said Alex, turning over this new development in his mind. He knew Cass had photographed as Fred had recovered the evidence. He had their scene notes and there was no indication that either of them had accidentally ripped a glove while processing the scene. Then he remembered – both Cass and Fred had been wearing purple nitrile gloves, not blue. He held the phone closer to his ear, and used his free hand to open his email account.

Marie continued, 'The profile belongs to a male named Frank Reynolds. According to the file he is employed out of the Ryhope depot as a handyman and driver.'

Alex paused in shock, the information sinking in as his cursor hovered over the email from Marie. He thanked her for getting back to him, and hung up, thoughts whirling. Frank Reynolds? The odd bloke who did the runs between the depots and fixed things when they went wrong?

Holy crap. The shit's gonna hit the fan with this one.

Alex headed straight to the Chief Super's office, praying he hadn't left yet.

Chapter Thirty One

29ᵗʰ October, 1825 hours – Cass's Cottage

Cass was shattered. She felt bone tired and her mind was a jumbled mess of exhaustion. It was time to go home.

She tidied her desk on auto-pilot, and popped her head into the main office. The place was deserted so she grabbed a pen and paper and scrawled a quick note to Faith telling her she was leaving for the day, but that her mobile was turned on. She'd taken to leaving notes the second her promotion to CSM had kicked in. In the beginning, she'd felt a little guilty leaving her staff to battle through whatever was thrown at them on their own. She couldn't work all three shifts in one day, but the simple action of writing a note left her feeling a little less like she was abandoning ship.

She closed the door behind her, checked it was locked, then grabbed her bag and headed up to Alex's office. There was no one around, the ticking of the wall clock and the dull drone of the computer fans the only sounds in the vast office. Cass smiled to herself, half expecting a tumble weed to blow past.

She decided to leave Alex a note too and quickly penned that she was heading home and would see him when he finished. Her cheeks turned a faint pink as she signed it 'Cass,' then added a few kisses for good measure. She was still getting used to the fact that he was in her life, that they both had feelings for each other. After Jameson she'd thought she would always be on her own, had figured she didn't need the hassle of another unpredictable man. Not that Alex was predictable, but somehow she knew he would never hurt her.

She drove home on autopilot and it was only as she opened the front door that she remembered belatedly Ollie was with her mum. She missed his paws clicking on the hardwood floor as he came to greet her, her home's silence her only welcome.

Cass decided she'd make a cuppa and put the TV on. She hardly watched television, generally content to read or write her journal articles, but today she wanted something she didn't have to think about. She aimlessly flicked through the channels, finally settling on a re-run of the TV show, Friends.

She pulled her tatty blanket round her, inhaling deeply and grinning at the faint tang of Alex's aftershave. Letting the sofa wrap her in its comforting arms, she fell into a deep sleep.

30ᵗʰ October, 0010 hours – Cass's Cottage

It was freezing. The cold seeped into his bones as he stood outside her window staring in at her asleep on the sofa. She blurred slightly, and it took him a moment to realise that his breath had misted the window. Shifting position slightly, his eyes narrowed as he watched.

Doesn't she realise how stupid she is? How ignorant? I could have been inside and snapped her neck ten times over by now.

Her dumb mutt wasn't there. Her knight in shining armour was nowhere to be seen. It would be *so* easy.

One flick of the knife he kept in his boot and she would be no more.

Frank pushed back the urge. She would get so much more than a simple flick of his knife. He would make her pay, she had to understand that this was all *her* fault. And he had every intention of forcing her to agree – and enjoying it.

All the years of watching her run around the station, commanding people to do her bidding, himself included. All the years of barely noticing him. And now she had been solely responsible for making him mess up, distracting him from his task so that he had become careless and left vital evidence behind.

It was getting harder to keep the anger at bay. All he wanted to do right now was burst into that house and let his rage take care of his problems.

But he drew in a slow breath, he couldn't do it tonight. He wasn't ready.

Tonight was just for watching.

He shrank back into the shadows, and silently returned to his car.

Chapter Thirty Two

31st October, 0805 hours – Cass's Cottage

Cass awoke and stretched gracefully, working out the crick in her neck from the sofa arm. The sunlight was streaming in the window, offset by a clear blue sky. Smiling at the bright scene, she wiggled out of her blanket and made her way into the kitchen. A beautiful day like this deserved freshly brewed coffee and warm croissants, laden with strawberry jam.

She gasped as she saw Alex asleep at the kitchen table, his head curved into the crook of his arm.

Her first thought was how adorable he looked, her second how tired he must've been to fall asleep in that position. She worked quietly in the kitchen so as not to wake him. She had no idea what time he'd got in; she hadn't stirred all night.

Humming softly to herself, she pottered about the kitchen and prepped their breakfast.

The sounds from the kitchen eventually woke Alex from his stupor. He yawned deeply and sat up, watching Cass dance as she hummed, her back towards him. He was filled with a sudden rush of love, and silently he padded over to her.

She didn't know he was there until his arms clasped her around her waist and she felt his soft lips nuzzle her neck.

'Good morning,' he whispered against her neck, before turning her around and kissing her gently.

'Morning back,' said Cass kissing him again before focusing her attention on preparing the croissants. 'You must have been late back?'

'Yeah think it was around two when I rolled in. Sat down at the table and the next thing I knew you were here.'

'Tough day I'm guessing,'

'Really tough. Had meetings all day. The DNA result came through late afternoon. You know Frank, our handyman? The DNA from the glove section you recovered is his. We're still trying to establish all the links, but if that DNA is his, and we've established the link to all three murders using the triangles, there's no reason to believe he didn't commit them all. It's really bizarre thinking someone we worked with all these years could be capable of something like this. How could he do it and nobody in the nick be any the wiser?'

Everything was black and white to Alex and the thought that someone he worked with, a member of the police family, could do something like this made him sick to the stomach.

Cass didn't speak straight away. She wrapped her arms back around him and looked into his eyes.

'You're a good guy, McKay. You see the good in everyone. Why Frank did this only he can say. Not every police officer is bad, you know that. But there's always a bad apple in every barrel. You'll catch him though. That's what you do, Alex, you catch the bad apples and stop them hurting other people.'

He smiled at her, a little sadly, but still a smile.

'You're amazing, Cass. Thank you.'

2nd November, 2205 hours – Cass's Cottage

Frank was once again leaning against a tree outside the cottage. He had watched as the sex slave had turned tail and ran. Granted he was probably going to work, but Frank had been too pissed off to care.

He'd been practically living in his old man disguise now for four days solid. He had barely slept in the crap flat he'd chosen, thanks to the neighbours keeping him awake with incessant music, if it could be called that, playing constantly from dusk 'til dawn. He hadn't tried to access his bank accounts, presuming they would have been frozen the moment his identity had been revealed, and despite having plenty of cash with him, that made him angry.

The money was his.

He wondered whether the police had visited address he called home, the address he had shared with his mother.

I bet they have. They'll have kicked the door in and rifled through my stuff.

He felt his blood boil.

They'll have been in my shed! How dare they. That's my place. Who the hell do they think they are?

'Her fault,' he said into the dark.

He knew what he was going to do. He couldn't go home; he couldn't go to his unit. He knew the police were crawling around. But, he'd found the perfect location to take care of Cass. The perfect place to make her pay for ruining his life. The only place that was right.

And nobody would find out, not until it was too late.

Then he might send a piece of her to Alex. A small part. Just enough to make him know he'd been beaten by Frank, that he hadn't been able to save his lover.

Frank wanted to see him squirm. He wanted to watch Alex's face as he opened the package and read the note. But that couldn't happen. As soon as he was done he would be heading to the airport with the fake passport he had acquired from one of his many 'contacts' from the dregs of Sunderland.

It would take a little more prep time, but he would be ready soon. And then she would pay.

Chapter Thirty Three

3rd November, 0305 hours – Ryhope Police Station

Alex had been called in to deal with a stabbing in the city centre – yet another incident caused by drink. The victim was going to live and had actually been shouting about revenge as he was wheeled down to the operating theatre.

It ended up being a big job. The kid had been stabbed near a bar in the centre, then staggered home where his girlfriend had called the emergency services. Alex had followed Johnny as he'd photographed the trail of blood – quite a feat when in the dark. He'd put the request in for daytime shots too – juries loved being able to follow the story all the way along.

The offender was a snip of a guy, short and skinny with a crop of ginger hair and a bad outbreak of acne. When Alex had spoken to him, he'd shown no remorse, merely said that the next time someone called him a 'ginga' then he would quite happily do the same again. The tattoos on his wrist and forearm indicated small-time gang affiliation – the victim had definitely messed with the wrong guy this evening.

Just another busy night in the town.

Working solidly, Alex prepared the file so it was ready to be handed over to the dayshift. He'd had a quick natter with the Duty Sergeant, updating him so he could hand everything over, and finally, he made his way down to the car-park.

He considered going to the flat and not disturbing Cass. He knew it wouldn't happen though. He wanted to be with Cass and Ollie at the cottage. He felt the now familiar flutter in his stomach as he thought about her. It had been strange at first, he had never felt this giddy when he thought about Helen; theirs had started as a friendship that just progressed into a relationship. He'd been happy for a while, content even, but he had never had butterflies in his stomach when he thought about her.

He frowned as he sat in the driver's seat without starting the engine. Since finding out that the serial killer was the handy man, he'd had a growing sense of unease. Something just out of his reach that was vital to the case. The links were all confirmed; the search team had uncovered a lot of circumstantial, as well as hard evidence in the place Frank called home. Images of torture on the home computer, links in the internet history of the websites he had visited, and a shed full of weapons and tools. Danny had asked the CSIs to perform an examination using high intensity light sources, and they'd stared in horror at the array of latent blood on all the wooden benches and surfaces. It had obviously been cleaned with a product containing a high percentage of bleach, but goodness knew what torture had occurred in that shed. The DNA results from the samples taken from the benches were still outstanding.

The industrial unit was still being searched but they had already found remnants of Scott's coffin. Alex had requested the DNA from Susan's foetus be examined against the sample recovered from the sea front, but he knew in his gut the baby was Frank's. He was still struggling with how the death of Albert fitted in, but the link was there somewhere. He just had to find it.

Alex turned the key and pulled his car out of the parking space and stopped as the heavy metal gates started opening.

This case could go on forever. There's so much left to do.

He was so lost in thought; he didn't spot the dark shadow of a man hiding in the tall bushes near the gate. As Alex's car disappeared round the bend at the side of the station, Frank nipped into the rear yard.

3rd *November, 0505 hours – Ryhope Police Station*

Frank hid some of his belongings in the boiler room in the station basement, accessible via a virtually forgotten entrance in the rear yard. No one used it except the boiler service men, and they had only been the month before. He knew that because he'd arranged it. They wouldn't be back now until March.

He'd altered the camera angles slightly, knowing where the blind spots were. The only other access to the boiler room was a door in the unused cells. It had been several years since they had been used and he would bet his life no one remembered what that door was for, let alone had a key. It had been there since the days before the refurbishment, when he had only just started at the nick. Back then, the door had been the access point to the boiler room. Part of the refurbishment had taken into account the requests of the various workmen, who felt uncomfortable passing through a melee of offenders and police officers every time something went wrong.

Frank smiled in the dull glow of the machine lights. This was indeed the perfect location – they would be searching all over the city for Cass when he finally took her. Not for one moment would they suspect she was literally in their own back yard.

He double checked his toolbox, making sure he had everything he would need, and left it in the darkest corner of the room while he checked his security measures.

Nothing but the best.

He'd invested in a couple of infrared lasers which would send an alert to his mobile if tripped. These were at the exterior of the boiler room door. A well-hidden CCTV camera installed above the door which had reasonably good views of most of the yard.

There was no one in the yard just now – time to leave.

This time his smile almost reached his eyes. He'd managed to lift the keys to one of the unmarked police cars – sneaking about unnoticed had become second nature to him and this time in the morning the station operated on bare bones. Marking the board to show the car was with fleet management for repairs meant that they wouldn't be looking for it. So he now had a completely untraceable vehicle not linked to him in any way, and better still, he could listen to the police radios and find out who was doing what.

His access card for the computers would have been disabled, but keys were easily copied and kept, even security keys, provided you knew the right people. It had come as no surprise to find all his own keys still worked, it would have cost a fortune to replace everyone's keys, and the North East Police were not going to waste money when there was a perfectly good CCTV system in place. The snivelling girl in front office wouldn't notice that the camera angles were off.

Checking his own camera again, he made his way out of the boiler room, edging along the wall to the alley that led into the back of the nick. He pulled his hat down over his face, fastened the police jacket he had lifted from the locker room and strode boldly to the vehicle he now had possession of.

As cool as you like, he drove up the drive and out of the gate.
Yes, I am a complete genius.

Cass sat in the meeting room with Kevin, Jason and the DI, cradling a cup of coffee.

'… So I have had to make a choice on what is the fairest way to make sure the jobs available are filled with the best people to do them. Some of the staff have had problems with sickness and lateness among other things. I have spoken with the union, as well as HR and it's been decided the best and fairest way to progress through the job cuts, is to re-interview staff for the positions. The decisions will be based on an amalgamation of performance, attendance and how they perform in the interview.' DI Hartside shuffled the papers in front of him as he finished speaking.

'Wait a second, boss. Did you just say you're re-interviewing staff? You're going to interview them for the job they already have? How is that fair? You might have members of staff who have been doing the job for years but are crap in an interview situation. That's just a way to put people under undue stress, surely?' said Kevin, disbelief evident in his tone.

'It is how it is, Kevin. As I said, this has been discussed with HR and the Union who have both agreed. This isn't a pleasant situation for any of us. None of us want to lose people from the department. But to meet the quota set by the government, it has to be done across the board, as cleanly and efficiently as possible.'

'Who's going to be conducting the interviews?' asked Cass.

'Well that is going to be down to the Supervisor for the area, and a member of HR,' said the DI slowly, his face already prepared for the onslaught.

Before Kevin blew a fuse, Jason intervened.

'That's not a fair process. We are all biased against all members of our respective teams. I for one, will not be telling my staff that I am interviewing them for their own position. Sorry, boss, but I won't do that.'

'It was agreed that one of the interviewers has to be well versed in forensics. You have to know the correct answers to the questions posed and be able to allocate points based on those answers. In order to do that, it has to be the supervisors. If need be, we'll assign each of you to do the interviews for different depots, that way you won't be interviewing your own staff per se.'

'And the staff who don't get the jobs, what happens to them? They get redeployed as call takers or front office staff? They take a wage drop and the force lets people who are trained with such skill, in a field that is so competitive and difficult to find a job in at the best of times, rot away in that role if they choose to stay with the police? That's an excellent use of trained resources, boss.'

Kevin's sarcasm wasn't lost. The DI narrowed his eyes before he said. 'It's not my decision. It is in fact out of my hands. We all have to make the best of a bad situation. I'm keeping you apprised at every step so that we can minimise the impact as much as possible. I would appreciate some cooperation during the process.'

Without saying another word, the DI got to his feet, reshuffled his papers again and left.

'I guess the fact he wants trained forensic staff performing the interviews is a good thing,' sighed Jason, pushing his chair back and standing.

'None of it's a good thing. We have an excellent set of staff, there's not many departments who have the camaraderie the CSIs have. There's not a whole lot of bitchiness, most people get on and are professional if they don't. And they all work their fingers to the bone. It sucks that the force won't see what will happen if we lose some of our staff. All it'll take is a couple of major incidents at the same time and there won't be the staff to deal with it. I just wish the DI could see that.' Kevin's words were heartfelt and Cass put her hand on his arm.

'I know, Kev. We'll just have to keep doing what we are doing and make the most of a bad situation. The counter-proposal has gone to the union for assessment so let's just see what comes of that. All any of us can do is hope for the best for everyone.'

4th November, 1300 hours – Ryhope Police Station

'Hey, you. How'd your meeting go this morning?' asked Alex as he walked into Cass's office and sat down, silently handing her a lunch bag.

She smiled at him, already knowing it would be her favourite chicken salad with coleslaw. It was funny how quickly they had got to know each other's likes and dislikes.

As she opened the bag she told him the short version of the meeting with the DI.

'So not great then. Sorry, love. You gonna be OK? What's happening with the CSMs? You said they were thinking of cutting two?'

'Yeah – dunno what's happening with that yet. They'll get round to telling us at some point am sure. I'll be fine, Alex, don't worry. It just sucks having to interview our own staff for jobs that are already theirs. How's the case coming?'

'Well we've pretty much finished with Frank's house and warehouse unit. The DNA has come back that Susan's baby was a paternal match for him so it looks pretty certain they were having an affair. Given how good Frank always was with cars, I would hazard a guess that it was easy enough for him to have access to her vehicle. We don't know where the old guy comes into it, but he used to drink in a local park, and having spoken to the park regulars, it appears that Scott and Kourtney were also regulars there. They used to drink and smoke weed on the bandstand apparently. It's highly likely they had interaction with or at least knew Albert – though how this ties in with the killer I don't yet know. The fact that Scott is at the Outreach centre ran by Susan's husband appears to be a coincidence. Some of the links are tenuous, I'm sure more will come to light when we finally catch up with Frank and get him in the interview room.'

'I never would have thought such a person would be living in Ryhope. I mean, I know statistically speaking there's as much chance of a serial murderer living here as anywhere else, but we in the UK tend to think of serial killers as American don't we? It's scary. What are the metal triangles all about? Do we know their significance yet?'

Alex shook his head, and they both looked up as Ben knocked at the door.

'Cass, this week's delivery has just arrived. I can arrange to have it taken downstairs, but it'll have to be later. There's a few people in the front office.' Ben paused, looking troubled. 'Is it true what everyone's saying about Frank? That he's a killer?'

'Looks that way, Ben. Don't worry though, we have leads. We will catch him,' answered Alex, shooting a quick glance of concern at Cass. Ben looked terrified.

'How can someone like that work for the police? How was it not found out? I mean, the police run vetting checks, right? He used to sit and have coffee with me. He's a killer, and he used to sit and chat like a normal person. How is that possible?'

'Sometimes we don't know the people we work with, Ben, all any of us can do is give people the benefit of the doubt, believe that they are nice. The alternative would have us all end up in the loony bin. You know if you ever need to talk you can ring me, you have my number, right? And if it's upsetting you that much, it might be worth ringing Occ Health and having a word with one of the counsellors. It's not wrong to need to talk about something like this. You're definitely not the only one struggling with the revelation.'

She nodded slowly. 'Thank you, Cass, yes I have your number. And I will give Occ Health a ring. Thanks again.'

Alex waited until he heard the entrance door to the front office click, before saying, 'It makes me sad to think of all the people in the nick who won't talk about this, all the people this will affect. Frank was practically part of the furniture here. The fall out will be huge. Not to mention what'll happen when the press get hold of it. And that won't be long – these things don't stay under wraps for long.'

Chapter Thirty Four

7th November, 0105 hours – Cass's Cottage

There was already frost on the ground. The stars blinked in the night sky, the moon was in its last phase, yet it still shone brightly.

Frank watched from the tree line to the south of the cottage. He knew Cass's mum had returned the precious dog and that Cass had a tendency to walk him in the woods in the dark. He knew Alex was at work, in fact he had made sure he would be. The murder in the town was quick and easy to complete. A single stab wound, strategically placed to the left of the female's chest. One day women would learn not to walk the streets after dark. She'd just happened to be in the wrong place at the right time.

He'd returned to the cottage just in time to see Cass's mother drive off with her husband in their posh Jaguar, the engine purring as the alloy wheels sent a little gravel flying as he hit the accelerator.

He smiled in the moonlight as he felt the surge of adrenaline flood through his veins. He hoped they would be sticking around. It could only serve to add to his pleasure to know he had caused the devastation of them losing their child.

Frank's anger was getting harder to control. He felt the burn, the need to kill something more now than ever. But deep down inside he knew that killing Cass would be the one that would finally give him back the feeling of ultimate control, that same feeling he'd had as he'd watched the life slip from his own mother as he had held his hand over her mouth, silencing her 'good boy' comments forever. He still counted Susan as his first human kill; his mother didn't count. She'd had cancer, had begged for him to be a good boy and help her get through it, help her get back to the church she had so cherished. And help her he had, though he was pretty sure it hadn't been what she had meant.

'Bitch deserved to die,' he muttered under his breath, the burst of steam almost causing him to take a step back. For a second he'd forgot he was outside. Taking a deep calming breath, he let the memory continue.

He'd felt *it* start burning in his stomach as she pitifully struggled, his gloved hand not having to apply that much pressure. Weak from the treatment, she was already having breathing difficulties and had to wear an oxygen mask. Her eyes had widened in fear, staring at him, finally seeing him for the killer he was and not the good boy she had always tried to force him to be. As he watched her life slip away, he had quietly said, 'I saw what you did to dad. You made me who I am. You helped me realise who I wanted to be.'

He had watched a single tear fall from her eye, heard her whisper a quiet 'No,' with her last breath, and he had smiled as the last speck of life left her body.

Afterwards, he'd sat with her a while, revelling in the feelings. Mild horror, he had killed his own mother. Mild concern, how would he get away with it? And finally, satisfaction – complete satisfaction. This was the person he was born to be. And now he didn't have to look after her any more, he was free to do as he pleased, when he pleased.

A sudden, faint noise brought him back to the present. He froze, his head cocked to the left as he listened. He heard further rustling, still quite far away. Eventually, he heard the faint sound of Cass singing softly.

Readying himself, he pulled the syringe from his pocket.

It was time.

7th November, 0240 hours – Cass's Cottage

Alex shivered as he opened the door. The temperature gauge on his dash showed -5 degrees Celsius. Winter was definitely here.

He frowned as he found the front door unlocked. Since Jameson, Cass had taken to locking it if she was in. He paused as goose-bumps appeared all over his body and the small hairs on his neck stood to attention. Something didn't feel right.

Silently he made his way to the living room. It was still and undisturbed, the lamp still turned on in the corner. He pushed the heavy door into the kitchen, half expecting to see Cass sat at the table with a coffee, but it was completely silent. He noticed the absence of Ollie's leash on its hanger in the corner, and breathed a sigh of relief. She had taken the dog for a walk.

His stomach was still turning somersaults as he headed upstairs to pull on some joggers and a jumper. He would walk along the route she usually took and meet her coming back. His gut was still screaming at him that something was wrong.

The bedroom was flooded with light as he pushed the door open, and his eyes focused on Ollie, asleep on the bed, his lead draped over him. Attached to his collar was a photo.

Alex felt fear claw into him, where was Cass? Striding to the bedside, he stroked Ollie's soft fur. The dog was breathing deeply and didn't stir. He reached for the photo and the blood drained from his face.

It showed Cass, unconscious, in the back of a car with tape across her mouth. On the back the untidy writing simply said, 'You want her. I have her. Now find her.'

Alex felt his heart stop as utter terror threatened to overwhelm him. What the hell was going on? Who had Cass? Slowly realisation dawned, Frank. He had Cass. Why, he didn't know, but he was certain he was right. He tried to gather his thoughts. Why was Frank focused on Cass? She had been the one to attend all three murders, could it really be that simple? Had Frank just watched the progress and become obsessed?

He almost groaned aloud as his mind made another connection – the death of Jameson. It had been entirely too convenient for him to die in the middle of three murder investigations with links to the lead CSM. Alex almost kicked himself. This was his fault. If he'd realised the links sooner, put it all together, he might have seen that Cass was in danger.

His mouth set in a grim line, he might not have noticed the links straight away, but he would find Cass. He pushed the fear to the back of his mind. He couldn't allow his judgement to become clouded. Cass needed him.

Ollie groaned next to him, his feet scrabbling as he struggled to wake up. Carefully Alex lifted him into his arms, took him downstairs and placed him on the backseat of his car. Revving the engine, he tore out of the drive, leaving a trail of dust. Before he'd reached the A19, he'd phoned Ali and the Chief Super – the whole police force would be called in now. One of their own had been taken hostage, and if there was one thing the police did well, it was taking care of their own.

7th November, 0355 hours – Ryhope Police Station

'What do you mean I'm not dealing with the case? This is my case. This is Cass for god's sake.'

Alex's voice was well above the level at which one should address a superior officer, but having just been told to stand down he was understandably upset.

'Which is precisely why you can't be in charge, Alex. At your own admission, you love this woman. The fact she is in the hands of a serial killer has you worried sick. For that reason alone, I can't have you in charge of the investigation. Never mind any evidence that came to light would be under the microscope because you have a personal relationship with her. Even if you look solely at the fact that you haven't slept in practically thirty-six hours, you are not capable of leading this investigation. That's final. Now, I suggest you take the dog, and go home. I assure you I will personally call you the second something develops. Eckley is an excellent DCI, Alex, you know that. He's a trained negotiator with excellent skills. Let him lead. We will find Cass; I give you my word.'

The Chief Super's words did nothing to appease him. That monster had had Cass for some time. There was no saying what he'd done to her so far.

'Fine I'll go, but I'm going to the hotel to tell Cass's mum. Rose needs to know what's happening. And I will be back in shortly, Sir.' His reply was curt and to the point and for a moment, the Chief looked mildly annoyed.

Finally, though, he nodded silently, and watched as Alex left the room with the dog in tow.

Ollie refused to leave Alex's side. The dog knew something was wrong. He didn't remember what happened, but Cass wasn't with him and his new friend was upset.

When Alex arrived at the hotel, he parked the car quickly and stopped, taking in a few deep breaths. He was losing it. He felt like he was standing on the edge of a precipice and that one step would take him over. They say you don't know what you have until it's gone, but this wasn't strictly true. Alex knew Cass was his, had known since that first confused glance. He might not have been ready to accept it until recently, but now he had and his heart felt like it would break.

If he hurts her …

He felt his anger burn amid the worry.

If he touches her I swear I'll kill him.

Grabbing Ollie's leash, he entered the hotel, flashed his warrant card at the receptionist and demanded to know what room Rose was staying in.

By the time the elevator dinged on the third floor, he'd managed to steady his breathing.

Moments later he was inside the room, sitting on the chair in the corner, with Ollie at his feet.

'What are you doing here, Alex. What's the matter?'

Tears welled up in Roses eyes, already knowing something was wrong.

'It's Cass,' Alex paused, not quite knowing where to start.

Rose's scream filled the room and she collapsed into Roger's arms. Was Cass dead?

'No. Rose, listen, you need to let me tell you what happened. Cass is alive, she's alive.' Alex had gone straight to her side, his hand on her arm, praying he was telling her the truth.

'You...tell...me. Tell me what's happened to my daughter,' stuttered Rose, poking Alex in the arm.

He took a deep breath.

'She's been kidnapped. Did she tell you about the murders we've been having?'

Rose nodded, confused. 'She calls me every time she's called out in the middle of the night. So I know where she is. There's been a few hasn't there?'

'Yes. It was established that they were all by the same person, a person we work with called Frank Reynolds.'

'Are you telling me someone Cass works with is a killer?'

'Yes. We think he has Cass, we don't know why yet, but Rose, we have every officer in the force looking for her. We will find her.'

'Can I ask you something, Alex. If everyone is looking for her then what the hell are you doing here talking to me?'

Her anger surprised him a little. Almost in shame, he hung his head.

'The boss took me off the case. I'm too close, Rose. Being in love with Cass means I don't have a clear head with which to find her.'

'I know you love her,' whispered Rose, patting his arm a little, 'but you're the best officer they have. You should be working this case. You *know* Cass. You know this Reynold's guy. You have to find her. Find my daughter, Alex, please, she's my little girl.'

Emotion took over again, and Rose wept for a moment before pulling herself together.

'OK, enough of these tears. Roger, up and dressed, Alex, give us five minutes and we will be coming back to the station with you. I am not leaving that incident room until my daughter is found. And I'd like to see that Chief of yours try to stop me.'

Chapter Thirty Five

Cass was confused. Her eyes were refusing to open, her head felt filled with cotton wool. For a moment she thought she'd woken with a cold. She fought against the thick blanket struggling to hold her under and forced her eyes to open.

As she did, she realised her hands were tied, heard the dull drone of machines working, and felt the cold and damp concrete underneath her left cheek. She tried to open her mouth to scream, but it was held closed by something.

Tape. It must be tape.

Her first instinct was to panic, but then her mind starting working more clearly. She tried to struggle against the bonds holding her wrists, and swallowed hard as she felt her breathing quicken in response to the surge of adrenaline.

Where the hell am I?

The fog dispelled further and she tried to remember what had happened. She recalled hearing Ollie yelp and rushed to him as he fell over. She also remembered a sharp prick in her neck, and had vague recollection of seeing shoes as her consciousness drifted away.

Where is Ollie?

She moved her head from side to side, searching the floor she could see for her dog. Suddenly she stiffened, sensing someone behind her. She heard the shuffle of his feet on the concrete as he walked around her and knelt on one knee. The light was dim and she could barely make out his features. She tried to pull back as he came at her once more with a syringe, grunting against the tape and struggling against her bindings.

Cass yelped as the needle entered, this time to her upper arm. And as the darkness called her back as its own, she thought of one thing.

Alex.

Somehow, despite the stress, Alex had managed to fall asleep, the caffeine hit from the multiple cups of coffee rapidly wearing off. He was half curled on one of the chairs in the corner of the incident room. His mere presence had caused a heated argument between him and the Chief, but he'd stood his ground, backed by a very angry Rose who stood beside him.

The Chief had eventually caved and allowed them to stay in the incident room, on the proviso that they didn't interfere with the investigation. It wasn't normal procedure and if it had been anyone but Alex, the Chief wouldn't have agreed.

The majority of the serving officers were now out doing enquiries and knocking on doors. The Chief had already spoken to the media and the revelation that there was a serial killer in their midst had been met with anger. Cass's picture was spread over the morning editions of the newspapers, and had featured on the local news.

Alex hadn't intended to fall asleep, but he'd been awake for nearly two days straight. When he had finally dropped off, Rose had put Roger's coat over his shoulders and left him where he was. She couldn't settle though. She'd walked up and down the office so many times she had practically worn a track in the carpet. She'd read the information on the white boards so often that the words were practically embedded in her head. The police ID photo of Reynolds fused into her mind. She was holding it together, but frankly she didn't know how. That monster had her child; it didn't matter how old they got, they were always your baby – and he had hers.

Rose knew if she got her hands on him, she would kill him. Drawing in another shaky breath, she wandered to the kitchen to make yet more coffee. She'd always found it best to keep busy when under stress, and the officers that were manning the phones were appreciative.

She carried in the coffees, handing them out without speaking, and watched as Alex pulled himself from slumber.

'Here you go, son,' she said softly, handing over a steaming mug.

'I fell asleep?' he asked, shaking his head in disbelief.

'You're exhausted, Alex, it's understandable. You've only had an hour or so, don't worry. That Chief of yours came in but has gone again. Eckley went with him.'

Alex put his coffee on the nearby desk, feeling his frustration rise.

'I need to reread the files on Reynolds. There must be something somewhere that gives me a clue where he could be.'

7th November, 1015 hours - Ryhope Police Station

Cass felt herself clawing her way back to consciousness once more. The room was silent but for the constant hum of the machines. It was still dark in there, the only light the glow from the machine displays.

Her shoulders ached from being pulled backwards, and she felt the grooves in her cheeks off the concrete floor. Quietly, she struggled with the bonds, trying to loosen them. Her wrists grew sore and she figured it was probably cable ties or something similar so struggling was futile. Instead she pushed herself over onto her back and tried to have a look around.

She froze as she spotted the inert form of a man, lying on top of a rug facing the opposite wall. She cocked her head to listen and nodded to herself as she heard him snoring softly.

Cass manoeuvred herself into a sitting position and shuffled to one of the machines. The edge was rough, and quickly she began moving her hands up and down, using the edge to try and cut the ties to her hands. She gasped as she slipped and felt the metal cut into her wrist, the sharp pain quickly turning to a stinging sensation as she determinedly carried on.

Suddenly the man grunted, turned over and opened his eyes, staring straight at her. Cass recognised him this time, and watched as he registered what she had been doing. He got to his feet slowly, walked over to her and grabbed her viciously by the hair, yanking her head backwards. Cass yelped at the sharp movement on her neck, and she breathed in and out quickly, trying not to panic. The truth be told she was petrified, but she couldn't show him her fear. She'd read somewhere that killers fed on fear – it gave them the fix they needed. She'd be damned if she'd give him the satisfaction.

She braced herself as she watched him raise his fist, and flinched as he punched the side of her face. Cass tasted the metallic tang of blood in her mouth, the burn of the impact on her cheek, and waited for the next one.

Instead, Reynolds grabbed her face in his meaty hands, pinching her cheeks together hard, and put his face close to hers.

'This is all your fault. Don't you dare try to escape again. If you hadn't been such a busy body, interfering in my shows, then you wouldn't be here. But I killed your stupid dog, and I intend to kill you and send you back to your slave in pieces. This is your fault.'

She blinked as his spittle landed on her face.

She felt the lump in her throat threaten to choke her as grief took over. Tears pricked her eyes.

Ollie's dead?

Suddenly, in the midst of her panic, she felt a sense of calm. Cass knew Alex would be looking for her. She knew he would find her. The loss of Ollie she would deal with later, right now though, she had to find a way of letting Alex know where she was.

She blinked as a bright flash went off in her face. He'd taken a photo of her. He grinned as he stared at the picture. It was perfect. It showed her desolation, her grief, and the streak of blood across her face where he'd hit her.

Now the bitch is paying.

Yanking her upright, Frank threw Cass against the back wall, taking her breath away. In the impact, she felt the shape of her mobile phone in her pocket. With a groan to herself, she realised she'd turned it off last night before she took Ollie out. She had to figure out a way to turn it on. The inbuilt GPS would provide a location. And she knew her colleagues would be looking for it.

She watched as Frank walked towards a glow coming from behind one of the machines. It was out of her view, but she recognised it as the glow of a computer screen in a dark room. Cass stayed still, listening, and heard him tapping away on the keyboard. She didn't know what he was doing, but he was out of sight. She had to try and get to her phone.

Chapter Thirty Six

7ᵗʰ November, 1025 hours - Ryhope Police Station

Alex glanced at his mobile as it beeped, alerting him to the receipt of an email. It wasn't from an address he recognised and he almost ignored it, until he saw the heading.

'You want her. I have her. Now find her.'

He glanced around the room, checking where Eckley was, before pressing the open button.

'I have what you want. She is still alive, for now. But you follow my instructions to the letter or she won't be for long. I will contact you later. Do not show this email to anyone. I will know.'

He scrolled down the page and was faced with a picture of Cass. He could see a bruise already forming on her jaw line near her mouth, and there was a streak of blood across her cheek. But her eyes were open, defiant and bright they stared at him.

She's alive!

His composure threatened to break as he stared at the screen, and for a moment was tempted to do as the email said and not show anyone. *I have to tell the boss, I can't not.* There was no way Reynolds could know if he had showed anyone else. Nothing he had done thus far indicated a high level of technical knowledge.

Jumping to his feet, he strode across the office to Eckley and the Chief.

'Just received an email to my work email address. It's from him. He's put a photo of Cass on it.'

Quickly he opened the email on the work computer, showing the image.

Rose gasped as she saw her daughter on the screen. In shock she grabbed Alex's arm and he reached his hand across and held hers tightly.

'Emails we can trace. Get on to Tulley in the Digital Forensics Lab, he'll be able to deal with this,' said Eckley to one of the sergeants. 'Is there anything other than Cass in the picture we can use?'

They all leaned in towards the screen, searching for anything that would help with finding a location.

'Looks like a machine of some kind to her right, but there's nothing evident to indicate what kind of machine, or where it could be, is there?' Eckley's question hung in the air as they all stared at the image again.

Slowly they all shook their heads.

Alex pulled back from the PC, his heart full in his chest. For a moment there he had thought this might be what he had needed to find Cass. His disappointment was palpable.

He was surprised when Eckley put a hand on his shoulder. 'We'll find her, Alex. She's one of our own.'

7ᵗʰ November, 1130 hours - Ryhope Police Station

Cass had managed to move the phone in her pocket until it was almost on the verge of falling out. Frank was still sitting at the computer screen and seemed oblivious.

Knowing it would clatter as it fell to the floor, she knew she had to disguise the sound somehow. Looking around in the dark, she saw the outline of a broom leaning against the wall nearby. Carefully, she turned herself around, making sure the pocket with the phone was the closest to the ground.

She took a deep breath and kicked her legs outwards at the same time as jolting her body. To her, the difference between the two clatters was obvious but she grabbed the phone in her hand and held it tightly as Frank came back around the machine to face her.

Seeing the broom on the floor, he laughed. His smile passed quickly and he said, 'I told you not to try and escape. Now you're going to have to learn that I mean what I say. Just like I told Susan. I told her that we would only last as long as *I* wanted, and then she started whining and nagging, always wanting more.'

He chuckled again, momentarily remembering the rush as she had died.

'She didn't think for one second I would hurt her. You should've seen her face, begging me for help, pleading with me. Pathetic. It wasn't until I hit her that she knew I wouldn't help. Her scream was like a fox caught in a trap. But my knife made quick work of that, one small slice to her neck. That was all it took. She learned her lesson. And now you'll have to learn yours. You're lucky. I don't want you dead yet.'

His eyes steeled over, and Cass braced herself against the wall behind her. This was going to hurt.

Frank lifted one of his size ten boots, and kicked hard into her abdomen. Drawing back, he kicked her a couple more times, smiling with satisfaction as he heard at least one rib snap with a crack that sounded over the hum of the machines. Her breath hitched as she struggled to draw in breath, winded and bruised.

He bent down. 'Last chance, Hunt. Do not try to escape again. Do we understand each other?'

Cass nodded in acceptance, grimacing as he roughly pulled her into a sitting position and returned to the computer.

She curled her fingers around the phone, ignoring the pins and needles in her arm, and blocking out the searing pain along her stomach and ribs. She manoeuvred it carefully as her fingers felt for the 'on' button. She felt the vibration as it powered itself life.

Cass sighed, resting her head against the wall behind her. Hopefully it wouldn't be too long now.

7th November, 1345 hours - Ryhope Police Station

Alex could feel his concern gnawing at his insides. He'd turned down coffee for the last couple of hours, believing the caffeine to be responsible for the lead-like feeling in the pit of his stomach. But it was more than that. Reynolds had now had Cass for around twelve hours. Alex didn't know if she was still alive, or whether he had hurt her in some way. He was going nuts. For the first time, he realised how hard it was to be the victim – the person left behind to deal with the police when something happened. It wasn't pleasant, feeling completely helpless, not having a clue what to do next or where to turn. All he wanted was to find her, to hold her and tell her it would all be OK. But he couldn't.

The Chief had advised Rose and Roger to return to their hotel and rest up for a few hours, assuring them they would be welcome back in the incident room later. Rose had only agreed when Alex had promised to ring her the second anything happened. The Chief had then tried to force Alex to go home for some rest, but had been met with a steely determined gaze. There was no way he was leaving the station while Cass was still out there somewhere.

Eckley and the team were running down every line of enquiry, the uniformed officers still out and about on the streets. All rest days had been cancelled, everyone was helping with the search.

The CSIs kept popping up to the office intermittently, all of them concerned for Cass.

And all Alex could do was pace up and down, staring at the information on the white boards, and pray that Reynolds hadn't killed her.

Unable to pace any more, he grabbed Ollie's leash.

'I'm taking the dog out the back. Won't be long,' he said to Eckley as he walked out of the office.

They went down the stairs, and Ollie dragged him in the direction of the CSI offices, the smell of Cass lingering in the corridor to his highly sensitive nose. He poked his head into her office and then pulled Alex into the one opposite.

Faith and Deena were inside, sat in silence. They both looked up as he entered, their eyes softening as they saw Ollie.

'Hey, boy, come here,' said Deena.

Alex let the leash go, and Ollie went over to Deena, allowing her to pull him close. Alex heard her sniff into the downy fur on Ollie's ears, and watched as the dog began gently licking the salty tears off Deena's face.

He felt his voice turn husky with emotion, 'We are going to find her, guys. I promise we will get her back.'

Ollie gave Faith a quick lick too then turned back towards Alex, put his head down and looked so sorrowful that for a moment Alex thought his heart would break.

'Come on, Ollie. Let's go get some fresh air.'

When they reached the yard, he let Ollie off his leash. The dog needed to bounce around a little, let off some built-up energy. Ollie put his nose to the ground instantly and started running around the yard, sniffling as he went. Alex watched, losing interest rapidly. Normally he loved the dog's mad antics, but today he couldn't focus.

His face had two days of unshaved stubble causing shadows where usually there was none. He could imagine the dark circles under his eyes and felt the tension in his cheeks and mouth. He felt like he'd aged ten years in the last twenty-four hours. He hung his head, letting his guard down for just a moment, and let the tears well up.

Where are you Cass? Please come back to me.

They had to find her.

What would I do without her?

Ollie pulled him from his dark thoughts by barking and scrabbling frantically at one of the doors in the yard. It made Alex smile, in a yard full of concrete Ollie could smell a rat, or mouse or whatever the heck had caught his nose.

Still grinning, Alex grabbed his leash. Ollie fought the pull, twisting his head and woofing loudly. Alex firmly pulled the leash shorter. 'Come on, Ollie, I think that's enough fresh air for now.'

Ollie kept whining, trying to pull Alex back to the door, trying to tell him he knew something.

But Alex didn't understand, and led them both back upstairs to the office.

Chapter Thirty Seven

Cass could've sworn she heard a dog barking. The machines were loud and clanking, and she was set back from the door, but she was almost certain.

She sat listening, ignoring the ache in her abdomen and ribs.

When Frank appeared before her suddenly, she jumped. His eyes were glazed, almost as if he were lost in a trance.

'Too busy looking to see what's right in front of his eyes. Like Albert. Always sniffing round my mother, Dad didn't see. Dad couldn't see. But Mum did. She took care of it. Made sure Dad could never see anything again. Shooed off old Albert too. He knew though. He saw the bruises. He saw and he didn't do a thing. He could've stopped her hurting me. He could have helped. But he chose not to see. Now he doesn't see any more either.'

Cass was trying her best to follow his jumbled words. His control had slipped, and the sentences were bouncing all over the place. She thought she understood though. Frank's mum had beaten him. And she had quite possibly done something to his Dad. Who was Albert though? It took a couple of minutes for her mind to make the link.

The old guy from the cave, he was called Albert.

Was this the link Alex had been searching for? Her mind raced as she made the connections while Reynolds' mutterings continued. 'He was there, right outside. Stupid mutt telling him but he couldn't hear. Wouldn't hear. So close and yet so far. It'll soon be time for the curtain to start falling. Wouldn't want to miss the show.'

His eyes suddenly cleared, the mist of confusion leading the way back to anger.

That was close, too close for comfort.

Time to put his plan into action before it was too late. Time to have Alex running around like a headless chicken.

He felt the surge of adrenaline as he made sure Cass was sitting up straight, then brought his fist hard into her nose.

She didn't see it coming and the burst of pain was instantaneous as the cartilage gave way with a loud crunch. Stars swam before her eyes and she felt the blood start to pour from her nostrils, dripping steadily onto her top. She felt anger mingle with the fear, as Reynolds' words flooded her mind.

Suddenly, she knew. The dog she had heard was Ollie, and Alex had been with him. They had almost found her.

'Smile for the camera,' ordered Frank as another light flashed in her face, this time capturing the steely determined look in her eyes.

It was time to help Alex further, before Reynolds completely lost the plot and killed her. Her fingers numb, she felt her way to the number two key and pressed call – she'd plugged Alex in as the second speed dial all the way back when they were dealing with Susan's murder. She couldn't hear the ring, couldn't hear if it had connected, but she hoped it had.

She didn't have much time left.

7th November, 1410 hours - Ryhope Police Station

Alex looked up as Charlie shouted across the room, 'Eckley, Tulley's on the phone, says it's urgent.'

Picking up the receiver, Eckley said, 'OK. He's what? How? … Thanks, Tulley. I owe you one.'

He hung up and looked around the room.

'Listen up, people. Reynolds sent the email from his own email address. This we know – but he somehow managed to hijack the signal for the force wireless network – Tulley reckons he is close to one of the stations. Now we all know that's a fair few stations across the force area, but if we focus on those in Ryhope, and Sunderland city primarily. We know he's local, we know he had knowledge of the stations he worked for as handyman. Fingers out people, I want every neighbourhood within two hundred yards of the stations checked in detail. Now.'

Alex walked over as Eckley began gathering his stuff.

'What can I do?' he asked, his voice shaking slightly.

'I can't have you out canvassing, Alex. You're too close, not to mention you look like shit. Can you stay here? Field any calls coming into the office?'

Alex nodded with a sigh. Eckley was right, out there he'd be about as much use as a chocolate fire guard at present. He couldn't leave though, not until they found Cass.

He heard his mobile ring from the corner where he had been perched and quickly walked over, grabbing it from his jacket pocket.

Alex fully expected it to be Rose, checking in on what was happening.

When he saw 'Cass' flashing on his screen, he felt his legs collapse beneath him and had to grab the table edge to steady himself. 'Eckley, wait. It's Cass!' he said loudly.

He swiped the screen, his heart lodged firmly in his throat as he answered. 'Cass?'

The dull drone of machines was loud but there was no reply. He checked that the line was still open before speaking again.

'Cass? Can you hear me?'

'Clever girl,' said Eckley. 'Keep the line open, Alex, I need to speak with her mobile provider.'

Realisation was slow in dawning to Alex, but then he sat down. Somehow, she had managed to call him. She knew they would be able to get a location using track and trace software.

'She's a bloody genius,' he said to himself.

'Is the line still open?' shouted Eckley from his desk.

Alex nodded, giving him the thumbs up. He kept the phone to his ear, listening for any other sounds. The drone of the machines sounded familiar, but he couldn't place it.

'They're running a trace now – they'll get back to me in a few minutes,' said Eckley, approaching Alex. 'Can you put it on loud-speaker?'

'Yea, it doesn't work very loud though.'

'Here, put your phone in this glass,' interrupted Charlie, emptying her water on the floor and handing it to him.

He looked at her incredulously. 'Huh?'

'The glass provides a natural speaker, trust me,' said Charlie with a slight shrug.

Alex activated the loudspeaker and placed the phone inside the empty glass. The volume almost doubled and the whirr of the machines could be heard loudly.

Suddenly, they heard the sound of a muffled voice.

7th *November, 1420 hours - Ryhope Police Station*

He felt his anger burning, almost out of control. Frank couldn't rein it back in. He had the feeling this was a big mistake. Bringing her here, to the station. He should have just killed her in the woods and left it at that.

He cursed at himself loudly, his brain refusing to kick in when he begged it to tell him how to get out of this.

What the hell am I going to do?

He could just kill her now and leave her there in the boiler room to rot. But there were so many officers in and out of the back yard at present, he doubted he would be able to make it to the fleet car, let alone get out of the yard. He wasn't in disguise.

He cursed again, this was all *her* fault. If she hadn't made him focus on her instead of the task at hand, then he would have been fine. Irrationally, he was now blaming her for everything.

There was only one thing Frank could had left that he could control. He walked over, towering above her as she tried not to show her fear. He put the red toolbox on the floor in front of her and pulled it open, widening it out so all the trays were exposed.

He'd originally thought he would use the hammer, but now he wanted something quicker that took less energy. Suddenly, he was very tired.

He rubbed a hand across the top of his head before pulling the knife from the tray, and watching, Cass screamed through the tape covering her mouth. She felt the phone slip from her grasp as he came closer, her eyes widening as she focused on the knife. The mobile hit the floor with a dull thud and for a second she didn't think he had heard it.

But the sound had invaded his anger.

She had done something.

Viciously he pulled her from the wall, seeing the glowing phone screen on the floor, realising the implications.

'Bitch,' he screeched loudly, then he leant down towards the screen and softly said, 'You're out of time, McKay. Say goodbye.' He raised his boot and smashed it down on the screen of her phone, terminating the signal forever.

7th November, 1422 hours - Ryhope Police Station

Alex felt the blood drain from his face – Reynolds was going to kill her.

He looked up, helpless. Everyone in the room had fallen silent, all of their faces frozen, showing every emotion from concern to anger.

Eckley slammed his fist on the table, making everyone jump.

'We've still got time, people. Get back to it,' he barked.

Alex felt his shoulders slump, Ollie's head resting on his knee.

Absentmindedly he ran his hand gently over Ollie's head and ears. Men were supposed to be strong, the police even stronger. But all he felt was emptiness, swallowing him whole.

Chapter Thirty Eight

7ᵗʰ *November, 1435 hours - Ryhope Police Station*

Cass was confused.

She had thought Frank would flip when he saw the mobile phone, had braced herself for the physical onslaught she figured would come. But he didn't. He slapped her, hard, and then strode silently to the computer.

It's the calm before the storm.

She glanced around, desperation fuelling her thoughts. She needed to find a way to get out of these cable ties. Trussed up like a Christmas turkey, she had no hope of fighting back.

She knew that the track and trace would be useless now the phone was off, unless they'd already done it. It was time to stop relying on other people to get her out of this mess.

She edged along the wall a little, desperately feeling for something, anything, that she could use against the plastic restraints. Then a nail ripped into the sensitive skin on her forearm. Ignoring the stinging pain, she set to work, rubbing the ties back and forth over the sharp point.

7ᵗʰ *November, 1440 hours - Ryhope Police Station*

Frank sat in front of the computer screen, staring at the flickering wallpaper as his thoughts jumbled together.

There was no way out.

He felt a sense of calm as he considered his options. He would go to prison for a long time, possibly his whole life. They would practically throw away the key.

Not because of the murders, but because of *her.*

Everything always came back to her.

He'd felt great satisfaction as he'd slammed his fist into her nose, grinning as the red river had freed itself, running down her chin and onto her clothes. She would be finding it harder to breathe now, the blood clotting inside her nose and sinuses, her cheeks swelling and her mouth restricted by the tightness of the silver duct tape.

He really wished he'd taken her somewhere else. Hindsight was always 20:20. It would have been somewhere he could have taken his time, and enjoyed every iota of pain he inflicted on her.

So far, she was proving to be resilient. She hadn't cried, barely yelling out as he had split her ribs in two, and bruised her diaphragm. Cass hadn't once complained despite the pain she must be feeling with every inhalation of breath.

His mouth set in a grim line, he wanted to break her. He'd expected tears at the very least. Now he wouldn't have that luxury. It was almost time now for it to be over, almost time to finish it.

But he was struggling with his final decision.

Should he stay, or should he go?

7th November, 1445 hours - Ryhope Police Station

The phone on the DCI's desk rang shrilly.

'Eckley. Uh huh, uh huh. That can't be right. You ran it twice? OK.'

His broken sentence made little sense until he put the phone down and glanced around the room.

'The GPS trace is showing Cass's location as this address. She is somewhere in this police station, people – I want every member of staff in the nick pulling into this room right now. We work in groups, moving room to room. Let's go.'

Within seconds the room was packed. Eckley repeated the orders, quickly assigning everyone a floor.

He paused when he came to Alex.

'Don't you dare, Eckley. I *am* working this. I'm gonna take Ollie – hopefully he will sniff Cass out. I am *not* staying in this damn office.'

Eckley gave him a curt nod, 'Charlie and you two, you're with Alex,' he said, pointing at Deena and Ben.

Alex knelt down in front of Ollie, his grey eyes connecting with Ollie's soulful brown ones. Gently he stroked the dog's ears.

'Find Cass, Ollie, where's Cass?'

Instantly Ollie jumped to his feet and ran to the door, whining loudly. Alex kept hold of his leash but let it extend to the max. Without a pause the dog ran to the stairs, quickly followed by Alex and the girls.

Frustrated, Cass grunted against the tape. The stupid nail seemed to be cutting her arm more than the cable ties. She felt wet blood adding to the friction of her movements but she kept going.

She needed to get free.

She was concentrating so hard she barely noticed as Frank appeared in front of her once more.

'Stop,' he said, his face inches from hers.

'It's time. You need to know something though. This is your fault. Everything that's happened is down to you. You've walked around the station for years, pushing people about, bossing them and forcing them to run to do your bidding. Well no more. It just had to be *you* on the hill that night, had to be *you* attending Susan's death. Anyone else wouldn't have seen the slice to her neck, but not you, Cass. Little Miss CSI.' His voice had lowered to a menacing growl, and he paused a moment, grabbing her face in his hands.

Cass was afraid; Frank's eyes were cold, calculating. She knew there would be no changing his mind. He intended to see her dead.

'And to score you for Albert. Precious Albert, all alone in his cave. He didn't stand a chance. You scurried around, making the officers carry your gear, calling scientists in. The little redhead was hot. I should've looked in on her, let her examine her own blood patterns.'

Cass suddenly clicked. All the times she had thought she was being watched, the times the hairs stood up on her neck, it had been him. He had been watching.

'It was just luck when Scott came along when he did. The jumped-up little prick called himself Andy. As if I couldn't find out who he was. I can find out anything. I found out who *he* was, the bully you used to shag. I found who he was and I took care of him. He wasn't getting his mitts on you. You're here for me. You should have heard Scott scream, Cass, he had tape like you. But he at least tried to scream and beg. And he cried like a baby. Are you going to cry, Cass? Will you cry as I kill you? Will those tears fall as I watch the light go out of your eyes?'

Cass shook her head, there was no way on earth she would show him how scared she was. She had learned with Carl how to detach herself from what was happening, send her mind to another place so she didn't have to face what was going on. But she'd be damned if she would go down now without a fight.

She worked the ties again, hard against the nail, ignoring the pain as it scored her wrists. And she stared at Frank, making sure her eyes showed defiance.

Even as he retrieved the knife from rusted red toolbox, she stared at him.

Cass flinched as the knife cut through her joggers as if they were nothing more than soft butter. She felt the sting as it cut into the flesh at the top of her thigh, but still she stared into his eyes, willing him to let her go but knowing it was futile.

He pushed the blade in deeper, and twisted it. Slowly he withdrew the knife and she felt her leg quickly grew warm as blood poured from her wound through her trousers and onto the floor. She knew that he had sliced into her artery. Her leg burning, she watched as he sat down in front of her.

Her eyes widened as he drew the knife diagonally across both his forearms, his blood rapidly pooling beneath his fingers.

'I'm not going to jail. We will die together, Cass. We'll be bound for eternity by this very act. The final act. The curtains will soon be drawn. I'll see you on the other side.'

Cass watched as he seemed to fade in front of her, and she leaned forward, trying to stem the flow of blood from her leg by using her upper body. Slowly she closed her eyes, letting him think she had passed out, and for the first time in a very long time, she prayed.

Chapter Thirty Nine

Ollie dragged Alex to the door in the yard. He knew his mistress was behind that door. He'd known earlier but now Alex seemed to be listening. Sitting on his haunches, he opened his mouth and howled.

The sound was mournful, primal.

Alex couldn't help but stop, lost in it for a moment, then he pulled himself together and turned back to the girls.

'Deena, go get Eckley. Ben, do you know where the keys are for this door?'

Both girls nodded and ran back to the station.

Alex left Ollie howling and banged on the door.

'Reynolds, I know you're in there. I'm coming in as soon as I get a key. I swear to god if you've hurt her I will kill you myself. Reynolds!'

He was verging on hysteria as he banged his fists on metal door, hoping Ben could find the key. This was one door that wouldn't be forced using an enforcer – the metal structure and frame probably ten times stronger than the UPVC doors the tool was normally used on.

Footsteps sounded behind him as the yard filled with his colleagues, Eckley at the forefront.

'Someone get me a damn key for this door,' said Eckley. 'I need floor plans for this station – there must be another entrance to the boiler room.'

'The keys are missing. They were in the handy man's office. But there is another entrance, Sir,' said Ben. 'There's an access door from the old cells. It's never used but it's there.'

'Eckley, stay here and bang on the door, let him think we are coming from here. I'll head to the other entrance and try and get in that way. My team, you're with me.'

Without waiting for Eckley to respond, Alex sped off back into the station.

7th November, 1510 hours - Ryhope Police Station

Cass half-opened her eyes, trying to fight the feeling of darkness dragging her down.

Frank was in front of her, his eyes vacantly staring into the darkness, and she knew he was dead. It wasn't fair – he'd got off too easily. It wasn't fair to his victims.

A hysterical giggle burst from her lips.

Victims? I think I count as one of his victims now. Where are you, Alex?

She could hear banging, somewhere in the recess of her mind, and for a moment she begged it to shut up. Her leg was burning, it felt almost as if it were on fire.

That's a good sign right? That I can feel pain?

Cass felt tears well in her eyes, this was it. There was no way to let Alex know where she was, no way he was going to get to her in time.

'I'm so sorry, Alex,' she whispered as the curtains finally closed, and she felt herself drift into oblivion.

7th November, 1515 hours - Ryhope Police Station

Unnoticed by Eckley, Ben had left with Alex and his team. As they entered the cell block, she pushed her way to the front.

'Here, it's over here,' she said, pointing to a door.

Alex placed his ear to the door. The only sound from the other side was the drone of machines.

'Ben, stay well back, we don't know what weapons he has but you can be sure he has some. On second thoughts, head back out to Eckley and tell him we are here. Do you know if it's locked?'

'I don't know. Sorry, Alex,' said Ben.

'It's fine. You did great, Ben, thank you.'

Alex tried the handle quietly. The internal latch clicked off and the door loosened from the grip of its frame. He could hear Eckley banging on the exterior door and prayed that would be enough to mask any sound.

'Charlie, stay here in case he comes out, Bill and Pete head left. Darren, Mal, you're both with me. Batons out guys, we don't know what he has on him, and I'll be damned if we're waiting for armed response.'

Silently they entered the boiler room, their eyes taking a minute to adjust to the darkness.

Alex paused at the electronic set up – Eckley was full view on the screen, banging hard on the door. He felt his heart go cold as he saw the notepad application open, the words as dark as Reynolds himself.

'You wanted her. You found her. Too late.'

Slowing his breathing, Alex stepped around the whirring machines and felt his heart leap into his throat at the horror that stood before him.

Tears filled his eyes; he was too late. He'd never seen so much blood. It glistened in the dull light, and the metallic stench assaulted his senses. He knew he had to be the one who checked Cass.

He heard the external door click open, heard the rush of footsteps and the lights clicking on just as the room flooded with light. He heard a scream as Deena saw Cass. Someone herded her outside, and he felt the hush fall over his colleagues.

Reynolds was inert, backed against a machine, his eyes glassy and open.

Alex ignored him, making a beeline for Cass.

She was hunched over, almost in two, blood pooled beneath her. Her hands were stretched behind her back, and he bit his cheek as he saw the cable ties cutting into her pale skin.

Forcing himself to breathe, he gently placed two fingers against the side of her neck.

His eyes widened as he picked up the faint beat of her pulse.

'Ambulance. Someone get an ambulance. She's alive,' his voice was raspy, emotion clogging his throat. 'And get me a knife, something to cut these ties with,'

Eckley appeared from behind.

'Alex, move away. Move to one side and let me see to her.'

He placed a hand on Alex's shoulder, guiding him to one side, and took up position beside Cass. Someone handed him a pen knife and he quickly snapped through the ties, her arms falling limply to her sides.

Gently he manoeuvred her onto her back, checking to make sure she was breathing. Her breaths were shallow, her pulse weak, but definitely present. Working silently, he pulled the tie from his neck and fastened it tightly above the wound on her leg. The bleeding had started again as he moved her. Once again he thought to himself, 'Clever girl,' knowing instinctively she had leaned over to stem the bleeding.

Alex sat beside her, his face ashen, watching as Eckley worked.

'She'll be OK, Alex,' he said softly. He watched Alex weep and knew he hadn't heard the words.

Within minutes the scream of a siren wailed as the ambulance made its way to the Sunderland Royal.

Chapter Forty

7th November, 1545 hours – Sunderland Royal Hospital

Alex was sitting in the waiting area of A&E, not seeing the multitude of people milling around him. He didn't see the stares off the patients and other people waiting, didn't acknowledge their silent questions asking what had happened, and why was he covered in blood.

All he could see was Cass, her face pale and her breathing shallow.

She had been rushed into surgery the second she had arrived; a whirr of doctors and nurses pushing her along and shouting at her side.

And he had been left alone.

Through his fog he had managed to phone Rose, his voice almost breaking as he told her to come to the hospital. He didn't hear her reply that Eckley had already rang, or that she was in the taxi on her way. He'd somehow managed to phone Ali too, telling him that Cass was alive.

Finally finished with the phone, he put it back in his pocket and stared at the plastic cup of water at his feet. One of the nurses had placed it there at some point, he figured. His hands shook as he picked it up and took a sip.

The first he knew of Rose's arrival was when her arms wrapped round him and pulled him close, her tears dampening the shoulder of his shirt. He knew how she felt, didn't try to fight as his tears fell and he gave in to the comfort of her arms. Rose just held him, letting her grief flow with his for a moment.

'Thank you,' she croaked, pulling back and cupping her hands to his face. 'You found her, Alex, you found my baby.'

Alex couldn't speak, didn't trust the words to exit his throat. He shook his head, his eyes so full of pain that Rose had no choice but to pull him close again.

'She's strong, my daughter. A fighter. She'll get through this, Alex,' she whispered into his ear, then kissed him on the cheek.

Finally Rose pulled back and sat down beside him. Neither had noticed Roger leave, but he suddenly appeared with paper cups of steaming coffee.

He sat beside Rose, placing one hand on her knee in comfort.

'DCI McKay?'

The sudden voice invaded Alex's thoughts as loud as a bell. He looked up, registering the blue scrubs worn by the man in front of him. His heart in the pit of his stomach, he nodded silently, feeling Rose grip his hand hard.

'I'm sorry it took so long for me to come back to you. I know you've been here a while. During surgery, Cass's heart stopped beating twice. We had to give her a large blood transfusion, but we got her back. She's been moved up to ICU for the time being. She's not out of the woods yet, still in serious condition. But she is stable. If you'd care to go with Diane here, she'll show you to Cass's room.'

Alex barely heard anything beyond the fact that Cass's heart had stopped beating but that they had got her back. He shook the doctor's hand, and turned to the nurse, Rose still holding his hand tightly.

The nurse smiled quietly, 'She's a strong one that one, there was no way she was ready to give up. As the doctor said, she is still in serious condition. She has a couple of broken ribs, bruising and some minor internal bleeding in her abdominal area, and her face is pretty bashed up but all in all she's doing really well. She'll look worse than I make it sound though just to prepare you. Her bruising has already started darkening. She may well need some reconstructive surgery to her nose further down the line.'

Alex exhaled deeply as they followed her down the duck-egg coloured corridors. He still had the lead weight in his stomach, figured it would be there until he knew for certain Cass was OK. He could feel Rose trembling beside him, her hand still gripping his. He tightened his grip momentarily: he knew how she felt.

As they entered the side room, both Alex and Rose gasped.

Despite the nurse giving them warning, they weren't quite prepared for how bad Cass looked.

She looked tiny on the hospital bed, the cannula in her hand wired up to a drip of clear fluid. The oxygen mask disguised some of the bruising but all around both eyes was already a darkening shade of purple, and there was a blue hue beside her mouth, and a small cut to her lip. Both wrists were bandaged, hiding the marks Alex knew had been left by the cable ties. The heart monitor bleated steadily beside her, and her left leg was elevated onto a pile of cushions.

'I'll leave you with her. Talk to her. It'll help,' said the nurse.

Rose finally let go of Alex's hand and pulled a chair up to the bed.

Alex picked up Cass's hand, gently rubbing her soft skin with the pad of his thumb. He was so wrapped up in his emotion that he didn't notice the tears falling down his cheeks again.

8th *November, 0605 hours - Sunderland Royal Hospital*

Cass felt as if she was floating. She could feel the waves lapping at her, trying to pull her back under. She fought against the tide, and tried to open her eyes. She could hear loud beeping, steady and in time with her heart which was pounding in the background.

Her mouth felt as if it were full of cotton wool, and her body felt heavy, and somewhere in the middle of it all was the pain. Dull and throbbing in her ribs, aching in her stomach, stinging to her wrists and sharper, more acute in her leg.

Struggling, she pulled herself further into consciousness, piecing together the fragments from her memory.

What the hell happened? I feel like I've been hit by a truck.

Her eyes opened a crack, then closed as the bright glare of artificial light caused needles of pain, making her groan. She opened them again, forcing herself to accept the light and not drift back into the darkness.

Tilting her head slightly, she saw her mum, fast asleep, leaning on Roger whose head was against the wall, his mouth open wide as he snored softly. A faint smile passed over her lips.

Something heavy was on her hand, she couldn't move it. Momentarily she felt panic, but quickly realised that it was Alex's head. He was sound asleep, his hot breath gently swaying the tiny hairs protecting her skin.

She was safe. Alex had found her.

Cass suddenly remembered the date – 8th November.

Happy birthday to me. I'm still here, and I'm alive.

As she faded again, she had a passing memory of Reynolds and remembered he wasn't a threat to her any more. And as she felt her head relax back into the pillow, the morphine helped the dark curtains close once more.

A smile fluttered over her lips. This was one show that was definitely *not* over.

Epilogue

Alex stood behind the tree in the cemetery looking over at the funeral taking place. Hardly anyone had attended – there was only four people besides the vicar. He wasn't surprised. None of the police family would turn out to this funeral.

It was sad really, to be buried and only have four people present to say goodbye. Alex frowned – it showed the kind of man Frank had been. The only reason Alex was there was to make sure the bastard was dead and gone. Glancing around, he took in the small group, the detective in him not switching off for a moment. The two older women were well dressed, hadn't seemed particularly saddened at the thought of losing Frank, and hadn't shed a tear. *Probably from the church he went to.* The next was a man, probably late fifties, and had the kind of demeanour that men have when they hold positions of relative power – *his priest maybe?*

The last male had Alex perplexed. Younger, maybe only twenty, he'd stood with his back to Alex through the ceremony. When it had ended and he'd turned to leave, Alex had felt a shiver when the man made brief eye contact. In that moment Alex had gazed into an abyss, one filled with apparent anger at a life taken too soon. He wondered who the man was. Alex had tried to follow, but he'd lost him, the male ducking out of sight behind a large headstone then failing to reappear. Alex shook off the uneasy feeling in the pit of his stomach. It was probably nothing.

It was a good job Frank had killed himself before Alex had found his way into the boiler room – he dreaded to think what he'd have done if Frank had been alive. Would he have had some control? Or would he have lost it and kicked the living hell out of the man who had taken the woman he loved.

The woman he loved – that thought made him feel warm, despite the bitter wind now whipping around the graveyard. He loved her. And she'd survived despite everything. He'd known the second she'd come round in the hospital that he wanted to spend his life with her, or maybe he'd known before but that had been the moment he'd made the decision to get the ring. He'd proposed the next day, and she'd said yes. In spite of all the confusion and pain she'd been in, she'd known what he'd asked and cried.

Alex pulled the collar to his jacket up around his face, protecting himself from the elements, and turned to leave. He paused at the mound of earth that contained what was left of Frank Reynolds and smiled. *Got you, you bastard.*

Lightning Source UK Ltd.
Milton Keynes UK
UKOW01f0233221016

285887UK00002B/1/P